GRAVE MATTERS

Donna Fletcher Crow

MOODY PRESS
CHICAGO

ISBN: 0-8024-2711-1

1 3 5 7 9 10 8 6 4 2

Printed in the United States of America

To David Munro,
Who shared his beautiful country,
unveiled his ancestors,
and once spent a sleepless night above
Dr. Knox's office;
and
to his lovely Wendy,
a most gracious hostess

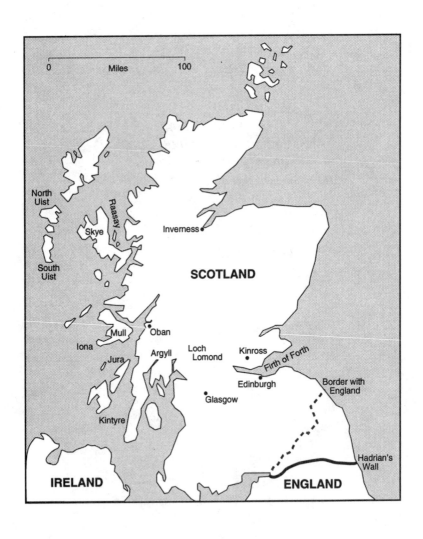

0   Miles   100

North
Uist

Raasay

Skye

Inverness

South
Uist

SCOTLAND

Mull Oban

Iona

Jura Argyll Loch
Lomond Kinross

Firth of Forth

Edinburgh

Border with
England

Glasgow

Kintyre

Hadrian's
Wall

IRELAND   ENGLAND

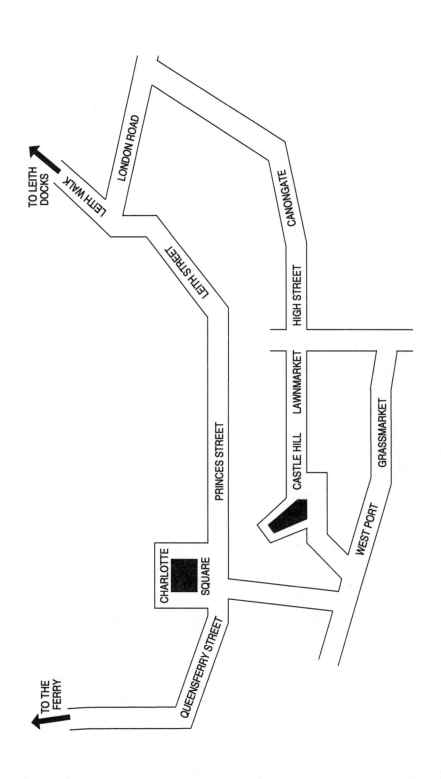

1

Lady Antonia Hoover gave a little shiver of excitement. Or was it of fear?

Lord Charles Danvers, her companion, in morning frock coat and stately tall black hat, looked at her with the softness only she ever saw from him, and a smile lit his craggy features. He patted the hand resting on his arm. "It won't be long now."

That was precisely what was worrying Antonia, but she smiled back and adjusted her deep-brimmed bonnet so that the lace and flowers would frame her heart-shaped face to best advantage. She was determined that if she was to be cut to ribbons along with thirty thousand other Londoners and foreign visitors, she would meet her fate looking her best.

Certainly the Crystal Palace was looking its best. It gleamed in the morning sunshine of May 1, 1851. This was the culmination of months, even years, of planning and work. Since the first of the year thousands of workers had been employed putting the finishing touches on the huge, elegant steel and glass building and arranging the fourteen thousand exhibits that came from all over the world. Within the space of three months more than one hundred thousand articles had been prepared for display in eleven miles of stalls.

All of Britain—indeed, most of the world—was Exhibition mad. Every shop and hotel in London displayed multilingual signs soliciting trade from foreign visitors. Hundreds of carriages of every condition filled the streets for miles in every direction. The capital was garrisoned with soldiers, and six thousand extra policemen had been called to duty in case any of the dire warnings of rampant and violent crimes so many prophets of doom had predicted the event would bring on their heads should come to pass.

Just that morning the *Times* had warned that when the model frigate on the Serpentine fired its guns in salute of the queen's arrival "the concussion will shiver the glass roof of the Palace and thousands of ladies will be cut into mincemeat."

But even such a dreadful augury couldn't suppress Antonia's spirits for long. Every time she looked upward at the gleaming crystal arch hundreds of feet above her head she felt again the shock of delighted surprise that had met her on first entering the great transept. At the far end two huge elm trees, giants of Hyde Park, rose far into the air. Their wealth of luxuriant green leaves was as free and unconfined as if still standing under the open sky. Just to her right the waters of the creamy-gold fluted glass fountain plashed from its many tiers, a gentle accompaniment to the orchestra playing at the far end. Everywhere she looked, Antonia's eyes were dazzled with tropical foliage, luxuriant flowers, rich carpets, and elegantly clad people.

Yet a tickle of fear remained. Could all this display of beauty, wealth, and power be swept away in a single moment? All these people be sent to eternity with the firing of a single salute? And then she looked at the tall man beside her. She knew that it wasn't the material things around her she feared most for, nor for the thousands of other lives thronging about them, nor even for her own. It was her dearest Charles who held the focus of all her days and all her life.

Since that autumn day two and one-half years ago when he had rescued her from abduction and brought their murderous acquaintance to justice, Charles had filled her formerly shallow existence with meaning—Charles and the faith they were growing in together. What if the great crystal dome should shatter down on them in millions of razor shards as predicted? Charles would protect her with his own body.

But she would not want to be protected—not to go on without him. She clung tighter to his arm, gripping it with both lace-mitted hands. Why had she been so head-strong? Why had she insisted that they attend the opening day? She had been insane to accept such a risk just two days before their wedding.

She started to breathe a prayer but was interrupted by the cheering of the crowds filling the park. The queen had arrived. A pause the space of three heartbeats brought a second roar of approval, telling those inside that the world-famous aeronaut Worthing Spenser, who had been waiting just outside the palace in his Union Jack draped balloon, had begun his ascent in honor of the queen—a feat he would repeat every few days throughout the Exhibition.

The orchestra stopped playing. All inside the Crystal Palace seemed to hold their breath. The only sound was the falling of water onto petals of blown glass. Then, like a gentle choir of high-pitched voices from all over the building, the many clocks included in the various exhibits chimed twelve o'clock.

It was time.

The guns fired their salute.

The roof held.

A soft sigh of relief breathed through the building.

"You weren't nervous, were you?" Danvers bent to speak in Antonia's ear.

She smiled back at him without comment. It was silly of her to worry, wasn't it? After all, they were young and happy and ready to start their life together in the best of all possible worlds—wasn't that what the Great Exhibition had been mounted to show?

From the first balcony the mighty organ now commanded attention as it pealed forth the opening strains of "God Save the Queen." Victoria—splendid in a satin gown, a tartan sash over one creamy shoulder and gathered ribbons in her coiled hair—entered on the arm of her regally uniformed Albert, who had been the guiding force behind the concept and organization of the Exhibition.

As a silent testimony to the queen's rejection of all doomsayers, she had brought two of her children with her as well. Princess Louise, wearing a pink satin frock with a circlet of flowers in her hair, clung to her mother's hand, while Prince Edward, in a diminutive kilt and with a plaid over his shoulder, strove to match his stride to his father's.

". . . Send her victorious, long to reign over us . . ." the crowd sang, and every knee bent and head dipped as the royal family progressed up the length of the nave.

Antonia was completely caught up in the glory of the moment, a moment that chased away all thought of the dire letters that had filled the *Times* for so many days warning that in attending the Great Exhibition the queen would be exposing herself to horrible conspirators and assassins, fraud and immorality, man-traps and spring guns. The invited guests of a lady's drawing room could not have conducted themselves better than this ardent throng.

The queen ascended the dais built in front of the fountain, surrounded by her ladies-in-waiting and some of the most illustrious statesmen of the day. At the end of the national anthem Prince Albert descended from the platform to read the report of the Commission.

The queen replied. "My dear people, the sight of this glittering arch, far more lofty and spacious than the vaults of even our noblest cathedrals, is so vast, so glorious, so

touching that one feels filled with devotion. One is overcome with a sense of mystery and must be reminded of
that day when all ages and climes shall be gathered round
the throne of their Maker."

Enthusiastic applause met her remarks.

"God bless my dear Albert, the author of this great
peace festival. God bless my dearest country, which has
shown itself so noble today. This is a day to live forever.
Let us all raise our gratitude to the great God who pervades
all and blesses all."

The Archbishop of Canterbury, in full ecclesiastical
robes of white and gold, stepped forward to lead in prayer.
"Make us truly grateful, our Lord and our God, for Your
many blessings to us individually and to us as a nation.
May it ever be said of this great land, 'Blessed is the nation
whose God is the Lord.' And God save the queen."

The archbishop had no more than lowered his hands
when the voices of the great organ, the two hundred or-
chestral instruments assembled, and a six-hundred-voice
choir sounded forth the "Hallelujah Chorus."

Now Antonia gripped Charles's arm not in fear, but
in ecstasy. Truly, as the queen had said, this was a day to
live forever.

"Hallelujah: For the Lord God omnipotent reigneth.
Hallelujah . . ."

The sun dazzled even more brightly through all the
crystal arches as Antonia choked with praise, gratitude,
and love. Nothing could go wrong now.

"Forever and ever . . ." The last "Hallelujah!" died
away to be followed by a fanfare of trumpets.

Queen Victoria stepped to the edge of the dais and
raised her hand. "I now declare this Great Exhibition to be
open."

Then the royal family led a procession through the
exhibition rooms on the first floor, leaving the thirty thousand other guests free to view the marvels of art and industry at their leisure.

13

Danvers started to lead Antonia toward the stairs to the first gallery, but her steps lagged. "Oh, Charles, it was wonderful. I hardly feel capable of—" She stopped mid-step, her face turning red.

There was no mistaking the familiar ruffle at her feet, rippling out the petticoats under her wide, ivory, striped silk skirt. How could it have happened? How could she, alone of all the thousands of visitors there have been the one to break the rules? The balconies were lined with policemen. Which would be the first to spot her malfeasance?

Always alert to her feelings, Danvers turned in concern. "Tonia, what's wrong?"

Wordlessly she pointed to the floor, just beyond the toe of her right foot, and raised her skirt a bare two inches. The rules were clear, the prohibitions clearly stated: No profanity, no smoking, no alcohol, no dogs.

"Tinker." Danvers shook his head at the nose of Tonia's golden terrier poking out from under her skirt. "How did he get in?"

"I can't imagine. I told him to wait in the carriage. I thought he did."

Danvers surveyed the crowd separating them from the nearest exits. "Well, there's little hope of getting him out now. I suggest we simply proceed as if we didn't know he was there. If one of Her Majesty's officers chooses to impound the little beast it'll serve him right."

"Charles, you're heartless." But Antonia could think of no better solution. Fortunately, as they progressed toward the wrought iron staircase Tinker seemed to decide that the safest course in such a crowd was to stay tucked well under his mistress's petticoats.

At first they merely wandered, carried along in the same direction as the crowd. The riot of color and textures burst on Antonia's senses like a Far Eastern bazaar: silks and satins; furs and feathers; jeweled weapons and saddles; clocks; cabinets; couches, chairs, thrones in ivory and zebra wood; adornments in jet, jasper, and jade; tapestry, embroidery, lace; leatherwork; gold and silver filigree; perfumes; tobaccos; exotic food, drink; china . . . At last she stopped, breathless, and leaned against one of the steel supports of the balcony. "Oh, wait. I don't think I can take in any more."

"Shall we choose a special exhibit to view and leave the rest for another day?" Danvers suggested, opening his official catalogue. "There is Prince Albert's Model Dwelling House over by the barracks. They say it is a clever, economic design which can make acceptable housing available to all—even those in the poorest slums." Tonia didn't reply, so he turned another page. "Brunel's thirty-one-ton, broad-gauge locomotive might make a change from onyx carvings and brocade."

Tonia laughed. "Indeed it would, my dear Charles. As would the model of the Liverpool Docks, complete with sixteen hundred fully rigged ships, or the raw materials section with piles of ores, timber, and ivory tusks. But I had something more restful in mind."

"Well—" Charles perused his book "—guns and models of warships and submarines don't seem to be quite the thing." He turned a few pages. "Second gallery: textiles, furniture, exhibits from America, Morocco, Scotland . . ."

Antonia looked upward to the top level of the great palace. It seemed that little of the crowd had made its way to the upper reaches as yet. Uncrowded domestic exhibits would be just the thing.

With typical enthusiasm, the Americans had reserved far more space than they could fill, so much of their display consisted of stacks of milk-churns, piles of biscuits—which they labeled cookies—and stacks of soap. Danvers did find some of their offerings interesting, however. There was a vacuum coffin guaranteed to prevent decay, a machine for turning over pages of music, and a model of a floating church.

Antonia was examining a gigantic piano designed to be played by four performers at one time when a family group with three exuberant little boys entered the exhibit. With considerable alarm she felt Tinker's tail beating against her leg. She knew the next moments would bring him bounding out with a friendly bark. "Heel, Tinker," she commanded sharply and walked briskly toward the Scottish exhibit from which the other party had apparently just come.

It was a perfect choice. Charles and Antonia had the room quite to themselves for the moment. Danvers was immediately taken with the display of a Dumfries hatter, which offered "Parisian hats for gentlemen."

"Oh, Charles, this is just the thing." Antonia pointed to a "Patent Ventilating Hat," which provided fresh air through a series of channels cut in thin cork and featured a valve fixed to the top of the crown that could be opened and shut at the wearer's pleasure to allow perspiration to escape. "Shall I order you one for a wedding present, Charles? I should think it might come in handy the next time Aunt Elfrida starts issuing orders."

"Thank you, my dear, but I shall endeavor to remain calm in the dowager duchess of Aethelbert's presence without the assistance of a cork hat. Tell me, though, what do you think of some of this fine furniture for our home?"

They moved to the side of the exhibit to examine a massive, black oak chair that had been passed and repassed through carving machines until not the smallest area of its surface remained flat—including the seat.

Antonia ran her fingers over the deep carving. "It certainly might be a good thing to own should we have visitors who are inclined to sit too long."

They moved next to a towering half-tester bed of immense size, as heavily carved as the chair. After a space of some four hundred years the half-canopied bed was suddenly back in vogue. The posts at its head rose to a height of eight feet. About three-quarters of the way up, projecting

16

scrolls supported the half-tester, which was draped in the white, red, and black Royal Victoria tartan that had burst into popularity when the queen sported a croquet outfit in that design. The floor-length side drapes sheltered a heavily-carved chest-shaped headboard, which served as background for the plaid-covered bolster and comforter.

Danvers shook his head. "That looks more fitted for a corpse to lie in state on than for a night's rest. Look —that footboard is so high it shuts in the sleeper like a prison. Completely impedes the free circulation of air."

"Oh, but just see how cleverly the headboard is designed to serve as a blanket press or storage for extra bolsters." Antonia moved toward the head of the bed, then paused. "And I do like the tartan hangings." She touched the soft surface of the fine weaving. "I read that the queen has had tartan carpets installed in her palace on the Isle of Wight. This is certain to become most fashionable."

Considerations of the future of Scottish weaving, however, fled from Antonia's mind the next moment. The hem of her skirt began churning like a pot at the boil. Suddenly Tinker sprang toward the bed with a yap and snarl as if one of the four bed posts had snatched a meaty bone from him and deposited it in the cleverly designed headboard.

Hearing a party approaching, Antonia made a dive to catch her errant pet. Out of the corner of her eye she saw Charles step forward and bow deeply to the approaching group. As her fingers closed around Tinker's jaws, muffling his growls, the significance of the situation struck her. Charles was bowing to his sovereign.

With a swiftness born of necessity, Antonia managed to stuff Tinker under the folds of her fringed silk shawl, turn to the queen, and execute a perfect curtsy. The fact that her curtsy was deeper and held longer in the dip than normal owed even more to her agitation than to her respect for the queen.

But Her Majesty seemed pleased by it, and she nodded in the direction of her dutiful subjects.

Then the queen's attention was taken by the enormous bed. "Albert, is that not excellent? Ah, my dear Scotland is a constant source of pleasure. We shall commission this furniture maker for Balmoral."

Prince Albert fingered the fine woolen plaid. "And the weaver too, I should think." He turned toward the placard beside the display. "Raeburn of Edinburgh." A secretary among the royal entourage scribbled a note.

Antonia, still frozen in her curtsy began to wobble. With a sigh of gratitude she relaxed against Danvers's strong arm circling her waist and raising her to her feet. Silently they moved to the back of the exhibit until the royal family and their attendants swept along the gallery to examine the exotic treasures of Morocco.

Antonia, who had been holding her breath as tightly as she had been holding her pet took in a great gulp of air with a gurgle of laughter. "Oh, Charles, I thought I was going to faint." She pulled back the fringes of her shawl. "My poor Tinker, have I smothered you?"

The slight loosening of her grip was all the little terrier was waiting for. He sprang from her arms and leaped at the bed. Antonia and Danvers both lunged toward him but were turned back by the ferocity of his bared teeth and the earnestness of his barks. This time there was no muffling him.

Torn between concern for her pet and fear of offending her sovereign should Tinker's barks reach the royal ears, Antonia tried to insert herself between Tinker and the massive headboard, which seemed to be the focal point of his barks. She was only vaguely aware of a crowd gathering behind her as she spoke soothingly to the dog and flung out her hand in an attempt to prevent his leaping up onto the bed. She miscalculated her gesture and struck the spring clasp securing the lid.

The lid flew up.

Tinker bounded onto the bed and into the chest, as the figure that had reentered the room stepped forward

18

with a snap of her imperial fan. "Oh, charming. A most practical design. Do you not agree, Albert?"

The queen, who had apparently returned for a second look at the bed she wished to have installed in her Scottish castle, advanced as Antonia sank in yet another deep curtsy. Her Royal Majesty took one long look into the chest from which Tinker's growls were emanating. Turning with the regal authority of one who ruled two-thirds of the world, Victoria Regina addressed the nearest of her attendants in a clear voice. "There is a person in that trunk. Please have him removed. He appears to be quite dead."

2

And he smells abominably." Her lace and ivory fan over her nose, Queen Victoria turned from the unpleasant exhibit. Three of her retinue scurried to summon police officers from their guard duty.

Following her sovereign's example, Antonia held one corner of her ivory shawl to her nose while the efficient officers quickly cordoned off the exhibit. A wave of stale putrefaction and alcohol filled the room as the body, snugly wrapped in a tartan far different from the royal-patterned bedclothes, was lifted from its casket.

Danvers stepped forward to offer his assistance. A ruddy-faced, blond policeman turned to him, and Charles's eyebrows rose. "Well, well, Sergeant Futter, isn't it? What brings you all the way from Norfolk?"

"Thank you for remembering me, your lordship. Actually it's Inspector now. And high time it is for me to be thanking you for it too. That spot of bother you helped us clear up at Stanfield Hall was what produced the step up."

He pulled his round-domed hat from his head, revealing an unruly shock of straw-colored hair. "Come to London on locum for this exhibition. Hope the criminals in the rest of the country don't take it into their heads to run amok while most of the nation's police force are keeping order here." He looked at the body on the bed. "Well, attempting to keep order, that is. Rum thing, Her Majesty findin' the likes of him tucked up here. It'll be more than our jobs are worth if we don't get to the bottom of this. And quick, too."

Having reminded himself of his own duty, Detective Inspector Futter began directing the men under his command. First he appointed a sergeant standing at rigid attention to get himself off to Saint Bartholomew's Hospital to summon the medical examiner.

Then he turned to an egg-shaped constable standing behind him. "Diggings, get busy questioning everybody you can find who's been in this exhibit this morning." He turned to Antonia. "If we could just start with you, your ladyship?" Then as a movement of the air brought another waft of stench, "And try to locate those who worked here in the last few days. Get the chairman of this exhibit."

Constable Diggings, nodding his red hair and freckled face as fast as he scribbled down his orders, saluted with pencil still in hand. "I'll find him, sir." He started to leave.

"Her ladyship first, Diggings," Futter reminded him.

The earnest constable pulled a large, white cotton handkerchief from the pocket of his dark blue uniform and mopped his forehead. Antonia thought he would also have polished the brass buttons lining his chest if he'd dared.

She had little to contribute in answer to his questions, however, other than the misconduct of her pet. Tinker was now curled docilely at her feet, although he occasionally lifted his nose and perked his ears toward the bed.

Danvers turned from the group around the bed. "I can add little to Lady Antonia's statement other than to observe that the body had apparently been in the chest for a number of days. The fact that it was wrapped in a length of this distinctive tartan"—he directed their attention to the length of heather-colored wool intersected with lines of gold, black, and white—"suggests his sojourn began in

Edinburgh with the bed. But I'm sure Sir Sidney Simpson can tell you more when he arrives from Saint Bart's."

Futter joined them. "There don't seem to be any marks of violence about the body. Looks to me like he crawled in the chest to sleep off his drunk and suffocated."

"Do you have any idea who he is? Are there any papers in his pockets?" Antonia asked.

Futter turned back to his men still examining the body. A tall, thin man shook his head. "Not a shred, sir. No coins, no papers."

Now over her initial shock and interested in the bizarre situation, Antonia took a step toward the bed. The movement brought her closer to the bad air, however, so she drew back. "Is there anything else in the chest? Perhaps something fell out of his pockets."

Turning away from the body, Futter followed Antonia's thoughts. The deep, dark wood chest, tucked behind heavy curtains, took some moments to explore fully. At last the officer turned with a triumphant flourish and held an empty bottle of Scotch whiskey aloft. "Aha, just as I thought—sleeping off a drunk."

Danvers nodded slowly. "Odd, though, don't you think, that he should have wrapped himself so tidily in a plaid while in such an advanced state of inebriation?"

"Probably cold." Futter shrugged. "Dismal bad weather in Scotland, I'm told."

Antonia, though, found the question more intriguing than a mere matter of climate. While part of her mind wanted to explore the puzzle, even found appealing the idea of working together with Charles to find a solution as they had in Norfolk, the rest of her mind was saying *No, no, no*. They were to be married in two days. She had no intention of becoming wrapped up in matters of death so near to this time of joy. Already she had been feeling the need for uninterrupted time with her beloved. What had become of the rambling walks and quiet philosophical talks they had so enjoyed? If they were caught in the de-

22

mands of an investigation there would be even less time.

"Yes, I'd be delighted to offer any assistance I can." Danvers's deep voice interrupted her reverie. "I understand how short-staffed you are with all this Exhibition brouhaha. But then, if the chap merely crawled in the trunk and dozed off to meet his Maker as it appears, it shouldn't take you long to wrap it up."

"Sir, I told you this exhibition is closed."

All heads turned at the sharp command of the officer guarding the entrance.

"And I'm telling you it's not closed to me. His lordship will be wanting my services." At the sound of the lilting Irish voice, Tinker bounded forward with a yap of greeting. "Ah, and so that's where ye got off to is it, ye wee beastie?" The portly intruder, wearing an unfashionable, bottle green coat, scooped the terrier into his arms and sailed past the protesting policeman.

Inspector Futter took one glance at the newcomer and nodded to his agitated guard, while Danvers stepped forward. "Hardy, I should have known you'd be here at the first whiff of excitement. But how on earth did you find out? And who's minding my cattle?"

"Ah, the poor wee bobby was without transport to Saint Bart's, and here were your fine, high-stepping horses just longing for a mite of exercise. I knew you wouldn't be denying their service to an officer on duty, m'lord. I delivered him right fine, then hurried back to offer my services." He paused to return Tinker to the floor, then added hurriedly, "After finding a right bright lad to watch your horses, of course."

"Yes, and after pumping the poor officer for every scrap of information, I've no doubt. It's just as well you've come, Hardy. The police are dashed overworked—it just might be that you can help them. You remember our old friend Futter?"

Danvers's man and the Inspector exchanged greetings, then Hardy bent over the colorfully ensconced corpse while Futter and Danvers explained the situation. Hardy looked over the body, paced around the bed, peered into the headboard chest, took a long whiff of the empty whiskey bottle, and turned to make his pronouncement. "Seems clear enough. He was burked."

Antonia laughed. "Hardy, whatever do you mean? Is that another expression of your Irish grandmother's?"

But Futter answered for him. "No, miss. It's an expression we use. Means he was done in without leaving marks of violence—most-like smothered. Like that there Burke and Hare did in Edinburgh back when there was a brisk business in bodies for dissection."

Now Antonia shuddered. "You can't mean it? Surely you don't think this poor man was murdered and smuggled all the way from Scotland to be used in a medical lecture?"

"No, no." Futter held out his hand soothingly. "Sorry to be worrying you, ma'am. There's no need of that now. They changed the law close on twenty years ago. Hardy here just meant to suggest the appearance of a natural death when it wasn't."

"Yes, yes. Natural death, of course it was." Sharp thumps of an ebony walking stick emphasized the newcomer's words. "Couldn't possibly be anything else with Her Majesty involved. Wouldn't be the thing at all to have the queen's name bandied about with murder. I say, what can any of you be thinking?"

Everyone in the room turned to the imposing entrance of a man well over six feet tall with broad shoulders and rotund chest to match his importance.

"Sir Sidney, thank you for coming so quickly," Futter greeted the chief medical examiner.

"Quite right. You did quite the right thing to send for me immediately. We can clear this matter up in no time. No need to make a fuss, I'm sure. No need at all." Sir Sidney Simpson handed his silver-tipped walking stick, white kid gloves, and tall black beaver hat to Sergeant Diggings and proceeded to the bed in two strides.

He felt the cold wrist and neck of the form on the plaid covers. "As I thought. He is dead. Quite dead."

Futter nodded earnestly. "Yes, sir. I rather thought you'd find him so."

Sir Sidney's aristocratic nose assessed the air. "None of your men drinking, are they, Futter?"

"No, sir. No. It's . . . er . . . the subject."

"Quite so." Sir Sidney adjusted his monocle and took several moments to run his fingers through his luxuriant, gray-peppered sideburns. "And what is your assessment, Futter?"

The Detective Inspector's naturally ruddy complexion grew redder yet, clear to the roots of his hair. "My theory, sir, is that the subject, under the influence of alcohol, crawled into the trunk and thereby suffocated."

"And where did this unfortunate mishap take place, Detective Inspector?"

Futter looked at the placard on its scrolled wrought-iron stand. "Er . . . Scotland, I would say, sir. Edinburgh."

Sir Sidney adjusted his monocle in the direction of the name card. "Yes . . ."

"Er . . . Raeburn Woolen Mills, Leith, sir."

Futter received a hearty slap on the back from his superior. "Well done, Detective Inspector Futter. You'll go far. I shall write my official report accordingly, and you can return this inconvenience to beyond the border from whence it came." He strode to the door, then turned. "I shall notify Her Majesty that I have dealt with the entire matter precisely as she would wish."

"And so turn the wheels of justice," Danvers commented as the important back disappeared. Then he turned again to the bed. "Seems a pity to ship the poor fellow off without a name. Must be some next of kin somewhere who'd like to know what happened."

25

He observed the limp form for several seconds before standing back and shaking his head. "Ordinary sort of fellow. Worker's clothes." The folds of the luxurious tartan made a sharply contrasted background to the coarse weave of the man's rumpled dark trousers, linsey-woolsey shirt, heavy jerkin, and loosely knotted neckerchief.

"A dustman, perhaps?" Antonia suggested.

Danvers pointed to the wrinkled hand. "Not well-groomed by any means, but no ground-in grime or callouses. Not a heavy-laborer, I'd say—and yet not a clerk either."

"How old do you think he was?"

Danvers's lofty forehead wrinkled thoughtfully. "Hard to say with his features shriveled. Not much gray in the hair—maybe approaching fifty—no more. Maybe less."

Just then a policeman who had gone out at Futter's instructions earlier in the proceedings returned, shadowed by a stooped, gray, skeletally thin man who seemed to be focusing all his energy on wringing his hands.

"Oh, dear, that such a thing should have happened on the very first day of our glorious Great Exhibition." The bony fingers wrenched around three times. "Oh, dear me, that it should happen in my very own section of the hall. Oh, my. What our dear prince shall say I can't imagine. And after he took such great care over every detail. Every smallest detail. And in my section too. Oh, dear, dear."

Mercifully, Futter interrupted before the fellow could completely dislocate his knuckles. "No, no. None of that now. No one is blaming you. Just some routine questions. Nothing to get into a stew about, I assure you."

The hand wringing continued, but at a less violent pace. "Oh, my, yes. Yes, of course. Anything I can do."

"Very well." Futter signaled Diggings to take down the man's statement. "We just need to know who received the merchandise, who worked on the exhibit, and when the bed was set up."

Antonia had not thought it possible that the man's pallor could turn whiter yet, but it did. "Oh, dear. Names.

26

Yes, the names of the workers. I have them all, you know. I keep meticulous records. I assure you, meticulous. I just don't see how such a thing could have happened."

Futter cleared his throat. "Names of workers, Mr. . . ."

"Philbin. Montmorcey Philbin."

"Yes, Mr. Philbin, names of everyone who worked on the Scottish exhibit."

"Yes, yes. My records. It's all written down. I'll need to refer to my records."

"And what can you tell us about when the bed was set up?" Futter prodded.

"Oh, a terrible worry it was." Philbin was so overcome at the memory that his hands suddenly hung limp. "I thought it would never arrive—the centerpiece of the whole exhibit—I can't imagine what we would have done."

"So it arrived late?"

"The very last minute—just two days ago—massive, heavy thing to get all the way up the stairs, and the draperies to arrange to perfection. We did it though—well, almost perfection." He gave a jerky glance toward the bed.

With a wave of his hand Futter sent Philbin, who had begun hand wringing again, off with Diggings to check the records.

"Sounds like our man must have been dead for about a week—about what I would have guessed, given that he came from a cold climate in a sealed chest." Futter nodded. "Of course, now that Sir Sidney's declared the case closed I don't suppose we need have bothered poor Philbin. No harm in having the record complete though."

Hardy cleared his throat. "Not wanting to press, sir, but I could just nose around a bit for you when we're on the other side of the border. Be seeing if I could find out anything more for your records. It's certain sure I am I'll have time on my hands while my betters are lollygagging around." He turned with the impish grin that always reminded Antonia of a leprechaun. "No disrespect meant, your lordship."

"No offense taken, Hardy. I have every intention of lollygagging to my fill. But who invited you along on our honeymoon is what I want to know?"

"And who'll be ironing your shirts and brushing your coats and polishing your shoes if not me, *I'd* like to know?"

"This is hardly the time and place to settle this matter, Hardy, but let me remind you that we shall be at a remote rural lodge for fishing and rambling. There will be no need of your spit and polish."

"Ah, you'll not be finding the Scottish the barbarian lot you're thinking—closely related to the Irish they are. You'll be happy for a spot of proper valeting, mark my words."

"Later, Hardy." Danvers quelled his man with a seldom-used tone of command and turned to offer his arm to Antonia, who was still looking thoughtfully at the form on the bed.

"Poor man, it seems so awful to die unnamed." She took Charles's arm and turned away for fresher air. "What will the Scottish authorities do with him?"

Futter shook his head. "I couldn't say, ma'am. Could put an advert in the paper, could launch an investigation. Most likely, though, they'll send the body to the medical school for the students to practice their dissection on—if he isn't too ripe by the time we get him back. Well, lads—" he turned to his men standing around "—you heard Sir Sidney. Get 'im in a box—he's got a train north to catch. And see what you can do to pretty up this exhibit a little— maybe spray some ladies' lavender water around. Don't want the public thinking the Crystal Palace is some kind of morgue."

3

"I take thee, Charles Frederick Arthur Emory of Danvers, to my wedded husband, to have and to hold . . ."

Antonia's clear voice filled the classic sanctuary of Saint George's Church, Hanover Square—just as the vision of the tall, elegant man in impeccable black formal wear filled her eyes, and as thoughts and dreams of their life together had filled her heart for the past two and one-half years.

He took her left hand with his own long, strong fingers and slipped on the engraved golden band that had been his grandmother's. "With this ring I thee wed, with my body I thee worship . . ."

Antonia felt the quick tightening at the back of her throat that those beautiful words always produced. She tightened her clasp on his hand and breathed a deep thank-you that they had found each other, that from this day forward their lives would be one.

Then the minister bound their hands together with his fringed stole. "I pronounce that these two be man and wife together, in the name of the Father, and of the Son, and of the Holy Ghost."

Then as the organ played softly, and Antonia's wide, ivory-silk skirt rustled, and the train fanned out behind, the bridal couple moved a few steps forward to the kneeling bench. Candles in the dim sanctuary turned Antonia's Honition lace veil and orange blossom wreath into a halo around her auburn hair.

"May Almighty God pour upon you the riches of His grace, sanctify and bless you, that ye may please Him both in body and soul, and live together in holy love unto your lives' end."

And Antonia was certain that God would grant exactly that.

As if in a dream, and yet with a reality that was far better than any dream, to the peal of the organ recessional Antonia and Charles led their wedding party and guests down the aisle and out the Corinthian portico of Saint George's. There the beribboned, flower-decked carriages waited to take them to the wedding feast at Danvers's home in nearby Grosvenor Square.

It was fortunate that they had a journey of only a few blocks to accomplish. Even now, with the church bells ringing twelve o'clock over their heads, the streets of London were jammed with people making their way toward the Great Exhibition. Indeed, Brook Street, the most direct connector between Hanover Square and Grosvenor Square, was so congested that the wedding procession was obliged to go up to the wider Oxford Street in order to make progress.

For most of the journey their advance, though slow, was steady with the flow of traffic. Only at the intersection of Oxford and New Bond streets did they come to a complete standstill in what appeared to be a hopeless snarl of carts, carriages, and pedestrians.

"Glory be, and we won't be getting out of town a minute too soon, m'lord," Hardy called over his shoulder from beside the driver of the Danvers's carriage. "The whole world is converging on London—if not right here on Oxford Street."

"I shall forbear inquiring what you intend by saying 'we' are getting out of town. Let me remind you that it is Lady Danvers and I who are going north this afternoon, Hardy. But for the moment, please make yourself useful. Run ahead to see what can be done to untangle this snarl."

With a sprightliness unusual in one of his round proportions, Hardy sprang from the seat and darted off into the crowd. He was gone only a few minutes before the Gordian knot ahead of them began to unravel itself. By the time he had leaped back to his seat, the carriage was rolling forward.

"Well done, Hardy." A ripple of ivory lace brushed Antonia's cheek as she leaned forward. "What was the trouble?"

"Proper coil it was. Horse down in the street. Everyone said that beggar-fellow Hare spooked the beast. That's as may be, but I gave him a shilling and set him back on his own side of Oxford Street."

"What beggar?"

"Oh, now your ladyship wouldn't be knowing about the likes o' him. Been begging here right onto twenty years, they say, ever since he saved his neck by turning evidence against his partner." Now traffic was moving easily. The driver clucked to the horses, and Hardy continued his narrative to the accompaniment of the clip-clop of shod hooves on pavement. "Him I was telling you about at the Exhibition the other day that burked all those poor beggars—poetic justice, my granny'd call it. He weaseled off to London after Burke's hanging, but some construction workers caught him and administered their own form of justice—threw him in a vat of lime. He got out, but left 'im blind. How what I say is—"

"Hardy, that is quite enough of your cautionary tales!" Danvers held up his hand. "This is our wedding day."

"And what better time to be thinking of the momentous destinies of life?"

In spite of the fact that her wedding had been leading Antonia to somewhat similar deep thoughts of late, she laughed now at the heavily solemn countenance that came over Danvers's man. His mercurial moods changed as quickly as the climate of his native Ireland.

The gleaming white columns of the Danvers home faced a leafy green square. The Ionic marble pillars were ringed with white-ribboned yew garlands, while pots of white tree roses, forced into bloom in a greenhouse, lined the portico in welcome to the bridal couple.

Upstairs in the first floor reception room, while a string quartet played Liszt from behind the potted palms at the far end of the room, the new Lady Danvers stood beside her husband and greeted their guests without the least hint of the impatience she felt to be off alone with him. They had had none of the quiet time together she had longed for in the days before their wedding. But now, quiet weeks in remote, rural Scotland spread before them.

Out of the corner of her eye Antonia glimpsed her gentle, gray-haired father, the baron of Breene, engaged in a seemingly cozy conversation with Danvers's tall, craggy-featured father, the earl of Norville. Undoubtedly her father was pursuing his passion and seeking to enlist another convert to the philosophy of Mr. John Stuart Mill. Norville seemed to be handling her father's zeal affably.

The earl was always the complete gentleman, perfectly at ease. And yet even now Antonia noted, as she had since she had come to know Danvers's father better, a stoop to his shoulders and a tightness around his eyes that indicated the earl of Norville bore certain worries.

"Antonia, how charming you look in your mother's wedding gown." Agatha, Charles's long-faced older sister, kissed the air beside Antonia's cheek. "You'll likely start a rage for wide-puffed sleeves and tight belts again." Agatha's own heliotrope satin gown was designed with the latest in long sleeves that spread to a fan just above the wrist and an up-to-the-minute, pointed-waist bodice. Agatha would

32

never be seen in less than the latest fashion, although she kept her daughters Susan and Mary in unbecomingly youthful styles. Antonia smiled at sixteen-year-old Susan, who bobbed a curtsy, making her long ringlets bounce.

But Agatha had more to say on this great family occasion. "And Saint George's was the perfect choice of churches. Of course, they always say that anyone who *is* anyone is married there. I created an absolute scandal when I chose Saint Marylebone, but then I always did think for myself, and I simply felt that the stigma left by Lady Hamilton—and that after the duchess of Kingston's bigamy trial—well, my dear, it just didn't seem quite the *thing* since they had been married there. Now, of course, with the duke of Wellington marrying off another niece at Saint George's every week—well, things are quite different, aren't they?"

"And how sweet Susan and Mary are looking," Antonia attempted.

"Yes, they are dear things. But of course, Arthur Emory will be going up to Oxford next year. I shall be quite desolate to lose my only son—but such is a mother's lot. And now that Charles will doubtless be producing an heir, Arthur knows he can't rely on his inheritance. Not that I begrudge a thing to any child of my brother's, you understand. But, my dear, when you are a mother you'll understand my heart."

Antonia smiled weakly and let her eyes rove the room. There were Margaret and Eleanor, Charles's delightful younger sisters, and his brother, Greville, who had just come down from Oxford for the day. Surely they could come rescue her from Agatha. Charles, whose closer duty it was, was suddenly conspicuously absent.

Then the sharp rap of a walking stick announced a newcomer. "That is quite enough of your jabbering on, Agatha. It is my turn to talk to Antonia now. I'm sure you've fatigued her quite beyond endurance as it is."

"Aunt Elfrida." Antonia turned gratefully to the dowager duchess of Aethelbert. She had seen the great lady in her high-necked lavender dress and high-coifed gray hair at the church but had no opportunity to speak to her earlier. "How good to see you, Your Grace."

"Humph. Quite so. And about time that care-for-nothing married you, Antonia."

"I wish you wouldn't call him that, Aunt Elfrida. He cares for quite a few things."

"And a good thing you're one of them. A tonic you've been for him, my dear, a tonic. But you can never be too careful where men are concerned. Just look at Norville." Antonia followed the dowager duchess's order and saw where her husband had disappeared to as well. He and his father were in a corner apart. Father and son, a tall, lean, perfectly tailored duo, bent toward one another. The earl spoke, his brow deeply furrowed, and the son nodded gravely. Norville drew a slim, black leather volume from his breast pocket and handed it to Danvers.

But such actions were not what concerned Her Grace. "A striped cravat. Whatever can he be thinking of? He wouldn't have gotten away with that when he danced with me at Almack's, I can tell you." When she turned with a sniff the brilliants and pearls encrusting the lace yoke of her dress sparkled in the light of the chandeliers. "And now Danvers tells me you're to honeymoon in Scotland. Why you should take a maggot into your heads to go off to foreign parts I can't imagine. Cold, dreary place. All they eat is oatmeal. And their national dish—cooked in a sheep's stomach—disgusting."

Antonia broke the monologue with laughter. "Aunt Elfrida, have you ever been there?"

"Once, my dear. Once. But it was quite enough to last a lifetime."

And the subject of the dowager duchess of Aethelbert's personal history was closed as she returned to the newlyweds' plans. "Since you seem quite set on it, however, you may as well take Gilchrist into hand while you're up there."

Antonia blinked with the struggle to keep up with the rapid shifts in conversation. "Er . . . Gilchrist?"

"My nephew. Gilchrist Morris—studying medicine at the University of Edinburgh. All nonsense, I say, when we have perfectly good universities in our own country. Why he should go up north to study with a lot of heathen I can't imagine."

"Hardly heathen, Aunt Elfrida." A blond, open-faced young man with bright blue eyes bowed over the dowager duchess's hand. "Edinburgh well lives up to its name 'Athens of the North.' For over a hundred years the University of Edinburgh has been the leading medical school in the world. And—I might add—I still hope for the honor of a tutorial from Monro *tertius,* grandson of the Father of the Edinburgh Medical School."

"Gilchrist. Where have you been? Impertinent young man." The dowager duchess peered at her nephew through her lorgnette. "Answering back to your betters is precisely what I should have expected from one living among barbarians."

"But Aunt Elfrida, aren't you going to introduce me to the bride? I believe we must be some sort of distant relation which is probably far too complicated to sort out."

"And which Antonia will never claim if she has half the sense I credit her with. But I suppose we must make allowances for your mother, Gilchrist. I told Osbert there would be trouble when he took a Scottish bride. Laird of Lochiel's daughter, indeed. It's just lucky the queen is so fond of things Scottish, or we'd be disgraced." She turned back to Antonia. "And mark my words, if this rapscallion doesn't mend his ways, we will be yet. See if you can talk sense to him, Antonia."

The dowager duchess swept off toward Danvers and his father, leaving Antonia to smile at the attractively shy Gilchrist. "I understand the weather is very chilly up north."

35

"Yes, it is, rather. But I never think of it. The people are absolutely top of the mark. Don't listen to Aunt Elfrida."

Antonia laughed. "I never do." Then she noted the slight blush on Gilchrist's cheek. "Oh, did you mean people in general or a certain person in particular?"

The blush deepened, and the blue eyes twinkled.

"Well, how very interesting. I must find an opportunity for you to present her to me when we're in Scotland. And what is the young lady's name?" Antonia added as an afterthought, since Gilchrist appeared quite tongue-tied.

"Oh, name—yes. Madelyn—Madelyn Raeburn."

"Madelyn. Very pretty." But Antonia frowned in the back of her mind. Why should the girl's name ring an uneasy note?

Then all thought of relatives near or distant, difficult or charming, was swept from Antonia's head. All except thought of her newest and dearest—her husband. The string quartet began "The Emperor Waltz," and Charles swept his bride to the center of the floor.

Toasts by each of the fathers and by Danvers's brother were followed by a response from the groom. Then more dancing, and dining from the sumptuous buffet set in the adjoining room. Antonia was having a final dance with her new father-in-law, who in his day had been a far better dancer than his son—in spite of his slight limp from wounds received at Waterloo—when she saw Hardy deliver a message to Danvers. Charles consulted the gold watch he pulled from his vest pocket, then nodded to his man.

At the end of the dance, he claimed his bride. "Hardy reminds me with a certain urgency that we must be off if we are to catch our train north. He has our cases in the carriage."

Antonia gave a fond final embrace to both their fathers and a dutiful hug to Agatha, then turned to go.

"And you may kiss me," a crisp voice behind her said.

36

Antonia and in a full voice, only slightly off-key, sang the lover's aria from *The Marriage of Figaro.*

Antonia smiled even as her eyes filled with tears. The dowager duchess had been right—she was a tonic for this complicated, wonderful man. It seemed such a short time ago that he had indulged his passion for opera with only the somberest tunes. As the song came to its lilting, jubilant conclusion, she held out her arms.

Radiant, with the wind ruffling her veil and coils of auburn hair hanging in tendrils around her face, she grasped his hands. "I take thee, Charles Frederick Arthur Emory of Danvers, to my wedded husband, to have and to hold—very tightly forevermore!"

4

Oh, what a beautiful city!" Antonia smoothed the folds of the simple dove gray traveling dress that had been in the case Hardy rescued for her and looked out over Edinburgh. It didn't seem possible that so much could have happened to her in less than twenty-four hours. And yet, there was her dear Charles surveying this lovely scene beside her, so it must be true.

The excitement of their escape from London in a balloon . . . the quiet early evening journey above the spring green English fields and pastures . . . the relief of catching their scheduled train . . . followed by the surprise of discovering that, instead of the first-class compartment she had expected, Danvers had laid on an entire private car for their wedding journey . . . and now this breathtaking sight.

It had been a perfect journey in spite of the fact that, contrary to her expectations, they had talked little. After his initial outburst of high spirits, Charles had been quiet, even to the point of seeming worried, and yet he was always the kind, thoughtful man she loved. It was undoubtedly her growing love that made her increasingly sensitive to his moods and produced this groundless concern.

"Edinburgh Castle." Danvers pointed across the vast green ravine that sloped from the south side of Princes

Street, where they stood, to a mammoth stone castle atop a great volcanic stone precipice. Carriages rattled along the cobbled street behind them. To their right rose the two-hundred feet high, Gothic-spired monument Edinburgh had erected only thirteen years before to their most beloved citizen, Sir Walter Scott. "Only two hundred eighty-seven steps to the top. Would you care to ascend, or shall we continue our journey?"

They had breakfasted in the elegant, red plush comfort of their railway car, sipping coffee served steaming from a silver pot and ladling tangy marmalade onto crisp toast, but already Antonia was thinking of the distance they still had to cover before they ate again. "Another time, perhaps."

Danvers took a few more moments to direct her gaze a mile to the east beyond the castle. "You can't see it from here, but Holyrood Palace is that way. Last year Her Majesty spent several days there on her way to Balmoral."

Antonia held up a gloved hand to shade her eyes. Her sunshade was in one of the cases Hardy was to bring. She had an impression of a pointed green mountain rising above craggy rocks just beyond the place Charles indicated.

Danvers followed her gaze. "Arthur's Seat, I believe they call that. George the Fourth rescued it from destruction by the earl of Haddington, who quarried there for road metal."

Antonia laughed. "What an amazing wealth of information you are."

"Haddington was one of my father's Edinburgh acquaintances. Father spent some time up here as a young man. I understand Haddington did very well selling the park to the government, but he complained about it to his dying day."

Antonia turned, still shaking her head in amazement at Danvers's widespread connections.

Charles handed her into the carriage he had hired to take them to their retreat on the shores of Loch Leven. Then they rolled along Queensferry Road through little villages

43

of tile-roofed, stone houses set right alongside the narrow, cobbled road. Russet and brown chickens squawked and flapped away from the approaching vehicle, but the frequently encountered herds of cows, some driven by young girls and some by old women, continued their measured, leisurely pace, moving no faster than a London traffic jam. And then on to stretches of lush green countryside where farmers strode through their new-turned fields, casting seeds for the summer growing, as their wives and children followed behind shooing the hungry birds.

At last they reached the shining, blue Firth of Forth, dotted with tall-masted ships, and beyond that the green points of the Lomond Hills. From the ferry Tonia also noted the many islands in the estuary. They sailed by a tiny one entirely covered with a building. "Oh, that looks interesting. What is it?" she asked the ferryman.

"Ach, that's naught but Inch Garvie. But now Inchcolm, a wee bit over there"—he pointed to the east—"is a fine sight indeed. An auld abbey, some say of the blessed Saint Columba himself."

Tonia clapped her hands. "Oh, I'd love to see that."

"Well then, you shall, my love," Danvers spoke in her ear. "I shall take you one day."

She smiled at him, and they stood at the rail, while the sea breeze ruffled their hair and gulls called above their heads.

Once the ferry deposited them on the north shore and they began their journey into the Kingdom of Fife, Antonia felt she was entering another world. Here it was somehow greener, more distantly rural, older and closer to the earth than English farms and fields. Birds sang from the forest; the carriage rattled over narrow, arched, stone bridges that crossed rivers rushing over rocky beds; and Antonia leaned deep into the padded cushions of the seat and sighed with pleasure.

Only rarely on the journey, at such quiet moments as these, did the disturbing scene she had witnessed in Hyde

Park niggle at the back of her mind. But each time that occurred, as now, she shooed it away, unwilling to have their idyll intruded upon by disturbing thoughts.

As they traveled, the earlier so-sparkling sun dimmed and disappeared behind clouds that were at first white, then a threatening gray. Their estimated twelve miles from the firth stretched to fifteen and fifteen onwards as the carriage wound again and yet again around curving country roads arched over with beech and sycamore boughs while the darker, less-branching Scots pine and holly filled in the background. It was a good thing Antonia had chosen not to climb the Scott Monument, for it would be a very late luncheon, indeed, that awaited them at Loch Leven Lodge.

The threatened rain never made its appearance, but a slight moistness, too gentle to be called a mist, filled the air and freshened Antonia's cheeks. At last they rounded a curve, rolled down a short hill, and the blue-gray waters of Loch Leven spread before them. The loch was edged with grasses and trees, and a more substantial mist than that in the air hung over its far shore, where green hills rose. And to their left lay the welcoming, sturdy brownstone walls of their honeymoon retreat.

Their host, Sir Graham Grahame, another of Norville's connections from younger, wilder days, must have been watching for them, because he came striding across the smooth green lawn that ran down to the loch. Wearing tweeds and deerstalker, he looked a natural part of the scene. His thick, russet sideburns were almost met by a swooping red mustache, a style that would have been hopelessly out of fashion in London but seemed perfectly suited here where the mountains were higher, the rocks more craggy, and the gardens less pruned. "Welcome, welcome. And come ye in." He extended a hand in greeting.

When they entered the broad front hall of the lodge, lined with dark wainscoting and hung with hunting trophies, Antonia expected to be turned over to the services

45

of a butler or lady's maid, but apparently Sir Graham Grahame ran his bachelor lodge with a minimal staff. He led them up the heavy, wooden staircase himself.

The top of the stairs opened onto a broad landing, which their host crossed, and he threw open a door onto a huge suite containing a bed almost as massive as that in the Scottish exhibit. But fortunately the heavy carving of this headboard concealed no hidden trunks—or anything more ominous yet. Indeed, the room could not have been more perfect for its bucolic setting. The wide, polished floorboards were carpeted with a rug woven in several shades of green and rose, a theme picked up in the heavy draperies that bordered windows looking out over the loch.

"Take your time settling in." Their host looked doubtfully at Antonia's single case, then repeated heartily, "Take your time."

Danvers hurriedly explained what had happened to their luggage.

"Och, that's an excellent story! Excellent story. Well, take your time. The meal is ready when you are. Our Scottish air will give you an appetite."

Antonia had little more to do than wash her hands, remove her bonnet, and smooth her hair before she was ready to accompany her husband back down to the dark-paneled dining room just beyond the entrance hall. Here the walls were decorated with double rows of oil paintings featuring fish and fowl in fields and on sideboards, interspersed with pastoral scenes of cows in pastures and majestic views of mist-draped, heather-covered, towering mountains unlike any Antonia knew in England.

Their host was as good as his word. Their repast was indeed ready for them. The entire table was spread with a confusing assortment of sausages, cheeses, Scotch eggs, roast fowl and beef, oatcakes, wheat bread, and fruitcake. Antonia felt that if this were a typical meal it would certainly be necessary for the Scottish air to produce a prodigious appetite if she were to do justice to their host's table.

46

When his guests were seated, Sir Graham Grahame stood at the head of the table, clasped his hands in front of his chest, and in his usual hearty voice addressed his heavenly Father. The God of the universe was thanked in ringing tones for everything on the table, for everything on Sir Graham's estate, for everything in Fife, for everything in Scotland. Antonia was beginning to suspect that it wasn't the Scottish air, but rather the length of the prayers, that developed one's appetite when he came to an ardent finish, thanking the Divine for the presence, safe journey, and blessed marriage of Lord and Lady Danvers, the children of his old friend who must be blessed as well.

"Now eat up, eat up," he admonished. "And take your time. Plenty of time to enjoy all God's gifts here. Take your time."

The meal progressed as they were served by Molly, a rose-cheeked, freckle-nosed girl with reddish-gold locks slipped under the starched crispness of her lawn cap.

Steaming pots of tea and bowls of tangy, dark red raspberries with a pitcher of thick cream ended the meal.

Tonia remarked in surprise at raspberries so early in the year.

"One of my bachelor indulgences is a little hothouse. Our country pleasures are simple but not to be scorned, I think."

After several scoops of the excellent berries, Grahame set his spoon aside, pushed his chair back from the table, and folded his hands over his tweed-vested chest. "Now, Danvers, you must be telling me about your father. Always I hoped he'd come up for the fishing and shooting —keep his crusty old friend some company—but he had his new bride in the south, and then his family duties, and after the unhappiness here—but you wouldn't be knowing about that. Long ago—all long ago . . . Still, it's a great joy to me to have ye young ones at my lodge."

He came abruptly to his feet. "Now, nothing to follow that meal like a good brisk walk. Our evening air is

47

almost as fine as early morning. Heavier, often wetter, but fine. Invigorating."

Antonia was getting the impression that everything in Scotland was invigorating.

"I told Cook to set dinner back, so no hurry. Take your time—plenty of time."

Antonia also hoped everything would be as unhurried as was their host's philosophy of life.

"Or would you prefer a row? Saint Serf's island is just at the end of the loch." Grahame waved with a gesture that indicated miles of water covered in the briefest—yet unhurried—amount of time.

Antonia looked doubtful.

"Quite right. Quite right. Save the row for morning. Before breakfast, perhaps. Lovely on the loch then. Fish jumping everywhere. Loch Leven trout—premiere sport fishing in Scotland. Best angling in the world here. In the world." He turned from the window. "Nothing else like it. But yes, a nice stroll for now. To the kirkyard, I'd suggest." He gestured out the left of the window along the lakeshore. "Perfect view of Loch Leven Castle from there. Mary Queen of Scots imprisoned there, you know. That's where she was forced to abdicate in favor of her son James. Then she made a daring escape. One of the servants got the keys of the castle to her under a serviette at dinner. They had a boat waiting to take her across the loch after dark. Brave. Very brave thing to do." He coughed. "Course, it was rather ruined by the fact that she chose to throw herself on the mercy of Queen Elizabeth after that. Still, brave lady— poor, brave lady."

Poor, silly lady, Antonia thought, but she held her tongue.

"Well, off you go then."

The honeymooners looked at their host questioningly.

"Oh, don't you worry, I'll not be intruding on your lovers' stroll." His mustache bobbed as he laughed. "You two young things go off and enjoy yourselves. And take your time."

Antonia slipped to her room to gather her shawl and bonnet. She was just wishing for a sturdier pair of shoes when Molly knocked at her door.

The maid bobbed a curtsy. "Begging your pardon, but Sir Graham thought . . ." Molly blushed as she indicated the ladies' boots she held. "I'm sorry. They are awfully out of style. But as your cases haven't arrived . . ."

Tonia thanked her warmly, not taking time to wonder where Sir Graham should have acquired a pair of lady's boots. She was ready for her stroll in a moment.

And so they walked, hand-in-hand, across the late-day grass that still felt morning-dew fresh underfoot. Tonia took in great breaths of the wonderful air and felt her cheeks glow. She knew she'd never been happier. And yet—it was her very happiness that brought uneasiness.

At the edge of the groomed lawn they picked up a narrow, curving dirt lane that took them to the peaceful kirkyard sleeping under its beech and pine. In the center of the yard, on a slight knoll, rose the brownstone church with its solid, square tower and slate roof, looking as if it had grown on that spot as naturally as any of the trees or hills surrounding it. They walked a zigzag path around the graves to the low stone wall that bordered the churchyard only a few yards from the lapping waters of the loch. A hardy crop of thistles grew in the sandy soil beyond the wall, and from the steely waters the promised Loch Leven trout jumped for low-flying insects.

The castle from which Mary Queen of Scots made her daring, ill-fated escape when she was no longer queen lay low and solid, surrounded by vegetation and desolation. The sun had now abandoned any attempt to fight against the gray damp of a misty evening that would soon be upon them.

Tonia shivered, and Danvers drew her closer into the circle of his arm. "Shall I take you in? You mustn't take a chill—" Suddenly his arm tightened around her with urgency. "Oh, Tonia—"

She knew immediately what he feared—he was remembering the lovely Charlotte, their mutual friend, Danvers's first betrothed, for whose death he had so long blamed himself until they learned the truth.

She lifted her head and placed a kiss in the hollow of his cheek. "No fear, my love. I have no intention of leaving you." She felt the tiniest hesitation. "But I would like to talk. Perhaps a more sheltered spot?"

Charles pulled her back from the dampness of the loch and led their steps to the right toward a little house built against the wall, overlooking the graveyard.

Tonia glanced at the stone monuments as they walked among them. The name on a particularly fine one with double marble urns caught her attention. "Jonet Grahame and infant daughter. That must be a relative of our host."

Danvers nodded and gestured toward many stones bearing the Grahame name. "An old family hereabouts, I believe."

He tried the door of the little house and found it unlocked. The door creaked on rusty hinges as he opened it. The room was bare save for two wooden chairs and a straight-backed bench, but the kindling and coal in the small fireplace were dry. In a short time he had a low blaze going.

Antonia looked around. "What a strange place. What is it?"

"A watch house." Charles drew her to the bench before the fire. "Built late last century, I'd guess. Families used places like this to keep watch on the graves of their loved ones to guard them against the resurrectionists."

"Resurrectionists?"

"Grave robbers, sack 'em up men, as they were called. Big business hereabouts—digging up freshly buried bodies and selling them to the anatomy professors in Edinburgh. Biggest medical school in Britain—all students were

50

required to attend at least two dissections in order to qualify for their degree, and yet it was almost impossible to come by bodies legally, so . . ."

"So they set out to rob graves, and families went on the watch to protect their own."

"They tried to. It didn't work very well, though. People couldn't live by a grave all the time, so the body-snatchers slipped in before the watchers arrived—or waited until they left."

"I guess that's the way of it, isn't it—in the end we really can't do a lot about the momentous things of life. Oh, we like to think we can—isn't that what the Great Exhibition is all about? How powerful we are and how in control of our destiny—steam engines, model housing—"

"Beds with built-in trunks?" Charles attempted a note of lightness, but it was lost in Tonia's shiver. "Oh, my dear, have I upset you by referring to that unfortunate scene?"

"No, you know I've always prided myself on having a strong constitution. But it has set me to thinking—or increased the thinking I'd already been doing. I think it's really you, my dearest love, the great joy we've found together, having so much, that makes me realize how much I have to lose. And here, in the midst of a graveyard, I'm so reminded of how tenuous it all is in spite of our great industrial strength."

She settled into the curve of Charles's arm as he said, "I suppose that was part of the great horror people had of resurrectionists and dissection. Especially up here. The Scots have always held a strong, literal belief in the resurrection of the body at the final judgment—and woe betide anyone who dares shatter the peace of the grave, no matter how unpeaceful life may have been."

Antonia rested her head on his shoulder and made encouraging noises for him to continue.

He did. "A rather alarming example of that is the butcher Davis who stabbed his wife to death, then blurted out to the constables, 'I have killed the best wife in the

51

world, and I'm certain of being hanged, but for goodness sake don't let me be anatomized!'"

Tonia nodded. "Yes, so incongruous it's humorous, yet how many commit less violent acts every day that still endanger their immortal souls while they are preoccupied with material things that will molder into dust?" After a moment's pause she slipped her hand into Charles's. "It shouldn't surprise me, my love, because you always seem to know everything, but you are remarkably well-informed on this resurrectionist topic."

She meant it as a compliment. She was surprised that her words should bring a gauntness into his face and that he should draw away from her. "Charles, did I say something wrong? When I said earlier that realizing how much we have makes me realize how much we have to lose, I didn't mean—oh, I don't know—I think I'm just afraid of not being grateful enough. Anyway—" she forced a smile "—anxiety for the future isn't what one is supposed to feel on their honeymoon, is it? Especially when one has the bravest, strongest, most intelligent husband in the world."

He regarded her for a moment, then returned her smile. "Don't forget most handsome and possessed of the best singing voice."

She laughed. "Indeed, my love, life is much changed. We have had many good effects on each other." She thought fleetingly of how in the past two years he had come to smile more, and she had put off her frivolous facade; of how he had renewed his faith, and she had found a new joy in hers. But some things didn't change. "My love, I will grant that you sing more. But you still don't sing on key."

He muffled her laughter with a kiss, and her unease was stilled—until she realized that he had sung only once on their honeymoon.

52

5

Two mornings later the honeymooners lingered over porridge and oatcakes in the small breakfast room off their suite, indulging thoroughly in Sir Graham's urging to take their time. Antonia shook back the deep, creamy lace sleeves of her peach silk morning gown and poured Danvers's third cup of coffee.

Hardy had arrived the evening before with the full complement of trousseau luggage, and Antonia reveled in changing from the very limited wardrobe that had accompanied her on their impromptu balloon ascent. She knew that the rich tones of the gown brought out the best of the amber highlights in her hair, hanging in ringlets over each cheek, and that the luxuriant lace draping her shoulders enhanced the ivory purity of her skin. And that none of the effect was lost on her husband.

She handed him his cup and smiled at the pleasure she felt when their hands touched, until the mood was broken by a small rap at the door.

Molly, crisp in white starched cap and apron, but with springy wisps of hair escaping around her plump cheeks, entered with a bobbed curtsy. "Sorry I am to be bothering you, but the young lady seemed so distressed, and she said Sir Graham wouldn't be doing for her at all,

53

thank you—even if I were to fetch him in from the loch with your Mr. Hardy—which I'd be more than happy to do with just a ringing of the bell if you thought—"

"Molly" —Danvers broke her flow— "what young lady?"

"Just knocked at the door, she did. Arrived in a frightful flurry all the way from Edinburgh this morning. Doesn't seem possible—must have started before daylight." Molly held out a small silver tray.

Danvers took the card and turned it over. "Madelyn Raeburn."

Antonia wrinkled her forehead, reaching for a memory, then gasped. "The weaver?"

Molly nodded. "Raeburn Woolen Mills. Very fine. Everybody's heard of them."

A second memory brought Antonia to her feet. "Oh, *Madelyn.*" She turned to Danvers. "That's Gilchrist's young lady. By all means, we'll see her."

Apparently the young lady had followed Molly onto the first floor landing, because she was before them in seconds. In spite of the girl's obvious distress, a sweetness of manner prevented her forcing her way. Smooth, dark brown hair showed beneath the deep brim of her lace-trimmed, lavender bonnet and framed the creamy skin of her round face. The bonnet's satin bow, tied just under her left ear accented the point of her perky chin. Rich brown eyes flashed intelligence but were quickly covered by thick lashes as apparently the alarm that had brought her on her anxious errand returned.

Antonia was drawn to her immediately. She took the girl's hand and led her into the room. "Refreshment for Miss Raeburn, Molly. Tea, I should think."

"I'm so sorry to intrude on you—a stranger imposing on your honeymoon—quite unforgivable, I know, but Gil . . . er . . . Mr. Morris said—" Madelyn choked a sob.

"You were quite right to come if you have need." Tonia motioned the girl to a chair. "Gilchrist spoke to me of you. I told him he should present you, but I had no idea—"

"No! No one could have had any idea. Never in a hundred years could anyone imagine . . ." She began fumbling in the folds of her skirt and cape for her reticule.

Danvers produced a large silk handkerchief from his breast pocket, and the fumbling stopped with a grateful nod and a glance of appealing, upturned dark eyes. In a moment she was composed again.

"Now, try to explain it all to us," Antonia encouraged.

"Gilchrist. He came back on the train yesterday. It was lovely to see him, even though he'd been gone for only a few days. You see, we're—we're very good friends . . ."

"I quite understand. Please go on."

"Well, last night a policeman arrived from London. It seems he had *followed* Gil all the way from London. And when Gil came straight to see me the sergeant marched him right off for questioning. He said the queen was involved."

"You mean Gil was *arrested?*" Antonia asked.

"No." Suddenly the dark eyes widened in a new alarm, then the lashes covered them. "No, I'm sure he wasn't. I think the officer took him to his lodging in the Meadows and questioned him most severely there. The police seem to think Gil had something to do with some man that died in the Crystal Palace."

"Did the officer accuse him?" Danvers asked.

Madelyn shook her head doubtfully. "I think he just warned him not to leave town. But I'm so afraid. It could happen any time."

The tea tray arrived, and Antonia gave the girl a well-brewed cup fortified with milk and sugar, then nodded for her to continue.

"That's all I really know. This morning a lad from the Meadows that often carries notes for Gil arrived just at dawn. Gil didn't know who else to turn to. Papa will be furious if there is trouble with the police—it's so bad for business." She held out a lengthy, crumpled missive. "Gil said I should try to get this to you."

Danvers took it and smoothed the folds. He looked up after a moment of reading. "Oh, I see. I wondered how he knew to direct you here. Apparently he overheard Aunt Elfrida upbraiding my father on the unsuitability of our honeymoon location, so he knew where to find us—lucky thing, that." He read further. "Yes, I should think implication in a murder charge would damage his incipient medical career. Hmm, heard all about the matter we cleared up at Stanfield Hall, hopes we can help him . . ."

"Well, we must, of course." Antonia was already on her feet. Then she paused. "But what does he mean—murder? I thought Sir Sidney was certain that poor man died by misadventure."

"It was quite clear that's what he wanted it to be." Danvers turned the note over. "Gil doesn't explain. Well, I suppose we must see what can be made of this."

Madelyn took a wavery, deep breath. "I'm so sorry—on your honeymoon and all. But I'm very grateful."

Antonia was already moving toward her dressing room. She spared only a few seconds for a look at the loch. Midday sun was shining on it, making the gray waters a deep blue. Yellow wildflowers bloomed in the long grass by the shore, and two white butterflies flitted by. But duty clearly lay in Edinburgh.

Tonia did, however, find herself with an excuse for one last visit to the loch. She volunteered to go ring Molly's bell that would bring Hardy and Grahame in from their fishing. A bright patch of wallflowers scented the air as she entered a small thicket of trees, lifting her skirts so as not to snag her petticoats on the thick underbrush.

Antonia was just reflecting on how lovely it was to be there alone when a tall figure appearing suddenly in front of her surprised her so that the bell jangled in her hand. "Charles . . !" she began, then felt foolish when the man turned.

The tall, slim figure was a match for her husband's, but the reddish hair, aquiline nose, and ready smile bore little resemblance to Danvers. He removed his tweed cap. "Ross Dalkeith, ma'am. Sir Graham's factor. May I be of service?"

"I've come to fetch the fishermen." She indicated the bell in her hand.

"Allow me."

She yielded the bell to his long fingers and returned the smile in his kind eyes. Then with a lingering farewell look at the loch, she turned toward their waiting brougham.

On the long journey back to Edinburgh, Antonia attempted to take Madelyn's mind off her distress by engaging her in conversation about her life there.

The girl responded with enthusiasm. "Oh, Edinburgh's very fine. In New Town, that is, of course. Papa doesn't allow us to go to Old Town at all—except to worship at Saint Giles."

"And right he is, I'm thinking." Hardy, who had returned from fishing on the loch in time to see his duty to go to Edinburgh, bobbed his head in approval. "Sir Graham was telling me only this morning that twenty percent of the people died there in the plague—but there's one close where one hundred percent of them just turned up their toes—like they were glad to be getting out of their miserable existence." Warming to his story, he leaned forward on his seat beside Madelyn. "The magistrates ordered it sealed off—but there's always one as won't listen to reason. There was one man and his wife who laughed off the warnings that were for their own good." Hardy accompanied his story with appropriate gestures. "Sitting reading their Bible on a Sunday afternoon they were. Suddenly the candlelight turned blue. Then a head appeared —suspended above the table. Then a naked arm holding a lamp. And ghostly, dancing feet . . ." Hardy's feet moved in a tapping rhythm.

Tonia turned to rebuke her husband's irrepressible man, then saw the flicker of amusement in Madelyn's eyes. "Oh, and for sure. I fear your good Scots host has been having a wee bit of fun."

"No, no. He swears to it."

"Well, yes, but that's all imaginings, long ago. Did he not tell you the story of our more recent ghost—the young woman of good family who was . . . er . . . disgraced, and perished in a suspicious fire in the Canongate?"

Hardy shook his head, and Miss Raeburn continued. "The house was rebuilt in the middle of the last century. Again it caught fire. A young woman dressed in the fashion of a hundred years earlier was seen among the flames crying, 'Once burned, twice burned, the third time I'll scare you all!'" Madelyn held out her arms in ghostly fashion.

Hardy slapped his knee in delight at the story, and Antonia relaxed. Gilchrist's Madelyn was not the shrinking violet Tonia had at first feared. The girl's tremors had been from concern for Gil's welfare, not from an attack of the vapors. Indeed, as the carriage rolled on over seemingly endless miles of rutted roads, Tonia, who had urged her to remain at Loch Leven Lodge and rest before attempting a return journey, increased her respect for Madelyn's stamina. Only after the party dined at a rustic, but adequate, inn at South Queensferry did the girl allow herself to sink into the corner cushions and doze.

It was some time later, when the carriage rolled over a rut in the road, that Madelyn sat up suddenly as if startled. "Dougal MacTavish!"

Tonia blinked. "What? Were you dreaming?"

"Oh." Madelyn put a gloved hand to her cheek. "No, not dreaming. I just suddenly thought. It hadn't occurred to me before. Dougal—I wonder if he could be behind this trouble Gil's in. He's the man I'd have to marry if it weren't for Gil. Even so, Papa may well insist, I'm sure, but he goes more carefully because he knows I care for Gil."

"And do you think this MacTavish might try to make trouble?"

Madelyn nodded. "He's very—sly—that's the word. And he's even more determined than Papa to have the businesses combined. You see, the MacTavishes have more sheep in the highlands than the duke of Argyll. Combining that with our woolen mill would make Dougal ever so rich and powerful. He'd like that a very great deal."

Danvers joined in the conversation. "Where is this MacTavish now?"

"He's an advocate in Edinburgh, but he spends a lot of time on his family lands in Argyll and some island of theirs too."

An exceedingly rough patch of road interrupted the conversation as all were obliged to hold onto their seats.

When the way smoothed out, Madelyn continued. "You see, the mill was originally the MacTavishes'—in our grandfathers' time. Of course, it wasn't really a mill then —just a lot of very skilled weavers who worked at wooden looms in their crofts. Grandpapa won the crofts from Mac-Tavish in a card game, so then the weavers worked for him. It's said they loomed the best tartan in Scotland— brightest dyes, every warp and woof woven straight. Strong fiber that would never wear out. So when Papa decided to build a modern mill, he moved the weavers to Leith."

"So it wasn't ever really the MacTavishes' mill."

"Not really, but the weavers were MacTavish people —part of the clan, you see."

Being English, Antonia didn't really see, but she nodded anyway.

Madelyn, her earlier sleepiness apparently upon her again, closed her eyes and sank into a corner of the carriage.

The girl had traveled a total of nearly sixteen hours that day when at last the carriage pulled up before the classic, Georgian exterior of a home in Charlotte Square. The moment the brougham wheels slowed on the cobbles she was fully awake, ready to be handed from the closed carriage by a servant who had apparently been keeping careful watch.

She smiled at her guests as she led the way up the iron-railed, stone stairs. "I hope you will be comfortable. I fear Papa may be . . . may be Papa."

They had no more than stepped onto the fine, glazed tiles of the entrance hall than Papa descended the stairs of the inner hall and flung open the dark, wooden double doors separating the two chambers. "And so. There it is you are, miss." Thick gray muttonchops worked at the sides of his square jaw, and his bull-like shoulders hunched while his pale blue eyes glowered.

Madelyn tripped forward and planted a light kiss on the cheek just forward of his right sideburn. "I knew you'd be happy to see me, Papa. And I've brought the most charming guests." She turned with a flourish. "Lord and Lady Danvers, may I present Mr. Harold Raeburn."

The shoulders hunched again, and the bull snorted. But manners won the day. "Lord Danvers, Lady Danvers. Welcome to the house of Raeburn. Ye'll take refreshment?" He didn't wait for their reply. "See to their luggage, Jeffers." Hardy and the Raeburn servant both turned to do his bidding.

Raeburn turned back up the stairs he had so recently descended. Good, honest Scottish stone stairs, unnecessary to cover with carpet, especially as they received so much wear. "I'll leave you to explain matters to your mother, my miss." Raeburn's gravelly voice accompanied his daughter's entrance into the drawing room.

Mrs. Raeburn's pale gray hair was tucked neatly under a lace cap so delicate it was hard to tell where the lace lappets left off and her own pale skin began. She pushed an imaginary strand of hair under the beribboned flounce, then smoothed the skirt of her soft blue moiré gown, which might have looked faded had not the color so obviously been chosen to match the paleness of her blue eyes.

She kissed her daughter on both cheeks. "My dear, you've been gone an extraordinarily long time. Did you have a nice drive in the country? Moraig said you would. Although why you didn't take her with you I can't imagine. Gallivanting off without your maid simply isn't done, and your father has a position to uphold."

"Flanders is a fine coachman, Mama. He was all the escort I needed. I left Moraig for your comfort. I knew you wanted her to help wind your yarns today. Did you get on well?"

"Quite well, thank you, dear. But it is fatiguing work. Oh—" Mrs. Raeburn looked beyond her daughter and peered vaguely at the newcomers behind her "—oh, do forgive me. Whatever must you think? I did not realize we had visitors as well. My, such excitement all in one day. Come in, please come in."

Madelyn performed the introductions, and Raeburn returned from instructing his butler on the provisions to be made for their guests' refreshment.

In a few moments the rich Oriental carpet covering the heavily carved oak sideboard was spread with a selection of oatcakes and bannocks, cheeses and jellies, cold meats and molded macaronis accompanied by a tea tray further laden with shortbreads and sweetmeats and a side tray of stronger drink for the men. Once again the fabled Scottish hospitality had triumphed.

Madelyn played her trump card in winning Harry Raeburn to her visitors, however, when she asked Lord Danvers to recount his ballooning experiences for her father. Raeburn was hearty in his approval of Danvers's adventures. "And did ye know that the first ever ascent in Britain was made right here in Edinburgh?"

Indeed, Danvers did not.

"Aye, but so it was—our own Jamie Tytler—in that spare ground just beyond Holyrood Palace. Did it in a balloon of his own handiwork. Set a fire in his gondola to heat the air just like the Montgolfier brothers. Only trouble was the fellow couldn't make all the heat go upwards to the air in the balloon—het up his own pants pretty good too."

Raeburn paused for a sip of port. "Got hot enough to do the trick at any rate. Shot up into the air three hundred feet and traveled half a mile," he finished with a satisfied air. "Yes, sir. You'd think that family would have learned its lesson by now, but you'll still see Tytler cousins or nephews messing about with flying contraptions off Arthur's Seat. They'll get killed someday."

It was as well that Harry Raeburn enjoyed his tale, for Moraig's entrance the next moment did not bring him pleasure. "There's a person to see you, sir." She stepped aside to reveal Inspector Futter standing, hat in hand, cheeks redder than ever and hair looking paler than ever in the light of the oil lamps and fire flickering on the marble hearth.

Raeburn glowered from beneath his shaggy eyebrows. "Confound it! A policeman in a fellow's own home." He came to his feet, head forward and shoulders hunched. "I'll have you know this is a respectable Scots household. We have no truck with lawbreakers or those who deal with them."

Futter turned his hat around in his hands. "Inspector Futter, Scotland Yard. Sorry to bother you, Mr. Raeburn— and your family—most sorry. I just have a few questions, if you could be so kind. It's because I know you are law-abiding that I've taken the . . . er . . . liberty to call."

As his speech petered out, Danvers filled in the gap. "Mr. Raeburn, perhaps you would allow me to vouch for my acquaintance here. Or perhaps I'm the one you came to see, Futter?" As unlikely as that seemed, it was a happy suggestion, for it shifted the stigma from Raeburn.

Futter instantly took up the cue. "Thank you, m'lord. If you could allow me to intrude on your evening . . ."

Futter refused Raeburn's offer of port but smiled gratefully at the cup of tea Mrs. Raeburn poured for him.

"I take it this is about that incident at the Exhibition," Danvers prompted.

Futter nodded.

"But I thought that was all cleared up—unhappy accident and all that."

"That's what we hoped, sir. But seems some insolent reporter fellow got wind of it. You'd think, with all the Great Exhibition stirring London, the blighter could have found something better to write about." He produced three broadsheets from the leather folder he carried under one arm: the banner "Caledonian Commotion, Her Majesty Shocked" ran across the top of the first sheet. "The Strange Case of the Scottish Corpse," another read.

"Got my orders to clear it up." Futter shrugged. "If it can be cleared. Do my best—all I can do."

"Yes, yes. Man has to do his duty," Raeburn growled. "But why here, man? What are ye doin' here?" There was no doubt that Harry Raeburn did not inquire as to Futter's presence in Scotland in general but in his drawing room.

"I understand your company made the hangings for the bed in the Scottish exhibit."

"Well, of course, and who else would be making them but Harry Raeburn, I'm asking you? Fine piece of work—Royal Victoria. Best ever milled, finest mohair, soft as down. Good enough for royalty."

"Quite so, I'm sure, sir. But it's the other pattern we're inquiring about."

"Other pattern? Nonsense. Only one sett used. Like I said—Royal Victoria. Nothing else. Tell you what—call in at my mill tomorrow. I'll have my foreman show you all there is to know about weaving the finest Scottish wool the world has ever seen. That satisfy you?"

"Well, not quite, sir." Futter pressed ahead. He held out another paper. "Tartan Shroud Cloaks Mystery," it proclaimed. The news sheet was quickly followed by a pattern card reproducing the distinctive heather-colored design. "This was taken from the . . . er . . . winding-sheet. Afraid it's all we have. The original was somehow . . . er . . . misplaced. I'm just following the tartan trail, as you might say."

Everyone turned at Madelyn's gasp. "My birthday tartan!" She crossed the room and took the sample from Futter. "It was my special design. No one was even supposed to see it until my twenty-first party. What was it doing in London?"

More and more, that was what Antonia, who accompanied Futter to the entrance hall with Danvers, wanted to know. And especially, what had Gilchrist been doing with the tartan shroud in Hyde Park?

6

That apparently was what Futter, who had grilled all the Crystal Palace guards after he discovered the disappearance of the belatedly important length of fabric, wanted to know too. And why he had tracked his one lead—Gilchrist —all the way to Edinburgh and questioned him, somewhat unsatisfactorily, at the crack of dawn of what had been a very long day indeed.

It had been a day that led to many questions and no answers. For want of a better name, the subject had been dubbed "the tartaned corpse" and was duly delivered to the authorities of this city from whence he had apparently come. But no one had identified him yet or reported a suitable missing person. He had been sketched and examined, and, since nothing more was to be learned from him, tomorrow he would be delivered to Surgeon's Hall at Edinburgh University for the benefit of the anatomy students.

And Futter would continue to grope and probe. "But I'd sure be thankful to know what I'm looking for." He plunked his hat on his head and went out into the night.

In spite of their long day there were no lie-abeds in the Raeburn household the next morning. The larks were just breaking into song in Charlotte Square when the maid

65

knocked at the Danvers's chamber with their morning coffee. And Antonia's cup was still half full when the next gentle knocking announced Madelyn's call.

The girl must have been up for ages. Already she was perfectly groomed and gowned in a cotton day dress of a blue and green flowered pattern, its crisply tailored shoulder tucks softened by a round lace collar. "I am sorry to hurry you, I don't mean to, really . . . but I just thought I'd ask . . . that is, I mean . . ."

Tonia laughed and patted her hand. "I quite understand. Gil will be waiting. Shall we say one hour? Can you find occupation for that long?"

"Oh, yes. Thank you so much. There are always Mama's embroidery silks to be sorted. I shall be in the morning room. Don't hurry . . . or, rather . . . well . . ."

Tonia laughed again. "Don't rush, just please be swift. I do understand."

In fact, it was slightly less than an hour later when Antonia, in a lilac and beige dress trimmed with whitework embroidery, and Danvers, wearing his always-correct black coat and waistcoat with a narrow black cravat for day wear, accompanied Miss Raeburn in an open landau over the cobbled streets of Edinburgh. The castle stood sentinel, high on its mighty hill to their left, as they passed to the south side of Old Town and drove on to the university area.

Antonia smiled at the clear sky covering the fresh morning and took a deep breath.

"Oh!" She choked and put a gloved hand to nose and mouth.

Madelyn laughed. "I know. 'Auld Reekie' is supposed to be a term of affection, but I fear our city lives up to its nickname."

"What is it?" Antonia asked between shallow breaths.

"Hops. From the breweries. One gets used to it—sort of. But it's nicest when the wind blows the other direction."

Gilchrist was just emerging from his lodgings as they rattled to a stop before a multistoried stone building across from an open, marshy field where several small boys were kicking a ball around in the damp grass.

"Oh, well met." His clear blue eyes reflected the bright morning sky as he looked first at Madelyn, then at his other visitors. "Thank you for coming. May have been silly of me to spook so when I learned Futter had his eye on me, but he's a deep one. Anyway, I'm still free at the moment. Need to make hay while the sun shines—and in Edinburgh that's not so often. There's a dissection this morning. Want to come?"

Tonia's laughter at the inappropriateness of the suggestion made him blush. "Oh . . . er . . . I guess not. Being ladies and all that. Pity, though. Jolly interesting things, dissections. It's the body Futter brought back from London, you know. The one they call 'the tartaned corpse.' Rumor is Monro might come out of retirement to do this one."

"Oh, yes." Antonia nodded. "You mentioned him before. The medical dynasty."

"Monro dissected Burke, you know. Great honor."

Whether the honor was for the dissector or the dissectee was not clear, but Gilchrist—now comfortably ensconced on the seat next to Madelyn, facing Antonia and Charles, while Flanders followed Danvers's instruction to take them to the university—continued his monologue. "The judge ordered it, you know—after Burke was hanged he got a taste of his own medicine, as you might say—a public dissection. I've heard it told—dozens of times. Lots of fellows around here who attended. They say you never saw anything like it—so crowded the students with tickets couldn't get in even with the aid of the police.

"Monro worked on the brain for two hours. Enormous quantity of blood gushed out—the classroom had the appearance of a butcher's slaughterhouse by the time he was finished."

Tonia smiled weakly and reflected that it was certainly a good thing that Madelyn wasn't a fainting maiden.

Had she been, she would have swooned long ago at the enthusiastic spectacle her dear friend was conjuring up.

"Then a riot broke out among students who couldn't get in." The normally reticent Gilchrist seemed to find this vision even more invigorating than the gore of the dissection. "One of the professors finally got control when he devised a plan to allow them to enter in groups of fifty. They went on as long as the light lasted. Seven females went in too. Next day twenty-five thousand viewed the remains." He leaned back against the seat, satisfied.

"Prodigious," was Antonia's single comment.

The carriage rolled past Old College, designed in the last century by Robert Adam—the Golden Boy of Knowledge stood atop its white dome—and on into the gray stone enclosure of Surgeon's Square. They were flanked on the right by the long, gray buildings of the school. The infirmary and Surgeon's Hall lay in front of them. And on the left, among the houses built into the Flodden Wall, stood a fine building.

Gil pointed. "There it is—Dr. Knox's house. He still lives there, I guess. No one seems to know for sure—never see him—complete recluse. The whole scandal completely ruined him. Pity, too. Most popular medical lecturer in the United Kingdom. Handpicked successor to the great Barclay."

Gil went on to explain how Knox, never a part of the medical establishment of the university, had lectured ex camera, since private dissections counted for students' credits as well.

But Tonia wasn't really following all that. Instead she stared at the stark, sightless windows of Dr. Knox's house. She almost imagined she could see beyond the glass to the rooms that had once bustled with some of the brightest, most energetic young minds of the university. Now the chambers shrank into themselves, cold, dusty. Tonia shivered and raised her handkerchief to her nose again, imagining she could smell damp and decay—or was that merely Auld Reekie?

Then she turned again to the windows. That middle one on the upper floor . . . she was almost certain she had seen a face. A bald head—an impression of heavy features—the glint of light on heavy-lensed glasses. Could she have seen so much from across the courtyard? And yet surely she couldn't have imagined it all.

Gilchrist turned in his seat to direct his listeners' gaze again to Surgeon's Hall. "There. That was Knox's high temple. He taught five hundred students in one session— the session before the scandal ruined him, that was. Classroom only holds two hundred, so he lectured three times a day. Little wonder he didn't check carefully enough on the source of his specimens. Still, can't expect the public to be logical, can you? Especially when they're in fear for their lives. The outcry to hang Knox was powerful. Guess he was lucky to get off with his neck. Still . . ."

Antonia's eyes followed Gil's once again to the quiet, solitary house standing apart from the others.

The medical student shook his head. "Pity, great pity."

Madelyn seemed to be the only one concentrating on matters closer to hand. She brushed Gil's arm. "And if you were to be implicated in the affair of Inspector Futter's corpse now . . ."

Gilchrist squeezed her gloved hand. "True, my sweeting, true." Then he gave his boyish grin. "But for the moment I might as well make what profit I can from it. There're rumbles about Monro's ethics too—but his name bears weight. Might as well have his signature on my lecture card. Sure you won't come in?"

Antonia caught the gleam of interest in Danvers's eyes, so she said, "I would be most interested in seeing the world's premiere medical school. Perhaps Madelyn and I could accompany you to the hall, and you could secure an usher to provide us with a tour of the school while you two attend the . . . er . . . demonstration." Even with her pride in her steady head, the idea of attending a dissection held no charm for Antonia.

Inside the building an instant gray coldness seized her in the echoing stone corridors lined with slate-colored walls. Every footstep sounded and resounded as Gilchrist led the way up the stairs and along the passageways, pointing out an occasional classroom as being of some particular interest to his course of study.

Then they rounded a corner, and the emptiness vanished. Students were funneling through the open double doors of the theater from every direction.

Gilchrist saluted several of his friends. Then his face fell, and he turned abruptly.

"I say, what's that scoundrel doing here? He's not a medical student."

Antonia saw a tall, muscular young man with strong, ruddy features and curling brown hair, wearing a black suit with a high black waistcoat of the sort favored by members of the legal profession.

From behind Antonia, Madelyn spoke softly in her ear. "Dougal MacTavish. I told you about him. I hope he won't see me."

She had no sooner spoken than Dougal pushed his way across the crowded corridor, seized Madelyn's hand, and bowed over it. "Fair Miss Madelyn it is, and now the sun shines brighter on Loch Lomond."

"It may very well, Mr. MacTavish, but I'm sure none of us can see so far." Madelyn withdrew her hand and presented him to Lord and Lady Danvers.

MacTavish gave a stiff, correct bow. "Doubtless you know my father—the earl of Tavish."

Danvers returned the acknowledgement. "By reputation only. I believe I've heard a great many sheep accounted to him."

"Fair number, I think." MacTavish managed to look bored by the sheep. "I'm not sure just what beasts he runs. I have more pressing matters here in the city."

Antonia smiled. Earl's son or not, the young man had need of considerable polishing of his rough corners before the smooth manners he affected would sit easily on him.

Gil turned back to the group and gave Dougal a hard stare.

"Ah, Morris. The very man I had hoped to see before I was distracted by far more delightful company." He smiled at Madelyn, who was purposefully looking the other way. "My sources tell me our friends at the police station gave you an uncomfortable time of it last night. Not good for a promising young doctor—not good at all. If you should have need of a lawyer don't fail to look me up. There's nothing I wouldn't do for the friend of a friend."

"What do you know about this matter, MacTavish?"

"Always pays for an up-and-coming advocate to have his ear to the ground, you know. Can't have too many briefs coming one's way. Anyway, I know enough to know you might be in need of a friend with my not inconsiderable skills. Or my knowledge of sheep raising and special tartans, if you follow my drift. If you should need a quiet place to rusticate until this is all cleared up, I'd be more than happy to send an introduction to Dun Eilean for you. My name's all you'd need. Tavish is lord of the Isle. Good place to duck out of trouble—keep it in mind."

"MacTavish, go . . ." Gil stopped himself with a grinding of teeth.

"Go to the Hebrides, you were doubtless going to suggest?" Dougal's smile seemed unnecessarily broad. "That is just what I had in mind for you. But I forget—your people have a small holding thereabouts somewhere, don't they? Mother's family, what? Well, take heart, old man, even the best of families run out eventually. Can't be helped. Anyway, I've taken the trouble to write you a letter on a certain subject. Be good enough to peruse it when you're alone. But I advise you not to wait too long."

71

Gilchrist jammed MacTavish's sheet of paper into a pocket.

With alarm Antonia saw Gil's fist tighten. No matter how clear Dougal MacTavish's challenge rang, this was not the place to respond. She breathed a sigh of relief as Danvers cut in. "Gil, that fellow down front—is that Monro?"

Dougal left them with a final, sweeping bow to the ladies, and Antonia turned her attention to the front of the theater.

A tall, imposing figure stood beside a long, white-draped table. Monro *tertius*—luxuriant white hair framed his high forehead and sharp, aristocratic features, while his snowy shirt front and perfectly tied white cravat emphasized the impeccable tailoring of his black suit—held court in the hall where his family had reigned, father, son, and grandson, for 126 years.

"I say, Lord Danvers, if you would be so good as to present yourself . . . er . . ."

Danvers grinned good-naturedly. "I quite take your meaning, Gil. A little name recognition when the time comes around for recommendations?"

Gil's cheeks reddened. "Well, it might not hurt, sir. And I mustn't fulfill Aunt Elfrida's expectations and make a hash of it."

"I think that's the last thing she expects, but I'm happy to be of whatever small service I might." Danvers moved toward the front of the room, and the rest of the party followed.

Whatever effect the proposed introduction of Gilchrist's family connections to the Chair of Anatomy Emeritus might have had, however, was not to be known. Just as they reached the front, Alexander Monro whipped the white cloth from his dissection specimen. It was a gesture calculated to rivet the attention of the entire audience on the presenter's technique. The crisp white sheet billowed above the table, then descended with a sharp snap.

Antonia screamed.

7

But that's not the one." Her voice was perfectly distinct. She didn't feel the least bit hysterical, although Charles's arm around her did feel comforting. She didn't know why she had screamed. Except that Futter had said, and Gilchrist had said—they were very precise about it—that the subject for today's dissection was to be the poor fellow she had last seen wrapped in tartan on an enormous, carved bed in the Crystal Palace.

Inspector Futter himself had accompanied the body to Edinburgh and delivered it to the police station on Calton Hill. She was certain she hadn't misunderstood. "This is not the man," she repeated.

"What can you mean, madam?" Monro inquired from his imperious height. "What do you know about my subject which the vulgar press are calling 'the tartaned corpse'?"

"I know that this is not the man from the Crystal Palace." Antonia held her ground even when Monro raised his monocle and peered at her as if she were the specimen under consideration.

"The lady is absolutely correct." Charles supported her assertion.

Monro turned to the side of the room. "Warrender!"

A small man of perhaps forty years, his round head bald above a sandy fringe, with small, circular spectacles perched on his prominent nose, bustled forward. "Sir?"

"You were the doorkeeper assigned charge of this anatomic material?"

"Yes, sir. Yes, indeed. Delivered first thing this morning straight from Calton Hill. I signed the receipt myself." He began turning out his bulging pockets to produce the chit, but in spite of the plethora of candidates, the proper document didn't seem to present itself.

For at least a full minute the room watched while the man searched.

Antonia, standing just in front of him, noted the agility of his long fingers—so like a musician's or surgeon's—except for the presence of dirt under his fingernails.

"Never mind. The material is—immaterial." Monro stared at Antonia from under chalk-cliff eyebrows. "The room will please be cleared of nonparticipants. I shall begin."

The Lady Antonia Danvers was not accustomed to being cleared from a room like last night's tea tray. With a lift of her chin she took her full time inserting each finger into her lilac cotton day gloves, pulling the backs smooth over each hand.

Equally unperturbed, Monro continued his preparations, laying out his instruments in precise array. Next he placed his lecture notes on the stand to his right: a stack of much-thumbed, crinkled sheets of parchment. Odd that a modern medical man should choose such outdated writing material, Antonia thought. The focus of her thoughts rapidly shifted to making a dignified exit, however, as Monro brandished a silver scalpel inches from her ear.

"We begin," he announced.

At the back of the room Tonia and Madelyn were met by a young medical student wearing a short, black academical robe over his suit. He sketched a bow to the ladies. "Gil said you'd like a tour. I'd be most awfully happy to serve."

"Oh, thank you, uh . . ."

"Milton, ma'am—no relation." Young Milton's dark eyes reflected his smile as he flipped a mop of black hair off his forehead.

"Thank you, Milton. But shouldn't you be attending the class?"

"No, no. I've filled that requirement—thank goodness. Anatomy's necessary of course, absolutely essential, but—well, I've seen enough for a while." He opened the door to a classroom lined with anatomy charts. "Here, see what I mean?"

The charts were dated all the way back to the fifteenth century. One was of a skeleton with all the bones labeled in Latin, another with the body sectioned into three oval cavities filled with organs vaguely resembling various garden vegetables, and another, disturbingly realistic, of the dissected subject lying on a table, the organs of his body cavity drawn in detail, surrounded by sketches of his brain.

Antonia turned away. "Thank you, Milton. These have diverted us quite enough, I believe."

"Would you like to see the Museum of the Royal College of Surgeons next, ma'am?"

"Museum?" Surely that would be less lurid. "That sounds quite the thing, Milton."

Their enthusiastic guide led them upstairs and further back into the labyrinth of the school to a room filled with high glass cases. The first held documents from 1506, when King James IV, patron of the college, gave royal approval to the barber-surgeons. Queen Mary's Charter of 1567 exempted surgeons from carrying arms in battle. Tonia paused before the first textbook of surgery in English, written by Glasgow surgeon Peter Lowe, then continued on through the exhibits of surgeons and apothecaries from the seventeenth and eighteenth centuries.

"Now here's an Edinburgh doctor we're all justly proud of." Milton pointed to the next exhibit. "James Young Simpson. Revolutionized surgery and midwifery with the use of chloroform."

Tonia looked at the portrait of a square-jawed man with a twinkle in his eyes.

"He experimented on himself and his assistants—inhaled ether and all sorts of vapors until he hit on chloroform." Milton shook his head. "What a jolly show—and just three years before I came here. Wish I could have been in on it."

"But wasn't it dangerous?" Madelyn asked.

"Plenty of headaches and upset stomachs." Milton shrugged. "But chloroform's great stuff. Puts the patient out with a single whiff—they sleep right through the operation. Don't give the doctor any trouble that way, either."

"Do they drink it?" Madelyn's skepticism showed in her tone of voice.

"No, no. Just smell it straight from the bottle. Or soak a rag and clap it over the nose and mouth. Have to be careful, though. Too much could be deadly."

A striking portrait of a man in a black robe and full white wig next took Antonia's attention. She read the name of the subject. "John Monro? I thought they were all named Alexander."

"John was the father of Monro *primus*," Milton explained, once again flipping his hair back with a toss of his head. "He initiated the development of the medical faculty within the university. Most of us think he should have the title of Father of the Medical School rather than his son."

John Munro was followed with a bust of Alexander Monro *primus* beside the skeleton of one of his dissections. Tonia gave it the briefest of glances.

The next specimen, however, she felt somehow drawn to examine. "Skeleton of William Burke," the placard read. Beside it was his plaster bust, made from a death mask taken the day after Burke was hanged, showing the bite of the rope around his thick neck. The exhibit was completed with a wallet and tobacco pouch made from Burke's tanned skin.

Milton observed Tonia turning sharply away and offered his arm. "Ironic those are there, isn't it? Dr. Knox was the first conservator of the museum. He had to display the instrument of his own downfall for posterity." He then directed the ladies' steps to the lounge, where they had agreed to meet Gil and Danvers when the lecture was over.

Tonia sat on a straight-backed, horsehair-covered sofa. "I hear so many references to Burke and Hare, but I don't know exactly what they did."

"Sold bodies for dissection. Only trouble was, the subjects weren't bodies—not dead ones, that is—when Burke and Hare started with them." Milton sat at the end of the sofa next to Tonia.

Madelyn took an equally stiff-backed seat on the other side of the room.

"Sixteen victims they had—all in one year. Appropriately enough, they were found out on All Hallow's Eve." Milton's narrative continued in a congenial, conversational tone. The lady had asked a question, and he was happy to supply the information. "Their first victim was old Joseph, who was dying of fever but was hurried into eternity with the help of a pillow. Then a nameless Englishman who sold matches in Old Town. Their first woman was Abigail Simpson, lured to Tanner's Close with the promise of a drink. Burke told the police Dr. Knox especially approved of her on account of the specimen being so fresh. And he never asked any questions. Their agreement with Knox was for ten pounds for subjects delivered in winter and eight pounds in the summer."

Not wanting to hear more, yet unsure how to stop the eager recitation obviously meant for her entertainment, Tonia let her mind wander to more philosophical thoughts. "'The march of the intellect' for which their age was supposed to be distinguished was such an oft-repeated phrase

77

that it could almost be called the slogan of their times. And yet, for all its illumination, it seemed that the age must be characterized by some deeper and fouler blots than any that preceded it. It was as if the brighter spots that did indeed shine served to illuminate the darker nooks and corners where evil was condensed.

"... And then there was the old grandmother and a deaf mute boy. After they suffocated the woman, Burke broke the boy's back over his knee. They loaded them into a herring barrel and delivered them to Paterson, Knox's doorkeeper, for sixteen pounds. Then the poor old horse that pulled the cart collapsed, so they sold him to the knacker's."

Antonia had just made up her mind to intervene in the narrative when Danvers entered, looking as ashen as she felt.

But however nauseous Charles might be feeling, it did nothing to slow his vigorous stride. "Gil is finishing the lecture—said he'd meet you outside the lecture room, Milton."

Antonia and Madelyn thanked their escort, who departed with a bow to the ladies.

"Did you find the demonstration enlightening?" Tonia asked her husband with a mischievous grin.

He appeared to be in no mood for banter, however. "I had quite sufficient to get the flavor of the exercise. I think we should get on to Futter. Need to let him know about the mix-up of corpses here—unless he already knows. Maybe the police sent a different subject on purpose."

But when they found the Inspector at the Edinburgh police station, it was clear that the substitution of anatomical material had not been at the behest of the police.

"What do you mean not the same one? Of course it was. We sent it out late last night—right after I left you—so everything would be all ready for this morning." He turned on his heel and led the way back to a room that held three marble tables. The slabs were all empty.

"So if the tartaned corpse isn't at Surgeon's Hall, where is he? And who is Monro *tertius* cutting apart?" Danvers addressed the room in general.

Futter shook his head. "First we lose the tartan, then we lose the corpse. Not a very good record, I'm afraid. Her Majesty won't be pleased."

Lose the tartan. Antonia replayed the scene in Hyde Park in her mind. Futter had followed Gil all the way to Edinburgh to question him about the tartan. But what had Gil's answer been? She still didn't have any more answers —just more questions.

She knew she should tell what she had seen. But the thought of damaging Gil's career stopped her tongue.

Then a worse thought struck her. *Lose the corpse,* Futter said. What had Gil been doing last night? For the first time she wondered why he hadn't been at the Raeburns' when Madelyn returned from fetching them. Madelyn had been running his errand. Why hadn't he run the errand himself? Of course, if the police had told him not to leave Edinburgh . . . still . . .

8

As if following her thoughts about the tartan, Futter picked up his hat and started toward the door. "Well, only lead we have—and I can't see as how it's much of one—is the place that nuisance plaid was made. Think I'd better go take Raeburn's tour. Care to come along?"

Antonia and Danvers indicated that they would find that most interesting.

Madelyn hesitated. "Will you think me terribly ungracious if I don't accompany you? The place is rather dusty and noisy, and I really should spend some time with Mama today."

With assurances that they quite understood, Danvers handed Madelyn into her father's landau, then turned with Tonia to accompany Futter in the considerably less elegant conveyance furnished by the Edinburgh police.

The carriage rattled and jounced over the rough cobbles of Leith Walk, making the considerable distance to the Raeburn Woolen Mills near the Leith Docks seem even farther to Antonia. But once inside the dim, sprawling wooden structure filled with the noise and dust Madelyn had warned of, the discomforts of the ride seemed but a mild prelude.

They were met by the foreman, who apparently had been briefed by Raeburn to expect their arrival. The paunchy, middle-aged man introduced himself as Ferral and immediately set out at a stolid pace on his short legs to inform his visitors of the glories of industrial milling. His lecture, enunciated by heavy lips, boomed above the racket of row upon row of steam-driven looms. Tired-looking women sat working the treadles and heddles of the heavy iron machines.

Now Ferral shouted over the clack of the equipment, explaining the operation of the dressing machine—which applied sizing to the warp—and the efficiency of William Horrocks's machine for winding the woven fabric onto the cloth beam.

As he continued, Antonia was puzzled. Why did she feel as if she had met Ferral before? Of course that was impossible. She was certain she hadn't seen this man with the thin, graying sandy hair, high shiny forehead, and near-sighted squint before. And yet . . . who did he remind her of? Frustrated at her inability to identify her impression, she turned her attention to the colorful patterns each loom was producing.

Ferral pointed out the various tartan setts, noting how in each case the warp and woof were exactly the same pattern, as in all true plaids. Tonia soon saw how many were variations on the dark blue and green Black Watch design with only the addition of a colored line or two. And then there were the more colorful patterns based on a combination of reds and golds. But nowhere did she see what they sought—a soft heather pattern with delicate lines of gold, black, and white.

"But what ye're seeing here is really the end o' the process." Ferral headed toward a steep, wooden stairway at the back of the room. "We do our spinning upstairs—the most Crompton Mules you'll see operating in any mill in Britain."

Looking upward, Antonia saw myriad motes of fiber floating in the shafts of pale light falling through the high windows. The sight confirmed the tickle she had been feeling ever since she entered the building. An uncontrollable spasm of sneezing overtook her. Danvers took her gently by the arm and led her from the room. Their guide cleared a chair for her in a relatively quiet office on the ground floor and produced a glass of cool water. Antonia thanked him, dabbing at her running eyes with an embroidered lawn handkerchief.

When at last the choking and sneezing subsided, Antonia looked around her. And she saw it. Loosely wrapped in brown paper among other bundles on a table in the corner, the gold stripe shining like sunshine from its duller background.

"Oh, what a pretty pattern." She fingered the stuff and knew she had felt its softness before.

"Not for sale." Accustomed to talking over the noise of the looms, Ferral's voice rang in the small room. "Special design for Raeburn's miss. Don't know what it's doing back here. Had it all done. Thought it was delivered. Then some fellow brought it in yesterday, said it was soiled and snagged, needed redoing for her birthday. On the quiet-like so Miss Raeburn wouldn't be upset."

Tonia observed him from the depths of her deep-brimmed bonnet. He seemed to be telling the truth, and yet the squinty eyes were difficult to judge.

But it wasn't Ferral's veracity she was most worried about. It was her own. Even after Futter made clear he suspected Gil's connection, she hadn't talked about what she had seen in the park. Certainly she hadn't wanted to involve Gil in anything unpleasant—but if he had involved himself and then lied to Futter about it, as seemed apparent, it wasn't her place to cover for him. Earlier she could claim the distractions of the balloon ascent and their honeymoon as reasons for not speaking out—all true enough diversions—but now she had no excuse, except the discomfort of the mill. She would wait until they were outside.

The relief of leaving the noise and dust was so great that the rattling of the hard-rimmed carriage tires on cobbled streets was a near relaxation. Antonia turned more to Danvers than to Futter. "I should have told you sooner—don't know why I was so silly—but when we were stalled in traffic by the park . . ." She described the scene of Gilchrist's receiving a parcel in Hyde Park—the very parcel she had just seen in Ferral's office.

She held her breath. Would Charles be angry that she hadn't spoken sooner? Or hurt that she had held back from him?

Her answer came in his warm clasp of her gloved hand, letting her know he understood how hard the telling had been. "You were right to speak, Tonia."

"Quite right," Futter seconded. "Thank you, your ladyship. He denied it, but I knew we had the right man. Time I had another chat with young Gilchrist Morris. Take you back to Charlotte Square, shall we?"

The offer was tempting. It had been a tiring day, and their hostess would soon want to have dinner served. Yet . . . Tonia looked at Charles. He would never desert a friend, no matter what bothered him. She blinked at the thought. There it was again. What *was* bothering Danvers? All the quiet strength she so loved and relied on was there, and yet it was unlike him to be so silent, so inactive. For days now he had been her support, her strength, her joy—and yet he hadn't quite been there. When had it started, this withdrawal? She began to follow the thought, then realized Futter was waiting for an answer. "Oh, no. Thank you, but I got Gil into this. I must face him."

"He was in it already, ma'am."

Futter confirmed her fears, but she could tell by the warm glance Danvers gave her that she had made the right decision. Yet the fact that so many of the decisions lately had been hers worried her. It was unlike her dynamic hus-

83

band to take a backseat to anything. On the other hand, she had been so happy to find him more relaxed as their love grew. Perhaps she was just being silly now and worrying over nothing.

Her worry over the confrontation with Gil was to be postponed as well, at least for the moment, it seemed, for when Futter knocked at the door of his lodging it was Milton who greeted them. No, Morris wasn't there. He hadn't returned after the dissection. Milton looked for him outside the theater where Gil said he'd meet him, but without luck. "Awful crush of people after Monro's exhibition. Must have missed him somewhere." Milton shrugged.

"Perhaps he went to Charlotte Square to see Madelyn," Antonia suggested.

That seemed as likely as anything, and Futter directed the police driver to take them across town once more.

When they arrived at the perfectly shined front door, however, it was not to be met by the usual serene order of the quiet Georgian residence. The gleaming black door burst open, and Antonia was all but knocked off her feet by a red-faced Harry Raeburn.

"Eloped! The young fools! They've eloped!"

9

The horses, man!" Raeburn shouted at Flanders, his coachman, who came up from below stairs still buttoning his jacket. "How many times do you have to be told? We won't make Inverary before tomorrow even traveling all night."

Flanders dashed down the street toward the mews.

"Madelyn and Gil *eloped?*" Tonia shook her head. "Why would they do that? Where have they gone?"

"It's plain as a pikestaff. The scalawag was in over his head, had to outrun the police, so he hoodwinked my daughter into going with him. When Harry Raeburn gets done with him there won't be anything left for the police." He shook his fist. "Flanders! Where are my horses?" Raeburn paced up and down the street.

"Where have they gone? Where is Inverary?"

"Seat of the duke of Argyll, in the Highlands, beyond Loch Lomond . . ." Danvers started to explain.

Harry cut him off, however. "They haven't gone to Inverary. No place so civilized for Morris. That's where he's sure to change horses, though—best chance of catching them there. They must have a three-hour start on us, but I'll catch them, you can be sure of that, and when I do—"

Raeburn crumpled the paper in his hand as symbolic of what he would do to Gilchrist, then held it out to Danvers. "Here. She said to tell you—impertinent miss. Not a word to her mother."

Charles took the paper and smoothed it out. Antonia read over his arm: "Dearest Papa, Gone to Eilean. Tell Lord Danvers. Don't worry, Daddy. You know Gil and I love each other. Madelyn."

"Eilean?" Antonia asked.

Raeburn nodded curtly. "Tavish's island. Small one in the Sound of Jura."

"But why would they go there?"

"Good place to go if you want to get away from anything. Goodness knows it's remote enough." Raeburn strode to the corner and shouted for his coachman again.

Danvers took up Antonia's question. "I suppose an eloping couple would want an isolated spot. I heard Dougal MacTavish offer it to Gil. But I certainly didn't get the impression Gil would be likely to accept the invitation."

Raeburn returned. "Fine fellow that Dougal. Now if that were the one she'd run off with I'd not give chase. Just let them go for a good thing. But Morris! Why would my daughter choose someone so helter-skelter? I'll not have it!" He turned as if to shout for his horses again, but instead his gaze fell on Futter. "Ah, police. Well done. 'Bout time you fellows started turning up when you're wanted. No sense in all the fuss you make over stinking bodies— do your best for the living, that's what's important. You come with me and arrest this fellow."

Futter removed his hat and smoothed his straw-blond hair. "Well . . . er . . . what's the charge, sir?"

"Charge?"

"That's to say, what law has he broken?"

"Are you deaf, man? Been standing here all this time and you don't know? He eloped with my daughter!"

Futter nodded. "Very unwise, I agree. But there's no law against marrying in Scotland. Matter of fact, I believe it's somewhat easier to accomplish up here north of the border. That's why so many of our young'uns are like to make for Gretna Green."

Harry Raeburn looked as if he were in danger of exploding. "Thought I heard something about him not leaving town because you wanted to question him?"

"Yes—well, you do have a point. I just need to check a few things . . ."

"No dilly-dallying. Can't wait."

Futter looked relieved. "Of course not, sir. But just where is this place?"

Raeburn unrolled a map and pointed to an unnamed dot off the jagged western coast of Argyll.

Antonia was amazed. "But how would they get there? There're no towns—no roads—"

"Tavish would keep a launch, or they could catch a ride with the herring fleet from some village along the shore. Young fools probably don't even have it worked out yet."

It was still beyond Tonia's imagining. "But why would the earl of Tavish live there?"

Raeburn looked at her from under his bristling red eyebrows. "Because it's where his family has always lived. Good sheep land in the hills and glens on shore. Where else should he live?"

Danvers's considerations were more practical. He studied the map, then shook his head. "No chance of catching them before dark."

Raeburn struck the map. "No chance of catching them at all if that fool coachman of mine dallies any longer. But I'll do for them all right. They won't travel all night. I will."

Antonia was about to question the safety of traveling in the dark over such rugged country, when Danvers's next comment made even Harry Raeburn close his mouth. "We can get to the island before them."

Just then Hardy, who was never very long from the center of any excitement, came up from the kitchen. "You'll be needing me, sir?"

"Indeed I do. Find out the direction of this Tytler family—the balloonists Mr. Raeburn was telling us about. I find I have need of an aerostat. See what arrangements you can make for them to help a fellow aeronaut in distress."

"Aerostat!" Raeburn thundered. "Do you mean to say ye intend to journey to the Hebrides in a balloon?"

"I can think of no quicker or more comfortable way of accomplishing the journey. The trip by land appears formidable." Danvers waved his hand toward the map he had been studying. Every inch was intersected by jagged inlets from the sea or broken by long, thin lochs with only a bare minimum of lines indicating what must be the sketchiest of roads.

"I would, of course, not consider such an ascent before tomorrow morning. I assume the gas mains of Edinburgh can provide us with coal gas, Hardy?"

"You can just leave it all to me, m'lord. A right fine sailing that'll be. No chance we might just hop on over to Ireland, is there now? Very close we'll be, you know."

For the sake of Harry Raeburn's equanimity, Antonia was glad Danvers merely sent Hardy on his way without further banter. "It should be a delightful journey, Charles. And I shall go with you. Madelyn is sure to be in need of feminine support. I don't know—they are an impetuous pair, but I wouldn't have thought this to be a likely thing for either of them to do . . ."

"What are you suggesting, my love?" Charles gave her close attention.

"Nothing really. I don't know. I just can't help wondering whether this elopement is all it appears to be. Still, I should love to see the Highlands and western islands. I have heard it is greatly romantic scenery."

The clatter of carriage wheels on cobblestones interrupted further discussion as the harried Flanders pulled the Raeburn carriage into the square.

Just then Mrs. Raeburn descended the front steps followed by Jeffers, carrying two large baskets. "Harry Raeburn, you'll not go off into the western wilds without a warm change of clothes and a hamper of food."

Harry sprang into the carriage. "I can't be bothered with that, woman. Don't you realize your daughter has eloped?"

"If she has, it's her father she gets such wild notions from. Now there's a fine roast beef with pickle in that hamper, and see that you eat it, Harry Raeburn."

Moraig followed with a pile of warm travel rugs, which Jeffers piled in beside his master.

"So you'll not be waiting for the aerostat?" Danvers asked.

"Is Harry Raeburn the man to cool his heels waiting for a new-fangled contraption when he has the finest pair of horses in all Edinburgh in his stable, I ask you?"

Obviously he wasn't, for the carriage had disappeared around the square before any in the company could so much as wave him off.

"Best look sharp, my love. It's gone five a.m."

"What?" Antonia was too groggy to rub the sleep from her eyes. She wasn't even sure she had eyes at five o'clock in the morning.

"Sun will be up in an hour—we want to catch the best breezes to the west."

"Oh, yes, the balloon." She sat up, clutching the lace-edged, linen sheet to her in the cool, gray room. "Where's Hardy? I need a cup of tea."

Hardy was already out preparing the aerostat he had cajoled from the canny Tytler family for a considerable compensation, but Moraig soon arrived with morning tea and a brass can of hot water for washing. Antonia donned

her dove gray traveling dress, then chose her three warmest shawls as protection against the swiftly shifting Scottish weather.

Edinburgh slept in darkness. The carriage wheels
sounded hollowly on the cobbles as they drove down
Princes Street. Not even the most enthusiastic street vendor
was yet astir to offer his wares at the elegant homes. To
their left the castle loomed a great, black hulk against a sky
still pinpointed with fading stars. Here and there, though, a
torch flared along the ramparts, indicating that Her Majesty's
troops maintained their duty.

They left the carriage with the Raeburn undercoach-
man at the foot of the Salisbury Craigs, where the footpath
began its steep ascent to the crouching-lion form that was
Arthur's Seat.

By the time Antonia stood on the top of the great
green height, slightly out of breath but glowing radiantly,
streaks of red and gold were reaching out to her from
across the Firth of Forth. She looked down on Holyrood
Palace, nestled below the hill and out across the city now
showing signs of stirring itself awake.

A small ruffle in the grass at her feet made her focus
her attention closer. A tiny gray field mouse, frightened by
the activity around the balloon, was scampering straight
toward her. She started to jump out of its way, but at the
last moment the furry, round creature saw her and veered
off to the right. Following him with her eyes, Tonia suddenly saw that the entire hillside was alive. From first one
side of the hill and then another, a long-eared, brown form
would spring forward, then scamper away through the tall
grass. Each time Tonia would gasp and start to point, only
to be distracted by the next quick movement. At last she
gave up trying to follow the activity and merely stood smil-
ing at the rabbits scampering among the harebells.

"Whenever you're ready, m'lady." Hardy held out his
hand to assist her into the gondola attached to the blue

and purple balloon that tugged on its tether, anxious to be aloft.

A few moments later Charlie Tytler, standing sturdy on the ground, loosened the last rope, and the balloon soared upward, carrying Charles and Antonia and the faithful Hardy off on their rescue mission.

"I wonder how far Harry Raeburn got last night?" Antonia mused as she wrapped her second shawl more firmly around her shoulders. The sun now stretched golden behind them as they followed the ever-narrowing Forth westward far below. But for all the golden splendor of the sun gilding the clouds above and sparkling the busy waterway beneath, the air was bitingly chill.

Danvers looked up from the chart he was consulting. "If all went well, he should be as far as Loch Lomond by now."

"And when will we be there?"

Danvers turned from his chart to check various instruments measuring air speed, direction, and altitude, then made a few calculations on a pad of notepaper. "At present wind speed, we should be near Loch Lomond in three hours."

Hardy unfolded a small canvas stool, and Antonia settled herself on it. "Less, m'lord, I should think, if the weather holds."

Antonia had been so fascinated following the activity of boats on the Forth and the beauty of the green fields beyond that she hadn't noticed the fringe of dark clouds hanging on the northern horizon to which Hardy now alluded. "Are those likely to give us trouble, do you think?" she asked.

"Not if they stay put up north, m'lady."

Hardy's answer was less than perfect reassurance, but Charles's smile warmed her more than her paisley shawl.

For near to an hour the beauty and serenity of their journey aloft was matched only by the equally beautiful, serene countryside below them. Tonia thought she could never tire of watching the scene unfold beneath the balloon. Occasionally their shadow startled a horse in a field or a flock of geese, and frequently a farm boy would pull off his cloth cap, wave both arms, and shout a greeting as they floated over his head. Always Antonia waved back, happy that none of their observers were engaged in pheasant shooting as had been that party in Norwich that once shot Danvers out of the air.

Then the scene below them changed, and they sailed near a city built around an oval-shaped hill topped by a great, ruined castle. "What is that?" Tonia pointed and found she had to raise her voice, for the wind was becoming brisker and tended to blow her words away.

"Stirling Castle," Danvers answered. "It was often said that he who held Stirling held Scotland—situated as it was right in the middle of the country. And there's Stirling Bridge."

Tonia leaned over the other side of the gondola to see where Charles was pointing. She spotted a triple-arched stone bridge spanning a river not far from the castle. She nodded, but the site conveyed nothing to her more than an attractive, ancient bridge.

"Where Wallace, the great Scottish freedom fighter, gave the English a decisive beating at the end of the thirteenth century. Unfortunately Wallace was captured and given a rather brutal execution in London. Robert the Bruce carried the work for independence to completion after him."

Now Tonia nodded more decisively. "Ah, yes. That's a name I recognize. Robert the Bruce is the man King Edward won the Stone of Scone from."

"The very same. Edward got the stone, but Bruce won his country's freedom."

Tonia was long in thought, trying to imagine the clashing of armies, the raging of battle on the peaceful fields below her. At last she shook her head. "Odd, isn't it?

Edward was a very good prince for England—the perfect flower of knighthood."

Danvers nodded. "But something of a monster here, I fear, as the Hammer of the Scots—and the Welsh as well."

The quickening winds blew them ever faster westward with rising hopes for a speedy, successful accomplishment of their goal, even though the stronger currents required more attention on the part of the two men sailing the aerostat and sent Tonia shivering deeper yet into her shawls.

Less than an hour later her attention was taken by the sight of the most beautiful loch she had yet seen: deep blue waters dotted with a fascinating assortment of small islands, some rocky, others solidly wooded. The loch itself was surrounded by dark green woods and watched over to the north by a high green mountain.

"Loch Lomond." Danvers identified it for her.

Tonia smiled. What comforting reassurance. The first major landmark of their journey, accomplished in record time. Beyond lay Argyll, the Highlands, the Hebrides— words out of a fairy tale. She found it hard to remember that their pleasant journey was supposed to be a desperate dash to rescue Madelyn from the perils of a disastrous elopement, fully cognizant though she was of the fact that such a mad escapade would forever ruin Madelyn socially and Gil's medical career.

That was part of the puzzle. Madelyn had been so concerned for Gil's career, it seemed impossible that she would consent to an act that would mean sudden death for it. And yet any idea of the kind, shy Gilchrist forcing her was equally unthinkable. And there was certainly no indication that Madelyn had left under anything but her own will. After Harry's frantic departure, Tonia had questioned Moraig closely, and together they had surveyed the girl's room. Madelyn had clearly packed a small bag, carefully choosing sensible clothes for her destination. But there was no indication that her leaving, though hasty, had been anything but thought through.

A clap of thunder echoing off the lofty peak of Ben Lomond brought Tonia bolt upright out of her reverie.

"Saints preserve us." Hardy began lashing down the few loose objects in the gondola. "And didn't I ask the blessed Christopher to let us outrun that wee black cloud? You wouldn't be thinking that was too much to be asking of one so long sainted, now would ye?"

Tonia gripped the edge of the gondola and looked at the gray clouds rolling over them. An aerostat was not a desirable place to be in a Highland storm. Almost as quickly as it took her to form the thought, the craggy side of Ben Lomond disappeared under a curtain of mist. They were sailing now in a world of wet, gray cotton wool.

Danvers worked the valves, intent on sailing them well past the spot where the mountain had last been seen.

"Should we try to put her down, m'lord?" Hardy's words were flung back by the wind.

Danvers shook his head, then removed his hat and handed it to Antonia to hold before a fresh gust could blow it over the side. "Safer to stay aloft than to set down in who knows what loch or pile of rocks." He gripped the map in both hands to prevent its being ripped from his hands. "Let's keep as much northward as possible. Need to avoid those mountains. Soon as there's a break, we'll land." He looked grim. "We should have been only two hours from Eilean. Now who knows where we'll end up?"

The two hours Danvers had predicted stretched to four—the longest four of Antonia's life. She had not known that a wind could be so fierce or unbroken. Or that a sky could become so dark at midday. The golden sunrise over Edinburgh seemed to have taken place in another world, as vanished as the serene, green fields they had floated over in that other lifetime. Now the whole universe was a turmoil of lashing wind and rain and thick mist that isolated them from everything else in creation. Tonia wrapped her third shawl around her and tied the ends behind her back as securely as possible. Abandoning the comfort of her stool as far too unstable, she sat flat on the floor of the gondola, gripping its leather straps for some kind of anchorage.

At first she tried to keep her eyes open, feeling somehow that if Charles stayed within her vision all would be well. But then she abandoned the attempt, knowing that the best possible thing she could do—indeed, the only thing she could do of any use at all—was to close her eyes tightly and pray. She tried to form an ordered, coherent petition as she would have prayed at church or during family prayers, but she was now in a world where no order existed. *Help, God! Lord, save us!* was as ordered as she could get.

Then she felt the solid comfort of a body next to her own and opened her eyes to look into Charles's dark, rugged features. He sat beside her and took her hands in his. "Antonia, I'm so sorry to have gotten you into this. There was another matter I was worrying about, but now everything seems trivial compared to your safety."

She returned his pressure on her hand and forced a small smile. "Perhaps we should have had something like 'in safety and in danger' added to our marriage vows. At least we're together, my love." She didn't know where she found the strength to answer him so calmly in such a perilous situation, but she knew she meant what she said.

He sat beside her for some time, holding her securely while the balloon and gondola rocked in the lashing wind.

Hardy stood staunch at the lookout, although there was nothing to see. He occasionally reported, but instead of the break they had hoped for in the mist, the darkness and thickness increased.

"Just pray the aerostat holds together," Danvers said in her ear when the movement of her lips must have told

95

him what she was doing. "Thank God the Tytlers used the best netting and ropes."

It wasn't long after that that a whoop from Hardy brought them both to their feet. "A light. I'd swear I saw a light down there." He pointed, but Tonia could see nothing.

A moment later, however, a definite break in the mist revealed a small cluster of lighted buildings before the wind drew the veil again.

"Begin valving!" Danvers shouted with a ring of triumph in his voice.

Antonia was almost sure, but she had to ask, "Isn't the wind dropping? It feels less." And she was sure the rain was diminishing—the drops were still as large, but they stung less when they struck her face.

The balloon descended rapidly. Then suddenly a new sound of violence wiped the smile from Tonia's face. A mighty crashing and sucking sound, repeated again and again until the sound began to drum inside Tonia's head just as the rain drummed outside. The balloon was blown forward, then back.

"Valve harder," Danvers ordered Hardy, who was emptying the balloon of all the gas he could manage with the ropes he controlled. Danvers stood at the side, peering into the darkness, searching for a likely place to throw his grappling hook. "Appears to be all rock and sand," he growled. "Can't see a place that looks like it'd hold."

An even louder crash than before made Tonia turn to look into the darkness behind her. And there she saw the great white crest of a wave, flung foaming white on a shiny black rock. For a moment it seemed suspended in the air, then it fell backwards to the ocean. It was a frightening sight, and yet the power was exhilarating. She held her breath as the breaker roared forward again, crashed and flew upward, held, then was sucked backward by the weight of its own force. On the third forward surge she felt the spray and the jolt of a heavy thump as if the wave had driven the balloon itself onto the rock. And then she realized. They had landed.

Her instinct was to fling her arms around Charles and sob with relief, but she knew this was not the time. The danger was not over yet. Wind and water still lashed at the silk balloon, now flopping like a beached whale on the jagged shore. The gondola lay two-thirds on its side, held in a lava crag. Any moment it could shift and tumble them onto the sharp rocks.

A shout and the flare of a wind-whipped torch made Antonia look upward where she had the impression of turf-covered land beyond the rocky beach. Hardy answered the shout. In the confusion of wind and breaking waves it was several moments before Antonia realized they had not spoken in English. "What is it?" she asked in Danvers's ear.

"Gaelic," he answered.

"Gaelic? Where are we?"

But he couldn't tell her.

10

Wherever they were, however, it was only moments until strong hands were guiding Tonia from the stranded gondola and leading her toward what she could now see was a fine stone house set well above the crashing surf. Her relief was great when the door opened and a woman stood in the lighted doorway, welcoming her in English.

It was only a matter of minutes until she was taken up the stairs to a snug room where a peat fire burned on the grate and a white-capped maid was holding out a pile of white linen towels to her. Her case, rescued from the gondola, was brought up to her. In less than half an hour, Lady Antonia Danvers, with hair freshly arranged under a lace cap, sat dry-shod before a sitting room fire, being offered tea or coffee and toast with marmalade.

Danvers was still shaking his head over learning where they were. "Raasay? It doesn't seem possible we could have been blown so far north. We were heading for a small island off the coast of Jura."

Their host was Raasay himself, the lord of the isle, a stocky, dark-haired man who seemed to think their plight a great joke. "Oh, aye, we do have some fine storms up here, and that's the truth of it."

"We can't thank you enough for rescuing us and giving us shelter," Danvers said. "You've a fine house here."

"Oh, aye, it's fine enough, practically new-built. You see, my grandfather's grandfather was out in the Forty-five."

Antonia blinked, trying to figure out just where they were and what their host was talking about.

Danvers seemed to see her confusion and took advantage of their host's pause for a sip of coffee to explain. "My dear, we've been blown to a small island off the northern coast of Skye. After his defeat at the Battle of Culloden —just over a hundred years ago it was—Bonnie Prince Charlie took refuge here to escape the English troops who were hunting him."

"Aye, that's right," their host continued. "As I was saying, my ancestor, the tenth Raasay, stood for the prince with a fine troop, but he conveyed the estate to his son so there'd be no forfeiture of the property if the fortunes of war turned against Charlie's men, as indeed they did. But then, as the prince was known to have taken asylum in Raasay, the government burnt every house upon the island. The family house was just new then, with a fine three-storied tower. But the eleventh Raasay rebuilt it all, using the stones of the old house. So that's where you stop now, sir. The house of Raasay, risen like a phoenix from the ashes of the old."

He took another sip of coffee, then turned to his wife, a fine, sturdy woman in a flowered dress who sat on the other side of the room. "Ah, Flora, my dear, how long will it be till supper? Have I time to show our visitors a wee thing or two?"

Flora, Lady Raasay, assured her lord he had plenty of time, so he led Charles and Antonia to another room where he produced a small, green bottle. "It was my ancestor who went with the prince from Raasay in a boat back to Skye. They walked all night over the mountain until they found the next laird who would help his prince. Prince Charlie went as Raasay's servant, carrying a little

99

bundle and a bottle of brandy. When the brandy was drunk, the prince was for throwing away the bottle. 'No,' my ancestor said, 'since it served Your Majesty I shall hope to drink out of it yet.' It's been in the family ever since, as has this." Their host produced a small silver stock clasp, which had also belonged to the prince.

Antonia had the feeling the discourse could have gone on for quite some time, so was happy, indeed, when their hostess announced that dinner was set. Antonia knew no meal in her life ever tasted better than that supper of mutton chops, turnips, and tarts, which they consumed by a peat fire while the wind gusted against the shutters. In moments when the conversation lulled she could still hear the pounding of the surf on the rocks below.

Thankful though she was for their rescue and kind welcome, Tonia could not help but wonder how long such violent weather would keep them on this island when they should be rescuing Madelyn. Were they already too late? Had Harry Raeburn likewise been turned aside by the storm? Were the foolish young lovers even now married and the escapade beyond redemption?

In the morning, however, Antonia found that her fears for their delay had been much exaggerated. Although she had wakened several times in the night to the continued howl of the wind, the banging of a loose shutter, and the bitter tang of peat smoke as the draft was hurled back down the chimney, in the morning the birds sang, the sun shone, and the sea was calm.

After a very good breakfast of cocoa, scones baked with butter, and a bowl of curd cheese, Lady Raasay invited Antonia to a walk around her garden. Tonia could now see that they were on a long (about fifteen English miles, her hostess said), green island with cultivated fields all around them. Inside her walled garden, Flora Raasay grew all manner of garden vegetables as well as gooseberries, raspberries, currants, strawberries, and apple trees. Antonia praised her hostess's excellent provisions.

"Oh, aye, it's fine here. We've all we need. Although I do think it's a fine thing to go to Skye every year."

When further questioning revealed that Lady Raasay had been to the mainland only twice in her life, and never so far as Edinburgh, Antonia realized how truly adventurous her own life must appear.

A short time later the men joined them carrying the travelers' bags, and they all walked down to the dock. Now the waves lapped against the rocks, but did not pound to the sky above them as they had the night before. In the daylight Antonia saw that a tall, stone cross stood embedded in one of the rocks of the harbor. Their host told them that his ancestor used to offer his daily devotions at that spot, but now they found it more convenient to worship God indoors.

Tonia turned to thank her hostess.

"Oh, but I do wish you could stay longer." The lady gripped her hands warmly. "We should have a dinner with all the families on the island and a fiddler and a piper, and we could have a most merry ball."

Antonia genuinely regretted having to leave, but they dared not delay if they were to accomplish any good at all. Hardy had loaded into one end of the boat the wicker gondola and the lustrous mound of purple and blue silk that had been their brave aerostat. It was now his assignment to hire whatever conveyance he could—which would most likely be a farm cart once he was back on the mainland—and return it to its owner while Charles and Antonia continued toward their goal.

The sailing across the Sound of Raasay was smooth and pleasant. It was impossible to imagine that this could have been the same water that beat so violently on the rocks the night before. Antonia refused the offer of a seat in the little forward cabin and chose instead to stand at the rail beside Charles as they sailed into the Portree Harbour. There little white cottages ringed the waterfront below banks of green, tree-covered hills brightened with clumps of yellow and orange wildflowers.

Here they said good-bye to Hardy, who was to go on to the mainland with Raasay while Charles and Antonia took a carriage to the other side of the island, thence to find a boat that would convey them southward to Eilean.

Every time Antonia thought of the distance they had yet to go, she could feel impatience rise in her chest and lodge at the base of her throat. Such disquiet was useless. They were doing their best. They could do no more. And yet the sense of urgency persisted.

What a shame to be hurried through such magnificent scenery. Raasay advised Danvers to seek a carriage at McNab's Inn—the very place where Bonnie Prince Charlie took leave of his brave guide, Miss Flora MacDonald, before he set sail for refuge in Raasay. With tears in his eyes, the prince had kissed Flora on the forehead, given her a gold coin and a miniature of himself, and left with the expressed hope that they would yet meet once more in St. James's. They never saw each other again.

Danvers, however, met with success, although at first matters did not look hopeful. A carriage to take them to the other side of the island was out of the question. Impossible. There were no roads that would accommodate the use of a carriage. A cart then? Surely the farmers on the island used carts? Yes, to be sure. But MacNab's Inn was not a farm. And the comfort of such a conveyance for a lady . . .

In the end he hired two quite adequate saddle horses and the services of a boy to act as guide and return the horses. Antonia was perfectly happy to gather her skirts and settle herself on the sidesaddle that the inn owner unearthed from the back of his small barn and polished with rather more profuse apologies than actual success in the cleaning.

At first their way lay over high, rolling, green land broken with outcrops of rock, patches of wildflowers, and the ever-present sheep. To their left, water sparkled from sound and loch, while cloud-draped mountains hung in the distance to their right. The short-legged, sure-footed little animals they rode made good time on the rough dirt track, and as they turned west around yet another long loch, the terrain suddenly grew more rugged, and the mountains loomed closer. Jagged black hills rose steeply from a green river valley, and birds called from the bushes at the base of the treeless heights.

Although they ever pushed to make the best time they could, actual speed was impossible, so Tonia enjoyed the sense of companionship as she traveled this wild land beside Charles. "Tell me more about this Flora MacDonald one hears so much of, my love. She seems to be quite the local heroine."

"National heroine, I should more think—even to those who didn't support the Jacobite cause. Well, let me see how much of my history lessons I can recall." Danvers was quiet for several minutes as the party left the rutted track to make their way around a band of sheep lumbering leisurely along the path. The heather- and tussock-covered land they turned to ride across was actually smoother than the trail, but they were obliged to keep careful watch for sharp rock outcroppings that could damage the unshod feet of the horses.

Finally back on the trail, Danvers picked up the requested narrative. "As I recall, Flora's father died when she was young, and Lady MacDonald took her under her protection when Flora's mother remarried. The Donalds are the lords of Skye. After Culloden, Lady MacDonald was obliged to serve as hostess to the government troops on Skye—a role in which she could easily serve as spy for her defeated prince, who was in hiding on the isle of South Uist off Skye's west coast. When she heard that the government was going to make a thorough search of Uist, the lady enlisted Flora's help."

Again the narrative stopped while all gave attention to their riding. They guided their mounts across a tumbling stream that ran from a high waterfall streaking white against the side of the mountain, then rushing on to fall into the sound beyond them.

"Pray, continue, my love," Tonia urged when they were once again on somewhat level ground.

"Flora's stepfather was an officer with the government troops. She obtained from him a permit to travel with her maid Betty Burke. And so, with the prince dressed as her Irish maid, Flora rowed him to Skye. They were even fired upon, as I remember. To cross the mountains to the other side of the island, Flora hired a horse, and her 'maid' walked beside her all the way to Portree where they parted."

"What a marvelous story. Flora must have been in great danger."

"I'm sure she was fully aware of the risks she was running for her prince—capture, imprisonment, even execution. As it was, she was arrested and taken to London but later released."

"And then?"

"She married and lived in Skye. Had several children, I believe."

Tonia clapped her hands, which made her little pony pick up his ears. "So, a happy story."

"The happiest to come out of the shambles of Culloden. Scotland didn't get her Stuart monarch, but she did get a national heroine."

As they rode on beside the jagged Cuillins, Tonia became aware of a sense of brooding in the mountains—a feeling that darkness lay behind the sun and that at any moment they could be engulfed in thick gray mist. At the foot of a high, green, rocky hill they came upon a cluster of little thatched, stone houses nestling in the curve of the valley.

"Oh, what a quaint little village," Tonia said.

Their young guide shook his head. "Clachan."

Tonia started. It was almost the first word he had spoken on the entire journey, and she didn't understand it.

"Clachan?" she repeated. "You mean that's the name of the village?"

Danvers interpreted. "He means it's a clachan—simply a group of crofts, not a village."

"Oh. I was hoping they'd have an inn. Breakfast on Raasay seems a lifetime ago."

"Fortunately McNab provided a hamper." Danvers patted his saddlebag. "But perhaps we could find a goodwife to provide fresh milk to accompany it."

A woman was scattering feed to chickens in front of one of the cottages. Danvers greeted her and asked if he could buy three mugs of milk. The woman looked frightened, dropped her apron, dumping the remaining chicken feed at her feet, and disappeared inside the gaping black mouth that was the doorway of her home.

A moment later she returned, chattering in Gaelic to a young man who appeared to be her son. He approached the riders, then stood, feet apart, hands on hips, head thrown back defiantly. "We're leavin' within the hour." He pointed to a mound of bundles and parcels by the doorway. "The others have gone to bury Malcolm. The factor agreed we could do that first. There's no need to be burnin' the thatch over our heads."

Danvers held up his hand to stop the young man's angry flow. "No, you mistake. I'm sorry. I didn't know the evictions had come here. We just wanted to buy some milk."

"Sorry are ye?" He kicked at a clod. "Nae sae sorry as we be. Sure we're being cleared—more land for more sheep for more money for the fine laird who owns the land but cares naught for his people. We're the last in these parts. Now the sheep can have it all." He started to turn away, then stopped. "Milk is it ye're wantin'? Ye'll have nae luck here. They took all our cattle three days ago—overdue rents they said." He stomped back into the blackness of the hut where his family no doubt had sat around smoking peat fires for generations out of mind. But he would be the last.

Danvers turned his horse, and they rode silently on up the narrow green valley under the looming mountains. Around the next curve they came to a tiny, stone chapel standing alone on the hillside, where a small group of people huddled together. This must be the burial the young man had referred to. The body lay to one side in a crude pine box while the living dug a grave. They took turns digging with the oddest little crooked spade Tonia had ever seen. Its blade was shaped more like a plowshare than a shovel. The handle was an unsmoothed sapling, and partway up the handle was a pin for the foot to push against.

They paused to observe the strange proceedings. Every head turned away from them, all the mourners looking just alike in their dark, homespun clothing, the men in their caps, the women's heads all covered with black kerchiefs. Then Antonia caught her breath. It was the strangest sensation. From that little clutch of faceless figures one head turned toward her. He regarded her for only one moment in a long, malevolent stare, then turned away, and yet, impossible as it was, she felt a flicker of recognition. Broad, heavy features, sandy hair—far too vague for any identity, and still, something about the look . . . In the mill? At the medical school? Someone in Edinburgh, she was certain.

Once beyond sight of the mourners, they stopped for a hasty picnic from the hamper Danvers had had the foresight to bring with them. The boiled eggs, oatcakes, and cheese went down well with the small bottle of ale the innkeeper had provided, but Tonia couldn't help thinking it would have been much better with the fresh milk they had been unable to obtain.

They didn't linger after the meal. Aware always of the need to hurry, they pressed westward through green valleys at the foot of the magnificent, sawtooth-jagged Cuillin hills.

The sun was hanging low in the west when they rode across the flat top of a green cliff on the edge of the sea. Beside them the scattered cottages of the little fishing village of Elgol tumbled haphazardly down to the rocky coast. A few fishing boats and smaller craft rocked in the water. One larger ship rode at anchor close to shore.

"This is the village from which Bonnie Prince Charlie made his final escape from the island. They say he hid in a cave along the shore. The night he was to leave, the islanders gave him a farewell dinner in the cave."

Tonia shook her head. "I'm confused. I thought he left from the other side of the island."

"To go into further hiding. It is confusing. He wandered for a hundred fifty-seven days all over these islands. With a price of thirty thousand pounds on his head, any enemy could have betrayed him in an instant. Yet no one did."

But their sturdy, taciturn guide was not interested in a history lesson. He had a long way to go back to his inn in Portree. Danvers paid him well and sent him on his way with the horses, then turned to seek transportation for the last leg of their journey.

Antonia was beginning to feel distinctly travel worn. The great sense of adventure she had enjoyed that morning was now lost in aching shoulders and sore muscles. How she longed for warm wash water and a soft bed, rather than a spot on a stinking, rocking herring boat. She suddenly felt a great rush of kinship for Flora MacDonald. That lady's journey had been even more arduous than her own, with the risk of fatal danger at every turn. Surely Antonia could endure this last leg of the trip she was making to prevent disaster for her friend.

But even so, it didn't appear that it was going to be easy to accomplish this one final lap. Danvers shook his head after repeated inquiries up and down the steep little street that tumbled to the broad strip of rocks forming the shore. "The fleet is out. No one knows when they'll be back—it all depends on the catch."

"What about those?" Tonia pointed to the few boats rocking at anchor in the bay.

"Either they aren't seaworthy, or the skipper is indisposed—if they could sail they'd be with the fleet."

The sun edged closer to the horizon. They needed to be on their way. They couldn't wait here for days simply hoping the fishing fleet would return. The clomp of draft-horse feet and the rattle of a heavy farm cart made her look up the street. The cart's clatter was accompanied by a mournful, wailing song being sung in the strange Gaelic tongue by the load of dark-clad people in the wagon.

The horse plodded to the bottom of the hill, and the driver shouted over his shoulder to his passengers. He made no move to help them from the cart, even though many were elderly women or mothers holding small children, and all carried heavy bundles.

"I told ye we'd go. No need tae be gloatin' over the leaving."

Tonia jumped at the familiar, rough, thickly accented voice. She turned and saw the boy from the crofters cottage where they had stopped earlier that day. She started to protest her innocence of any gloating, but Danvers spoke. "Ah, the ship in the harbor. It's an emigrant ship?"

"And did ye think we'd be takin' it for a pleasure cruise? Soon there'll be nae people at all over hill and glen. Jest the sheep bringin' in money. And may you and yer kind have the good of it, I say."

Danvers chose to ignore the lad's blaming him for all the faults of the ruling classes and asked instead his question of more pressing concern. "Where does this ship stop, man?"

"America," the boy more spit than said the word.

"But does it not call anywhere else first?"

The lad shrugged. "Ask the captain." He turned on his heel to follow the sad little group to a small launch that would be rowed out to the ship.

Danvers turned to a tanned, toughened seaman who was just about to get into the launch. "Do you call at any more ports?"

The man gave a vigorous projection to the wad of tobacco he was chewing. "A few passengers for Oban, that's all. Then the open seas, and God give us good sailing."

The launch was crowded and the mate anxious to be off, but Danvers offered the clink of coins, so the man agreed to take them to the ship.

The clutch of passengers in the launch gave the finely dressed couple blank stares that Antonia found harder to bear than the young man's defiance. But they made room for them.

A few minutes of creaking and splashing of the oars manned by two crew members brought them to the ship. Tonia was the first to ascend the rope ladder up its curving wooden side. Danvers stood below her, holding the ladder as steady as possible, and yet the climb was a considerable feat in full skirts. The rough oakum prickled even through her gloves, the rope swayed and twisted, her feet groped for each unsteady step. Then at last she felt herself being steadied and lifted as muscular sailors handed her over the side and onto the deck.

As soon as he was aboard, Danvers approached a man in a blue uniform with gold braid, his gray mustache flowing into thick muttonchop sideburns. After a brief conversation, Danvers turned with a smile. "Captain Laing will be happy to welcome you aboard, my dear." He turned back to the captain. "My wife, Lady Danvers."

The captain tipped his hat. "The *Reliant* and all her crew are mighty proud to have you aboard, ma'am." He led the way to his private quarters.

The captain's cabin on the forward deck was paneled with polished mahogany and carpeted in dark blue. It was small but snugly fitted with a sturdy table and chairs, several chests, and a comfortable-looking bunk at the far end. Books, papers, mugs, and nautical instruments littered every flat surface, but the room was clean.

"Please, make yourself comfortable, ma'am. The first mate will be serving us a nice hot meal as soon as we've cast off. This final batch of stragglers were the last I had orders to wait for. Uncooperative lot they are, and after their lairds pay their passage and do all they can to set them up in a new life—still, can't expect gratitude from their sort, can we?"

He cleared some papers off a chair and offered it to Antonia before taking his bowing leave of her.

She sank into the seat gratefully. It didn't seem possible that the warm meal and soft bed she had dreamed of were about to become reality. "Well done, my love. What an excellent accommodation. I hadn't dared hope. How long will we be aboard?"

Danvers surveyed a chart on the wall. "Given fair winds and good tides, I should think we'd be in Oban early tomorrow morning."

Antonia closed her eyes with a soft sigh.

Sometime later she was aware of the gentle motion of the ship and the splash of water that told her they had set sail. Up from a lower deck floated the sound of a tune played on a tin whistle accompanying the chanted sing-song of a Gaelic lament. She opened her eyes slowly, aware of the golden glow of the setting sun filling the cabin. She looked to her right for a moment. An intense, burning ball glowed white and golden through a strip of fluffy cloud that hung just above the black, silhouetted ridge of a western island. The rays of the sun reached toward the boat in a ripply golden path. Surely this was an omen for the success of the rest of their task.

A sense of movement behind her made her turn. For a moment she was aghast at the look of contempt on the face in the window. But before she could cry out, it was gone. Instead she gave only a strangled sob.

"Antonia, what is it?" Danvers was by her side instantly. "Were you dreaming?"

"Yes, I must have been. That face . . . today at the funeral I thought . . ."

"What face?" Danvers strode to the window that looked out on the surrounding deck. "No one there now."

"No. I'm sure I'm just being silly. I was dazzled from looking into the sunset." But even later, while enjoying the captain's simple but tasty dinner, Antonia didn't feel as certain as she had sounded.

Danvers had asked the captain something about emigration from the islands and was getting a full answer.

"Ah, yes, took the first boatload from Skye myself, I did. Let's see, that'd be fourteen years ago. Took more than four hundred fifty to Australia that year. Three years later I took six hundred to Canada, and there'll be more, many more—it's the future. But it's always the same—the moaning and sobbing. They're going to a lot better life, but they don't know it. Costs two pounds five a head for passage—landlords pay it all—right generous of 'em I say—but the people will carry on so."

"I suppose one can understand it, though, when their families have lived on the land seemingly forever." Danvers helped himself to a second slice of the captain's roast lamb.

"Land's not good for farming—it was meant for sheep rearing. The good Lord made it that way. They have no business flying in the face of the Creator or the law. Perfectly within their rights, the landlords are, you understand. Crofting has no tenure rights, never has. People fall behind in their rents—ought to be thankful to have their passage paid, that's what I say.

"Of course, they used to pay their rents in service in the old days—made up armies for those warring Highland chiefs. All that's changed since the Forty-five, though. No need of private armies now—and a lot more peaceful it is too."

111

The first mate refilled the glasses with a full, red wine.

Below deck a plaintive song rose and seemed to swell with the rock of the waves. Perhaps the captain was right, and the people were going to a better life—Tonia hoped so. But she couldn't help sympathizing with these people who were being torn from their ancestral homes by faceless landlords and forces they couldn't understand. Thinking of the heavy hearts giving expression in such sad songs, Antonia glanced over her shoulder out the window. Then she froze.

Impossible. It was dark out there. She couldn't have seen anything. It made no sense that there should be a face glowering at her through the glass. Her imagination had never been highly excitable before. It was just the wildness of these islands. It must be.

11

As the major port gateway known as the Road to the Isles, Oban was a bustling town with an ancient, ruined castle on a wooded promontory jutting picturesquely into the harbor. Early the next morning Tonia thanked the captain for a most comfortable passage among the islands and only looked over her shoulder twice to see if the mysterious face was peering at her from the crowd. All she saw seemed intent on their own business. She had wondered if her intruder might be the belligerent lad from Skye who so unreasonably blamed Danvers for his misfortune, but she saw him nowhere and was certain he would be below deck with the other emigrants. The other passengers for the mainland had already departed down the gangplank.

Once again, though, Danvers did not have the easy time he had expected in securing the services of a boat to take them to Dun Eilean. It seemed that every time he told a boatman where he wanted to go, the man would suddenly lapse into Gaelic and inexplicably forget every word of English he ever knew. Yet Antonia was certain she had heard many of them speaking the queen's English—or a somewhat reasonable facsimile thereof—a few minutes earlier.

At last Tonia turned to a woman gutting fish by the side of the pier. Antonia pointed to Danvers and asked casually, "Why won't anyone rent a boat to that man?"

"It's the clearances. They won't be hiring to any of his kind."

"But he isn't a landlord. He isn't even—" Antonia stopped. She could see it was useless. These people were in solidarity with the crofters. They did not share the sea captain's blasé attitude. And they would not be moved by logic.

The woman shrugged and picked up another silver herring. Slit, slit, scrape, and it was done.

"Listen, my man, I don't care anything for your local politics. And don't you start jabbering at me in that heathen tongue, or I'll have an officer down here and see that he finds some reason to fine you. Now I need a boat, and when Harry Raeburn needs a boat he intends to get it!"

Antonia turned with a smile. She had never thought that Harry Raeburn's thundering would sound good to her.

"Now see you here. A good-for-nothing scalawag has run off with my daughter, and I mean to get her back if I have to buy your leaky tub of a boat and sail her myself."

The news that Raeburn was a father desperate for his daughter's honor, and not yet another hired strong arm come to burn out the crofters, brought the desired results.

The small open boat rocked in the choppy waters of the Firth of Lorn, and a sharp breeze pulled at Antonia's bonnet as gulls wheeled overhead. Danvers put his arm around her as she shivered, and she smiled at the thought that at last they were nearly there. Standing at the tall rudder, the boatman Harry Raeburn had badgered into service pointed to a small black mound in the distant water. "Eilean," was his single contribution to the conversation.

As the wind whipped the sail and the island grew in size, Tonia's spirits rose. All that remained of their goal was to talk sense to Madelyn and bring her away with them. Surely an easy task, as the girl would have had three days now to come to her senses and must be lamenting the rashness of her action. And even if not, Harry Raeburn was not the man to dawdle in such a situation. Antonia was certain he would simply pick up his daughter bodily and take her to the boat if necessary. How he would treat Gil, however, she shivered to think of—although the young man certainly deserved chastisement for his foolhardy action.

The island was beginning to take form when Harry turned around to talk to them. Its green shape appeared to be something close to a mile long from north to south, perhaps something less than that the other direction, but it was hard to tell. To the east it seemed to slope to a rocky shore curving in a small bay. Tonia thought she could just make out a small beach—probably where the boatman would land.

The back of the island, to the west, rose in a rocky shelf that must serve well to protect the land from lashing storms in the open waters beyond the firth. On the turf above the bay, what had at first appeared to be a massive rock outcropping gradually took the shape of a large stone house.

"Dun Eilean." The boatman added a second word to his vocabulary.

Raeburn nodded his head. "Fortress of the island, that'd be." He explained to Tonia. "*Dun* means 'fort' in the old tongue. *Eilean*"—he pronounced it *aylan*—"is Gaelic for 'island.'"

Tonia smiled. "So really the name is 'island island.'"

"That's about the size of it. The MacTavishes never were a very imaginative lot. Still—good, hardheaded businessmen. That's what counts. Good business with their sheep. And I'll tell you something. When I get this little matter settled with my miss I mean to see her married to young MacTavish, and there's an end to it. We'll have no more of this shillyshallying. And that's what I'll tell her as soon as I get my hands on her."

Tonia looked up in surprise to see the boatman veering to the right as if he meant to make for the steep, rocky back of the island rather than for the little bay below the house.

Raeburn noticed too. "What're ye doin', man? There's the harbor—make for it."

"Not the wisest plan if ye're nae expected." The boatman shook his head and gave a long, slow pull on his pipe. "There's tales they tell of the Tavish firing on uninvited boats. Not that I've ever experienced it, mind you, but I've no desire to be finding out."

Craggy spears of lava loomed out of the water. Waves broke white against them on even such a relatively calm morning as this. No peaceful cove presented itself on this exposed side of the island.

"Man, you'll smash us on the rocks!" Harry Raeburn shouted.

"Nae. I know my job, and I know my boat. I'd best be taking my chances with rocks I can see than with bullets I can't."

"Nonsense, man. Tavish is headstrong, but he isn't an outlaw—"

Everyone jolted upright as a gunshot sounded above the splash of the water. Tonia gripped Danvers's arm.

"As ye were sayin'?" The boatman nodded at Raeburn.

"Shooting rabbits, that's all. Cook'll be making rabbit stew for supper, you'll see."

"It's not I that'll be seein'." Then the boatman said no more as his full attention was required to guide the small craft through a narrow channel that was free of lava snags and up to a narrow, rocky shelf below a black cliff just wide enough to allow the passengers to disembark. "Used to come here when we were lads. A big sport to see if we could outsmart the auld laird—father of him that's the Tavish now. Fine game for lads tired of fishing. Bear to yer left. There's a path that'll do you all right." He glanced

116

at Antonia's boots. "I could be wishing that the lady was a mite better shod, but you'll do."

He sprang over the side. His rubber boots half covered with water, he waded ashore and pulled up the boat so that the others could land more or less dry-shod.

"Where do you think ye're going, man?" Harry Raeburn stopped him when he started to return to his boat. "We'll need transport back, I told you."

"Aye, you will. Like as not I'll pass this way again in a day or two. If Tavish hasn't hauled you off in his own boat, ye can light a beacon."

"Light a beacon?"

"Just pile some bracken on a high rock and set it alight. Someone's sure tae see it."

"Wait a minute—" Harry looked as if he would restrain the man physically, but the sailor shoved his boat off the shingle with one foot as he leaped over the side with the other. With a few strong pulls of the oars he was beyond reach.

"Good luck tae ye!" He lifted his cap and continued rowing.

Tonia was thankful that Harry's reply was indistinguishable to her ears.

Danvers surveyed their surroundings. "Looks like the recommended path starts just over here." He pointed to a steep, narrow break in the side of the rock. "I should say we'd best make a start before the tide rises." Already their beach was narrowing from the incoming water.

Head down, shoulders hunched, still emitting angry mutters, Harry Raeburn strode forward.

Tonia followed, thankful for the supporting hand Charles placed under her elbow. The ascent was incredibly steep, at times seemingly straight up, and the path so narrow she was obliged to gather her skirt from both sides and hold it tightly in one hand while she steadied herself with the other hand against the side of the cliff, doing who knew what damage to her gloves, not to mention what the scrapes from harsh lava must be doing to her finest goat-skin boots.

The view from the top, however, was worth the hazards of the climb. The sheltered side of the hill sloped down to a gentle, green, bowl-shaped valley dotted with wildflowers and sheep. Blue water sparkled beyond in every direction, and seabirds called. The only harsh note on the landscape was a clutch of four or five stone cottages in a hollow to their right. The remaining charred shreds of their thatched roofs stood silent witness to the suffering that had occurred there. The sheep the crofters had been removed to make room for grazed peacefully around the sightless cottages. Three figures with rifles moved in the distance on the valley floor.

Raeburn pointed. "See, what did I tell ye? They'll be the rabbiters."

As he spoke one of the three brought his rifle to his shoulder and shot into the bracken far below them. A stirring in the brush told them the hunter had missed. Then suddenly a form sprang forward from the largest of the broom bushes, and Antonia saw that it was no rabbit the men were hunting.

A scream rose in her throat, and she muffled it with gloved hands as a second rifle fired and the dark-clad male figure leaped to cover behind a boulder.

"Get back." Danvers pulled Tonia behind a protecting rock shelf, and Raeburn took cover behind a thick gorse bush.

"We must help him," Tonia said.

Danvers considered. "Perhaps. It's hard to know the right of it. Might be a thief—or worse. Tavish is the law here—he has the right to protect his property."

"Which he is known to do violently." Tonia shivered as the words of the boatman suddenly became real to her, and she realized that they too were trespassing. They could be the next ones fired upon. She drew further back into the cleft of the rock.

118

"Still, it's one apparently unarmed man against three rifles. We can't let him be shot down like an animal."

They were all quiet for several moments, surveying the land and thinking. If only they had a dog they could send to his aid, Tonia thought. Even a small pet like Tinker could offer some diversion. She considered the boatman's words about lighting a beacon but could see that would serve little purpose in this situation, even if they could build a pile of dry bracken without being fired upon themselves. She moved carefully from her hiding place to get a better look at the island. As she stepped forward her foot dislodged a pebble. It bounced harmlessly down the path behind them, but it gave her an idea.

"Charles, if you and Harry could creep along the ridge to our left to where you're more or less behind those men, and find a large boulder that you could push down the hillside . . ."

Danvers considered. "Might be just possible. It wouldn't actually do much, but it might distract them long enough for the fellow to get away."

Antonia didn't say anything, but her eyes pleaded for the unfortunate human being in the valley below. Whatever he had done, surely this wasn't the way he should be treated.

Danvers and Raeburn nodded at each other and moved carefully to the left, keeping behind rocks and bushes. Tonia peeked from her hiding to see what was happening below. Apparently the hunters had lost their quarry momentarily. They were standing, each gazing a different direction, but none at an angle likely to spot any movement on the top of the ridge. She pulled back into hiding and breathed a prayer for the unfortunate man, for Danvers and Raeburn, for Madelyn—for all of them.

When she dared look again she could see no movement along the ridge, so Danvers and Raeburn must be in position. Below her the hunters moved slowly forward, but none seemed about to fire, so perhaps they still hadn't spotted their victim. She held her breath, waiting for the next move.

She hadn't long to wait. She saw the granite snag just before she saw Danvers reach out to push it. It must have stood balanced there for hundreds of years of wind, rain, and sunshine. If their need hadn't been so desperate she would have thought it a pity to dislodge it. But the effect was marvelous. As if it were alive it leaped from its rocky footing, and Harry Raeburn, bless him, accompanied its crashing journey with as wild a war whoop as any that could ever have been issued by a Highland warrior.

At first the rock fell end over end, toppling smaller stones to accompany it in its descent. Then it fell sideways and began rolling like a fat, oval log, flattening bracken and gorse as it went.

At first crash the hunters had spun around and fired on the falling stone almost in unison, thereby loosening more rubble and increasing the effect of the rock shower. One of their number had then taken to his heels and run for the valley floor. The other two stood in undecided confusion. At last one started upward toward the place Harry's shout had come from, until, at a command from his mate, he turned and started back in the direction the rock was falling.

Antonia saw no more, for a rustle of brush and crunch of small pebbles made her turn to her right. The hunted man crashed through the cover, landing almost on top of her. At sight of Antonia, he stopped as if struck dumb. "*Tonia.* What are you doing here?"

"*Gil!* It was you! Why are those men trying to shoot you?"

Gasping for breath, Gil flung himself at her feet.

Before he could answer, Danvers and Raeburn returned. Raeburn took one look at the exhausted Gil and threw himself upon him, grasping him by the neck. "You! If I'd known it was you I'd have let them shoot you. Young good-for-nothing. Run off with my daughter! Shooting's too good for ye!"

Gil made a choking sputter, and Danvers drew Harry back. "We're too exposed to talk here with men prowling around below with rifles. I noticed a cave on the other side of the cliff. We should be safe there for a while," Danvers said.

Gil, rubbing his throat, nodded. "I don't think they'll believe I could have gotten over the ridge, so it should be all right."

No one talked until they were huddled in the shelter of the cave hidden behind a pile of rocks beside the path. "If a bird hadn't flown out of this on the way up I'd never have noticed it. Someone who knows the island well probably knows about it, but I think this will be safe enough for a time. They'll be pretty busy trying to figure out what happened." Danvers grinned broadly, obviously pleased with their exploit to rescue Gil. "Now, Morris, why were they shooting at you?"

Harry started to make another lunge forward, but Danvers held out a restraining hand.

Gil shook his head. "I don't know. I just walked up to the house to knock on the door, and they came after me." He wiped the sweat still pouring from his forehead with a large cotton handkerchief and looked at the incredulous faces around him.

"You mean you're alone?" Tonia asked.

"But why—" Danvers started.

"Where's my daughter?" Raeburn cut through all else.

Gil looked thunderstruck. "You mean she isn't in Edinburgh? What are you doing here? Did you come about the sheep too? Dougal said he wouldn't give the evidence to anyone else, that's why I didn't tell Futter. I suppose I'm in more trouble now for leaving town."

"That's the least of your troubles, my boy!" Harry broke past Danvers's restraining arm and grasped Gil by the shoulders. "I want my daughter back! What have ye done with her?" He began shaking Gil. Tonia feared Raeburn would slam the boy's head against the rocky sides of the cave. "How dare ye elope with her? How dare ye?"

Again Danvers intervened to curb Raeburn's fury.

"Elope? What are you talking about?" Gil managed to choke out when Harry Raeburn subsided. "I got a message from Dougal MacTavish. He said I was to go to their holding at Invercrenan—said he'd just had a message from their factor there that could clear me of any suspicions the police had." He stopped to shake his head. "It sounded far-fetched, but I supposed it had something to do with the tartan—it did seem to be a special wool, and I know Tavish experiments with fancy sheep—I don't know—it sounds pretty silly now, but it made sense at the time. I suppose if I hadn't been so worried about it all—and then Tonia said Munro had the wrong body, and I figured I'd get blamed for that too. Futter was sure to see something sinister in my being a medical student—I don't know . . ." He slumped against the side of the cave.

"So if ye went to Invercrenan, why are ye here?" Harry's threatening gesture toward Gil was obviously only for show. He wanted to hear the answers to his questions even more than he wanted to thrash the boy.

"Tavish was there. I showed him Dougal's message. He said he didn't know anything about it—he hadn't seen Dougal for months—but maybe Dougal meant Dun Eilean, and since the island's only a short sail from their mainland estate I might as well try that while I was here. He was very decent, I must say. Even had a servant row me over." He paused for breath, then looked at Harry. "But what do you mean about an elopement? Where is Madelyn?"

Tonia answered. "She left a note that she was coming here. It sounded like she was coming with you—she said she loved you." Gil gave her a grateful smile. "Anyway, we knew you were worried about the trouble you're in, and we heard Dougal offer you a retreat, so we thought—"

"Sir, Mr. Raeburn, sir." Gil turned to Harry, all the color drained from his face. "Sir, you can't think I'd do that. Yes, I hope to marry Madelyn, but I have the highest respect for her—I'd never sully her name . . ."

Harry Raeburn waved a hand his direction. "Yes, yes. I think I believe ye. And a lucky thing for you it is too." He paused. "But if you didn't run off with Madelyn, who did?"

They looked at each other. Tonia nodded. Only one answer seemed feasible—Dougal MacTavish. She looked at Gil. "Dougal sent you that message to get you out of the way. And we're here on his family's island . . ."

"And he's wanted to marry Madelyn for a long time." Harry looked crestfallen. "And I wanted him to." He shook his head.

"But where is she now?" Danvers asked. "Do you think she's in the house?" he asked Gil.

"I don't know. I didn't get close enough to see much."

"But why would Dougal try to have you shot? Eloping is a serious matter, but not worth killing over."

Gil shook his head. "I don't think they were trying to kill me. If they had been, I'd probably be dead by now. I think they were just trying to scare me away."

"So what do we do now?" Antonia asked. "I wonder if they shot because Dougal saw it was you. I mean, I wonder if I could walk up to the door and be received civilly?"

"Well, you're not going to find out, my love. We're not taking chances like that with your pretty head."

"Seems I saw a hay wagon in the field. When it gets dark we could creep up and push it against the door, then set it alight . . ." Harry Raeburn was ever the man of action.

"I don't think so, Raeburn," Danvers said. "We're not sure Madelyn is in there. If she is, I doubt that she's in any danger—unless we put her in danger by doing something like setting the house on fire."

"If we could just know what's going on inside there." Gil ran his fingers through his pale hair. "Can't go in with guns blazing since we don't have any guns."

No one seemed able to form a clear plan. At last they agreed that it would be a good idea if Danvers were to creep back up the path and see if there was any new activity in the valley.

For what seemed an eternity Tonia waited patiently after the soft crunch of Danvers's foot on the path faded. No one in the cave spoke. For her part, Tonia could think of nothing useful to say. But at last, when it seemed long past the time when Charles should have returned, she could take it no longer. "I'm going up there too."

Neither man protested, and in a few minutes she was beside Danvers, peering across the sweep of the valley as late afternoon shadows lengthened over the turf. Only sheep moved beneath them. At last Danvers stood up, still behind the rocks. "I've not seen a thing. The place may well be deserted."

"But we can't go without finding out for sure. Where do you think those hunters got to?"

"In having their supper, I suppose."

A rustle of brush announced Raeburn and Gil's joining them. "I say we go down there—the men, that is." Harry nodded to Antonia. "Lady Danvers can wait safely enough in the cave until we find out what's going on."

"Correction. Lady Danvers can step right over here where she'll be safe enough if you gentlemen behave yourselves." Three threatening figures stepped from behind the rocks to their left. One of them held a rifle leveled at Antonia's head.

12

Mr. MacTavish doesn't like unexpected visitors, but as long as you're here it'd only be right that ye pay yer respects, so to speak." The man gestured with his rifle toward the path to the house.

"Lower your gun." Danvers faced the man. "We won't give you any trouble. If Dougal MacTavish is here, I can assure you we want to see him even more than he wants to see us." He offered his arm to assist Tonia in the descent.

The man did not exactly lower his gun, but he dropped his aim so it wasn't pointed directly at Antonia. The party moved forward.

When they approached the massive stone house, the barking of dogs made Tonia turn to a large wire cage just inside the low stone garden wall. Three tall, yellow and brown hounds stood on their hind legs, clawing the wire as violently as they would claw any victim unwise enough to get within reach of those enormous paws.

"Mr. MacTavish turns the Finian hounds loose just before dark every night. Ye won't want to be out pleasure strollin' then." The tallest of their escorts, the one with cadaverous eyes that looked like black hollows, grinned horribly.

The house still appeared deserted, and yet Tonia couldn't suppress a shiver at the sensation that somewhere behind those black-looking squares of glass they were being watched.

She must have been right. No sooner had the heavy iron gate snapped shut behind them and they started up the stone-flagged path, than the front door opened. Dougal MacTavish stepped out, splendid in his red, green, and blue kilt. "Ah, what excellent timing. We are honored to have guests in so remote a spot as this. But what would a wedding supper be without guests?"

He held the door wide and gestured to his men. "Raymond, put the rifles away now. It'll soon be too dark for hunting. I'll need you and the boys to serve at table." He turned back to the newcomers. "It's most inconvenient. I would have canceled the servants' little holiday in Inverary if I'd known we were to have such distinguished company. Without doubt they'd have wanted to be here to serve you, if they'd only known. Of course, certain things came up rather unexpectedly."

No one moved to enter through the heavy, planked door he held open.

"Blast it, Dougal, why'd you have me fired on?" Gil waved a fist in his direction.

"Fired on, dear boy? You must be mistaken. It's early for grouse, I'll agree, but they are such delectable game, I told the boys just to see what they could do—this being such a special occasion and all."

Now Harry Raeburn moved—to place his nose within about two inches of their host's. "What are ye meanin' —wedding supper?"

Dougal took a step backward. "Well, I'll admit the term is just a bit premature. Pity about Parson Adams being delayed in Inverness with that big storm we had two days ago. But it really wouldn't do to have the service performed by any but the old vicar who has so faithfully served near to three generations of our family. No, in a case like this, Parson Adams is definitely worth waiting for, I say. But that's no reason to let an excellent roast go to waste, is it now, gentlemen?"

With that he turned and led the way in himself. "But we mustn't stand about any longer. We're keeping my bride waiting."

He led down a dark hall, then threw the door open onto a large room with a black oak-beamed ceiling. The walls were hung with tooled leather, and even the drapes at the tall windows were of leather, gold-embossed. In spite of the fire burning in the tall, marble fireplace and reflecting on the polished floorboards, the room still felt cold.

"Papa!" Madelyn jumped to her feet from a cordovan wing chair in a shadowy corner. "Oh, Papa, I'm so glad you've come!" She took two hasty steps forward, then stopped. "Gil! I thought—"

"That's right, my dear." MacTavish's smile showed white teeth. "Greet your father. Only too natural to want to have family with you on a happy occasion like this. How lucky it is when family and business matters can coincide so beautifully, isn't it?"

Madelyn walked obediently across the floor to her father but did not fling herself into his arms as it had apparently been her first urge to do.

"What have you done to my daughter, MacTavish?" Harry Raeburn thundered.

Dougal spread his hands out, palm upwards. "Why, nothing I haven't done several times before—which is to propose a most advantageous marriage to her. The happy difference is that this time she has accepted me."

"Madelyn, no!" Gil cried.

"Is this true, girl?" Harry asked. "He's done ye no wrong?"

"No, Papa. No wrong." Her voice was barely audible.

"And ye've accepted him freely?"

"Yes, Papa." Her head hung.

The room was silent for a moment. Then Antonia broke the stillness. "Well, then we must wish the bride well. I give you my love, my dear." She stepped forward to embrace Madelyn and kiss her on the cheek away from MacTavish's view. "Offer me your help," she whispered, then turned to their host. "You'll appreciate that I had no idea I was to attend a festive occasion, sir—thinking, as we did, that we were merely helping Gil seek evidence on a police matter. I'm afraid I must ask you to postpone your dinner a few minutes longer while I do what I can to improve my sorry appearance. Madelyn, my dear, you know how hopeless I am at arranging my own hair."

"Yes, I'll help you, Tonia. I believe I have a ribbon that will just match your dress."

They were almost to the door when it opened and a tall, long-faced, large-boned woman entered carrying a tray with a decanter and several small glasses.

"You must entertain the men on your own for a few minutes, Deidre. Lady Danvers and I will return shortly." Madelyn marched on, and Tonia was glad to see that the lift was back to her friend's chin.

Once in the hall, Madelyn held a finger to her lips and sped up the dark-railed stairway, then down a long corridor. She opened the door on a forest green room with a bed hung with maroon draperies. She turned the key in the lock, struck a match to light a lantern, and put a square of peat on the glowing embers in the fireplace. "There now, we can be quite comfortable—as comfortable as it's possible to be here. But we can't stay long. I don't mind Deidre too much, but I don't want one of those men he calls his 'boys' coming up here to fetch us."

"Madelyn, what is going on? We thought you'd eloped with Gil. Have you really consented to marry that dreadful MacTavish? Who is Deidre?"

"Deidre's his sister. I think she lives here. Anyway, she's here to lend me countenance. Good thing too, since there are no maidservants—or he got rid of them all—I'm not quite sure. Anyway, she's not too bad. I feel sorry for her. Of course, she obeys Dougal in everything."

"Yes, yes, but are you really going to marry him?"

Madelyn sank into a chair with a sigh. "I held out for a long time, but it really does seem best."

"But why did you elope with Dougal? We thought you'd run off with Gil."

Madelyn shook her head. "If only it could have been. Dougal said Gil had been arrested, but he had evidence up here that only we could get—something about my tartan the police were asking about. He said it tied Gil to a murder in London, and he had information here that the police would do anything to get their hands on. Proof that would hang Gil. But Dougal swore he'd destroy it if I married him."

"Madelyn, do you believe that?"

Madelyn bit her lower lip. "That he'll destroy the evidence? I don't see why he wouldn't. He only hates Gil because I want to marry him. If I'm married to Dougal . . ."

"No, Madelyn. I mean, do you believe such evidence exists? Do you believe Gil capable of doing anything terrible?"

For the first time Madelyn brightened. "No! Of course I don't. Oh, Antonia, thank you for making me see that. I've tried to keep my head, but I've been so frightened." Then her countenance fell, and she sank back into the chair again. "But I do believe Dougal capable of making something up that would ruin Gil even if it didn't get him convicted."

Tonia nodded. "Yes, I can easily believe that too."

There was a knock at the door and the muffled sound of a female voice.

"Deidre," Madelyn whispered. "I forgot about her." She pointed to the dressing table. "Just a minute, Deidre," she called.

Tonia sat at the stool before the mirror and began combing her hair.

Madelyn unlocked the door.

Deidre entered with a pitcher of warm water. "I don't see why you insist on locking your door, Madelyn. You're perfectly safe here." She poured some water into a bowl for Tonia to wash.

"You know I hate Raymond, Deidre. I won't take a chance on his coming in on me."

"Nonsense," the woman snapped.

"Thank you for the water." Tonia tied Madelyn's gray and blue plaid ribbon around a cluster of side curls.

Deidre gave her an unsmiling look. "You will be so good as to be down in five minutes. My brother is hungry, and he doesn't like to be kept waiting."

Antonia washed quickly. "Madelyn, you are not going to marry Dougal MacTavish. We are not going to let this happen."

Madelyn shook her head. "I don't see any help for it."

The meal was the most uncomfortable Antonia had ever sat through. Although the food, apparently prepared by Deidre, was excellent, the tension was so strong no one could eat—except Dougal MacTavish who took hearty servings of everything, accompanied by quantities of a deep red wine that he continued to urge on his guests.

Tonia prayed Gil could restrain himself from throwing a glass of wine in Dougal's face when he talked expansively of the joys of marriage awaiting him. She was certain Raymond kept his rifle just behind the serving screen, and she didn't want to provoke its appearance.

At last Dougal had eaten his fill, and Deidre started to rise to lead the ladies from the table.

"Stay, sister." Dougal stopped her. "I have something to say that I wouldn't want any of our guests to miss."

The ladies settled back into their chairs.

Dougal emptied his wineglass, and Raymond refilled it from the sideboard. "I believe everyone here is acquainted

with the fact that Madelyn's grandfather won his vastly profit-
able woolen mill from my grandfather in a card game—"

"He won the startings, man. The mill my father built
by his own sweat and toil—to which I've added my share
of the work and more. It's nae your mill and never was."

"Perhaps not. But I intend that it shall be now." Dougal smiled. "What none of you know, I'm sure, is that your
father cheated in that infamous card game, Raeburn."

Harry Raeburn's heavy fist thudded against the table.
"That's a stupid lie, man!"

Dougal appeared amused by Raeburn's anger. "It
was stupid, I agree. Mostly it was stupid of my grandfather
to be hoodwinked and of my father to take no revenge. I do
not intend to be stupid."

Harry pounded the table again. "Even if he did cheat,
ye couldn't be knowing it now."

"On the contrary. My father bribed your father's man-
servant to get the story. It seems your father's man was the
one to clear away after the game. He discovered that one
ace was missing from the pack—in the suit that had been
trump the last hand. Knowledge of that fact would have
been enough to give your father the winning edge."

"I believe your father bribed the man all right—bribed
him to make up the story."

MacTavish ignored his response. "Fortunately, I'm
not an unreasonable man, Raeburn. Goodness knows I'd
naturally not want to sully the name of my bride's family by
making such a scandal known, and, of course, in due time
the mill will come into my control as part of my wife's
property. But it occurs to me that we might just speed the
course of natural consequences if I were to give you a
chance to make reparation for your father's sins by agree-
ing to a return match—same stakes, of course."

"You mean ye want me to gamble with you for Raeburn Woolen Mills?" Harry growled.

"Precisely. I was certain I had made myself quite
clear on the point."

Harry considered. "Aye, and if I do, there'll be no need for ye to wed Madelyn."

"When you lose. True enough. As regards the mill, that is. There are other considerations, however."

"Dash ye, man. There are no other considerations, and well we both know it. 'Twas the only reason ye ever wanted my lass. I see it plain now. I'll play ye fair and square. But Madelyn goes home with us—however the game comes out. And there's an end to it."

"Done." Dougal raised his glass, and Harry responded with his in pledge of the terms. "Raymond, the bezique cards." MacTavish turned back to Raeburn. "You know, no doubt, that is the game our forebears played which today bears such consequence on our lives."

"I had no notion. But bezique will do very well."

Raymond placed two unopened packs of cards on the table.

"If you'll allow me." Danvers stepped forward, unwrapped each deck, and counted thirty-two cards in each. He then shuffled the packs together.

The others at the table withdrew to more comfortable seats. MacTavish maintained his place at the head of the table. Raeburn sat to his right. As self-appointed referee, Danvers sat to the left. A sudden gust of wind blew a blast of peat smoke down the chimney. The candles guttered, and the shutters rattled.

Harry won the cut and dealt the first hand of eight cards to each player. The next card was a heart. Hearts would be trump.

The play proceeded. The only sound in the room was the players' muttered declarations, the slap of the pasteboards, and a rumbling from Harry Raeburn as he won or lost each trick. Harry took the last trick, adding ten points to his score and thereby winning the hand.

MacTavish dealt next.

Antonia could sense a slight relaxation in Madelyn sitting next to her on the small sofa. But Tonia felt her own tension mount as the next hand progressed with Mac-Tavish seeming to take the most tricks, although she lost count. She was thankful that Charles sat at the table, watchdogging every card played. Whether or not Harry Raeburn's father cheated as MacTavish claimed—and there could be no proof either way—there was no doubt in her mind that Dougal MacTavish would do anything for his own advantage.

When Raeburn lost a rather large bid, Tonia glanced sideways at Madelyn and was amazed to see that the girl had hardly noticed. Then she saw the source of Madelyn's equanimity. Her full skirt billowed over the edge of the sofa, and Gil's chair, placed at a clever angle, just allowed the young couple to hold hands behind Madelyn's petticoats.

Madelyn, however, was the only relaxed person in the room. Tension grew as MacTavish won the next two hands. The earlier wind now lashed rain against the shuttered windows, and the pounding of the waves on the beach below sounded almost as if they were lapping the very walls of the house. Tonia wished she could be holding Charles's hand, but as he was out of reach she clasped her own together so tightly her nails bit into her flesh.

Harry won the fourth hand. Only ten points separated the players. The next hand would take one of them over the 1,500 game points.

It was Harry's deal: three cards each, two cards each, three cards each. Clubs trump—a seven of clubs, which in bezique added ten points to the dealer's score and an additional ten points to the score of anyone taking a trick with a trump. This would be a high-scoring hand. The chips marking the scoring points mounted as each trick was taken.

MacTavish declared a marriage on the first trick—playing a king and queen of the same suit, for twenty points. Harry took the next trick with a trump, which gained him the bonus ten points.

Tonia caught her breath as MacTavish played a bezique—queen of clubs and jack of diamonds—adding forty points to his score. The pile of chips in front of each player grew. MacTavish had the taller stack, but brisque points—bonuses for playing aces or tens—were only added at the end. She had seen Harry play several of each but had lost count of the actual number. All she could do now was wait and pray.

MacTavish took the last trick for a bonus ten points. He counted his chips first—1,650 points. Dougal MacTavish had gone over the 1,500 required to win by 150 points. He folded his arms and leaned back with a satisfied smile, which never softened his glittering eyes.

Harry Raeburn counted his chips—1,700 points.

Tonia let her breath out in a rush and leaned back against the sofa.

Madelyn sprang across the room and hugged her father. "Oh, Papa, well done! You won!"

Then Tonia saw that MacTavish's smile had not wavered. "I think not. I fear your declaration is a bit premature, my dear. There remains one last trick to be played."

At MacTavish's words, Raymond stepped from behind the serving screen with his rifle leveled at Madelyn.

"You monster!" Gil jumped to his feet but didn't advance as Raymond moved the gun a few inches closer to Madelyn's head. Gil sat down.

"I believe that settles the winning hand rather thoroughly." MacTavish pulled a legal document from his jacket pocket. "Foresight and preparation—invaluable tools the legal profession teaches one. Fortunately I brought them into play, and so I am prepared with the requisite documents at hand. So nice to avoid unnecessary delay, don't you think?" He tossed the papers to the table in front of Raeburn. "You will, of course, want to read these carefully to be certain that all is in order. You can be certain I have left no loopholes in the matter of immediate conveyance of the title of Raeburn Woolen Mills to myself."

Dougal rose languidly, took a box of cigars off the sideboard, and offered them around the room to the men. When all refused, he took his time selecting one, clipping the end off, and lighting it to his full satisfaction. After his second long draw, which added a heavier scent to that of the smoky peat and warm leather already filling the room, he turned once more to the sideboard and produced a nib pen and inkwell.

"Whenever you're ready, Raeburn. But don't let me rush you. I know a good businessman like yourself wouldn't sign anything without reading all the fine print. Danvers, if you'll be so good as to sign as witness. I could ask Raymond, of course, but he is rather occupied at the moment."

Harry finished reading, growled in his throat, looked down the black steel of the rifle barrel to his daughter's shining auburn hair, and reached for the pen. When he had signed he handed it to Danvers, who also signed.

MacTavish took the document and blotted both signatures before folding and replacing it in his pocket. "Thank you so much, gentlemen. A pleasure doing business with you. A real pleasure. I would offer to shake hands, but I somehow suspect you might decline, and that does create such an awkwardness, doesn't it?

"And now but one awkwardness remains. I fear I must impose a little longer on my dear sister's gracious hostessing and request that you all remain here until I've settled certain business matters in Edinburgh. But then, I know none of you would care to set out in tonight's inclement weather anyway. I would say it would be insanity for one not born and bred to these waters as myself. Fortunately, I've sailed them many times under worse conditions, so I will be able to meet my obligations in a timely manner."

"Obligations? What are you talking about, Dougal?"

Tonia started at Deidre's words. Throughout the game the woman had remained so silent in her far corner that Tonia had forgotten she was there.

135

Dougal turned to his sister. "Nothing for you to worry about, my dear. Just a little financial matter. Gentlemen's debt to be paid."

"Oh, Dougal, have you been gambling again? Mother always said you had Grandpa's disease and that it would be the ruin of you."

"Well, it seems she was wrong, doesn't it? I'm not the least bit ruined. As a matter of fact, I consider this a most successful night's work." He paused at the door. "Raymond, there should be no need to inhibit our guests' movements too severely. You will, of course, want to keep your . . . er . . . implement nearby, but as I'll have the only boat there's no danger of their straying far until I return for them."

He bowed to the room. "Have a pleasant stay. I'll delay no longer than absolutely necessary. Oh, and I'll take a message to Mrs. Raeburn, shall I? I know she'll be relieved to hear that you're all well."

"You stay away from my wife, you scoundrel!"

Deidre rose. "I'll see you off, Dougal."

The door banged shut behind them with a fresh draught from the wind. Raymond replaced his rifle behind the screen and began clearing the few glasses scattered around the room. Danvers crossed to sit by Tonia. Madelyn stood silently by her father, her arm around his slumped shoulders. No one spoke.

It was several minutes before they heard the tread of boots on the tiled floor of the hall.

"Dougal, please reconsider. It isn't too late." Deidre's voice reached them, but not Dougal's reply. The front door creaked on its iron hinges.

The silence lasted the space of three heartbeats. Then a blast of wind, a snarl of the dogs, and a protesting cry mingled to bring all to their feet. Tonia was never sure whether the shriek that followed was Deidre's, commanding the dogs to attack or objecting to what their savage instincts led them to do. Perhaps it was merely the whistle of the wind around the towers of the house. But she knew she would never forget that chilling sound for the rest of her life.

The moment the snarls and barks of the hounds mingling with the cries of Dougal MacTavish filled the room, Raymond grabbed his rifle and ran out. Tonia jumped with each of the three shots. Each was followed by a sharp yelping. Then all was silent again except for the lashing of wind and rain.

Deidre entered, as stony-faced as ever. The disheveled state of her sandy hair was the only sign that she had been outside her own parlor. "I warned him he was just like Grandpa, but he wouldn't listen. Grandpa was killed by his own dogs as well."

She turned and walked toward her room.

13

The next morning a watery sun shone on patches of gray clouds in the sky and pools of gray water on the land. But the Firth of Lorn lapped calmly on the sodden little beach of the bay below Dun Eilean.

Danvers was the first to see the small launch approaching. There was no need to worry whether Raymond would object to their meeting this visitor. Raymond was occupied with Deidre in Dougal's room, laying out the savaged remains as decently as possible. Raymond's two cohorts had gone to the field beyond the garden to bury the hounds.

Tonia walked down to the shore with Danvers, stepping carefully to avoid the puddles. She smiled when she recognized the pale tow hair and ruddy complexion under the dark blue domed helmet. They had been too long away from law and order in these wild islands. "Inspector Futter, how good to see you."

The next man off the boat was elderly and stooped, with a paunch stomach. He wore a broad-brimmed, flat black hat and cleric's collar. "Parson Adams," he introduced himself. "Such delays, such delays. All the way from Inverness. I do hope the MacTavish isn't too dis-

tressed with my tardiness. A marriage to perform, I understand?"

Danvers shook his hand. "Your timing couldn't have
been better, Parson. Just one change of plan. It'll be a funeral rather than a wedding."

"Oh my, oh my. Well, well. The Lord giveth, and the
Lord taketh away, what? Blessed be the name of the Lord."
He began patting his various pockets, then drew out a slim
black volume with a smile. "Ah, yes, here it is—'Order of
Service for the Dead.' Always prepared. That's what a good
servant needs to be. Always prepared." He began turning
pages in his prayer book as he made toward the house.

"Funeral?" Futter asked Danvers.

"Strange doings here last night, Futter. It'll make a
report worth the reading if you care to write it all down.
Nice thing for you is that MacTavish's Finian hounds did
all your dirty work."

"Not unless they cleared up this business about the
tartan corpse, they didn't. It's that scoundrel Morris I've
come for."

At that moment Gil and Madelyn stepped out the
front door.

The policeman strode forward. "Fat lot of good it did
to warn you not to leave Edinburgh, didn't it, young man?
Now do you want to come along for questioning nice and
quiet-like, or am I going to have to arrest you?"

"You have no idea how pleased I'd be to go along
with you, officer."

"Oh, is that so? And to give me some straight answers to my questions as well, I hope."

In the shortest time possible, they were sailing back
toward Oban. Madelyn and Harry Raeburn stood on deck
for a clear view of the myriad cloud-draped green islands
rising from the blue waters around them.

Inside the small cabin, however, Futter wasted no
time on sightseeing. He pulled from his pocket the card
bearing the reproduced plaid pattern and held it out to Gil.

"Now, Lady Danvers here had a very interesting story to tell me about you and a bolt of fabric of this precise description—a little something it seems she saw back in Hyde Park. I'm sure your memory will need no further jogging, sir, in spite of the many distractions that have taken place in the intervening time."

Gil dropped his head in his hands. "Oh, I know. I knew I should have admitted it." He raised miserable eyes to the inspector. "When you showed up in Edinburgh I knew I'd have to. But I couldn't do it to Madelyn. It'll break her heart. And now, after all she's been through . . . but the minute I read the description of the tartan in the *Times* I knew it was hers. She designed it herself and was so proud of it—who else but the daughter of the finest weaver in Scotland would have her own tartan for her birthday?— besides the queen, of course. And that was all they wove— just that single bolt for her dress. So of course I had to get it back. The guard was easy enough to bribe. But then it was in such bad condition—even smelled awful. If my sweet Madelyn knew where it had been and what it means—"

"And what does it mean?" Futter asked.

Gil ran his fingers through his blond hair. "I've been trying to work that out. Any way I go at it, it seems Harry Raeburn must be involved. But Madelyn mustn't know her father's mixed up in anything sordid—whatever it is."

"It seems you underrate your young lady, Mr. Morris. I informed her about the tartan just before you all set out on this wild goose chase up here. She held up fine. But I wonder how she's going to feel when she hears that you've been charged with murder?"

All the natural ruddiness drained from Gil's cheeks. "Are you charging me?"

"Not at the moment. I don't have it all worked out yet. But there's plenty going on here. I'm warning you, I will get to the bottom of it. And when I do, you'd better be right where you belong. If you set one foot outside Edinburgh I'll lock you up so tight you'll be gasping for air."

The next day they arrived back in Edinburgh. Antonia was as anxious to be alone to talk to Charles as she knew the Raeburns were to be together, so as soon as they had greeted their hostess they retired to their room.

It was an elegant guest chamber in what was apparently the typical Edinburgh situation on the ground floor overlooking the garden to the back of the house. The wide, velvet-draped bed was flanked on both sides by highly polished chests. On the opposite wall a warm fire of sea coal, blissfully not peat, glowed on the hearth before a pair of plushly padded chairs.

"Oh, Charles, it's so wonderful to be back to civilization!" Tonia interrupted herself with a small giggle. "Can you imagine what Aunt Elfrida would have to say to the Highlands and islands? She called Edinburgh barbaric." But after a moment of savoring her refined surroundings, Tonia turned to the larger matter facing them, which their recent escapade had done nothing to untangle. "Can you figure it out, Charles? Something horrid is going on. People very near to us are involved. And I can't make any sense out of it."

Danvers shook his head, and Antonia noted how the lines beside his mouth were deepened again—as she hadn't seen them since the Stanfield Hall affair. She placed a kiss on her fingertip and ran it down the side of his cheek. She cared far more about whatever was bothering him than about any mystery the police needed clearing up. And yet it all seemed so confused it was impossible to sort the problems or questions into categories.

Charles took her hand and touched her fingertips to his lips, then began an attempt at the sorting out. "Perhaps if we just listed the questions: Who was the tartaned corpse? What was he doing in that bed in London? Why was he murdered? How's that for starters?"

Tonia nodded. "And where is the body now? Who did Monro dissect? Who switched the bodies? And why?

141

All that quite apart from any questions about Madelyn's plaid and Gil's involvement, of course."

"Quite enough questions to occupy us for one evening, it seems."

The room was quiet for several ticks of the longcase clock on the wall.

"There doesn't seem to be any place to start," she said. "Except that it must have something to do with Raeburn's mill."

"Has to. The body was wrapped in a plaid exclusive to them. The bed the body was found in was draped in Raeburn fabric, then shipped to London from the Port of Leith . . ."

"Yes. But by whom? And why?"

Then one of those unusual—formerly unheard of—silences fell between them, silence that seemed to be getting longer of late. And it seemed that awareness of it stifled Tonia's ability to break it. At last Danvers turned to a side table and picked up a small black book she had noticed him reading earlier. "What is it, my love?"

He glanced up from under his dark eyebrows and seemed to weigh his answer before speaking. "Just something my father gave me. A sort of journal he kept long ago."

Antonia picked up a volume of poetry their hostess had placed in the room. But she found Robert Burns's dialect heavy going. Soon she closed the book and paced around the room on the Oriental carpet. Perhaps now she should talk to Charles, ask him what was wrong. Of course it was silly not to. They had always been open with each other. Now they were man and wife—surely that should mean a new closeness, less restraint. Yet she could not bring herself to probe. As long as the question remained unasked, she could tell herself nothing was wrong. Once spoken, the matter would have to be faced. And what if it were the unthinkable—that he was unhappy with his choice of wife?

"Charles . . ." Her voice was so soft she didn't think he could have heard her. But the dark eyes turned from the book to hers.

However, any answer he might have made to her entreaty was lost in a bumptious knocking on their door.

"Come."

Even before Danvers's answer was fully enunciated, the door opened and Hardy entered with a wave of triumph. "Sorry I am, m'lord, not to be here when you're needing me to see to your comforts—and missing you these days I've been. But I've been about your business you can be sure, and you'll thank me for it, I know—but not that you're needing to say a word."

He plumped down a slim white envelope on the table next to Danvers with a small bow that made his stout figure seem even rounder than usual and his cherubic blond curls to fall around his face.

Danvers opened the envelope and drew out two pasteboard tickets. *"The Anatomist,* a play by James Bridie, the lamentable comedy of Knox, Burke, Hare, and the Westport Murders. Adelphi Theatre," he read aloud.

"And right you are. Completely sold out, but I managed it for you. Knew your lord and ladyship wouldn't want to miss the hit of the season."

"Am I to take it, Hardy, that Lady Antonia and I are engaged to attend a dramatic performance?"

Hardy turned from the clothes press where he was assembling Danvers's night things. "And I won't hear of you paying me back for them—consider it a wedding present. Your pleasure will be my pleasure."

When the recipients of his magnaminity made no reply, Hardy continued. "And isn't this Edinburgh a right one for being a fine city? After your little trip north, ye'll want to be seeing the sights, I'm sure." He paused in his work to consider his lord and lady's silence. "The castle. You'll not have been to the castle? The kirkyard—Greyfriars? The

143

duke of Queensberry's house—where his eldest son roasted a kitchen boy alive on a spit and was found eating him?"

"*Hardy!*" The last brought Danvers to his feet.

"Begging your pardon. Supposing I did get a mite carried away. It's forgiving me you'll be, though. I'll set it all right tomorrow. A jolly day for sure."

Antonia looked doubtful. But perhaps it would be better than focusing on doubts closer to home.

Even with Tonia's best attempt at cheerfulness, however, when the candles were snuffed some time later, her thoughts returned to serious subjects. After stories of murder, grave robbing, and dissection, then the perils they had faced in the Highlands, now topped with Hardy's story of cannibalism, she could only be horrified by such blatant disrespect for the sanctity of life.

Surely man—God's highest creation—should be treated better by his fellow men. Certainly MacTavish's example wasn't the first to indicate that man could be evil. But wasn't man, created in the very image of God, capable of even more good than evil? If so, where was evidence of that good?

14

By next afternoon, though, Antonia had determined to put somber philosophy behind her. In a rich, brown merino day dress, fringed paisley tippet, and deep-brimmed straw bonnet, she held tightly to Danvers's arm as their landau jostled up the rough cobbles of Castle Hill. Although clouds gathered in the distance, the sun shone overhead, and the air held only the mildest tinge of its often-heavier reek.

"We were quite right to follow Hardy's advice, my love. It would be unthinkable to miss the most famous sight in all of Edinburgh."

As the carriage rattled across the visitor-dotted esplanade, Hardy turned from his elevated position on the cabriolet seat beside the driver to assume the duties of tour host. "And a fine parade ground it is, is it not? All peaceful-like today, but not always so, I can be telling you. This is the very spot where they burned Edinburgh's witches. More than three hundred found guilty of working for the devil were dispatched right here."

He gave indication of a desire to expand on those facts, but at that moment Flanders pulled the carriage to a halt beside another vehicle, and the party alighted. Antonia took special care with her suede leather halfboots on the uneven stones.

They made their way across a drop bridge cleverly designed so that an attacking army, should one have managed to scale the already considerable defenses of the rock, could be plummeted into the dry ditch below the castle. Fortunately the bridge was secure for the day, and they entered the sixteen-foot-thick walls of the castle under all six sets of portcullis gates.

Numerous clusters of visitors wandered among the tangle of gray stone buildings and along the batteries of cannon lining the walls. Officers and men of the various regiments stationed at the castle went about their work. A pair of Gordon Highlanders, one in full kilt and shako, the other in tartan trews and a plaid cap, were conducting a serious inspection of the artillery in spite of the enthusiastic hindrances of two small, ragged boys wearing pointed hats and carrying toy rifles. They appeared to have some notion of marching their smaller-yet sister around the cannon at gunpoint. The sister disagreed—noisily. A small, black, yapping terrier added to the confusion until their mother, carrying a squalling baby wrapped in a tartan shawl, picked up the girl child around the middle and marched down the esplanade with her, leaving the boys to follow.

Antonia made her way to the edge of the parapet. "Oh!" She drew a sharp breath and surveyed the grandeur before her just as, on her arrival in Edinburgh, she had looked up to where she was now standing. Her eye swept down the great green ravine and across to Princes Street, while Hardy explained to Danvers about the draining of the North Loch a hundred years before—depriving the depressed of Edinburgh of "the pot," a deep hole in the loch that seemed to have been used with some regularity for committing suicide when the city fathers weren't using it as a dunking pool to discipline lawbreakers.

Antonia, however, preferred to concentrate on the panorama before her: the Scot monument almost directly ahead, Calton Hill to her right, the classical order of New

146

Town and the leafy emerald green of Charlotte Square shining jewellike to the left. And then beyond it all, the sparkling blue waters of the Firth of Forth, busy with tall-masted ships. She gave a moment to think of the secluded, misty waters of Loch Leven and its pastoral countryside. While there, she had not thought they would have been torn from their secluded retreat so soon. But now she would enjoy what was before her, and surely matters would be settled soon so they could return to their idyll.

Hardy pointed out the new military prison, declaring it a model of modern penitentiary design, and led on to the Palace at the far southeast corner of the citadel. "And you'll not be seeing anything like this anywhere else, m'lady —only original crown in all of Britain. The Honours, they calls them. Seems some parson's wife hid 'em away and kept 'em out of the hands of that thievin' Cromwell, or they'd a-been melted down for his uses."

Two pair of Highland guards in kilts, sporrans, and cockaded hats stood with rifles at the ready on each side of Crown Square, unperturbed by the activity milling around them. Hardy gestured to a heavily grilled window to the right of the palace tower, indicating their goal.

They entered the palace under the recently heightened octagonal turret-tower supporting the castle's main flag-staff and followed Hardy back and up a narrow staircase. Most of the visitors had turned toward a small ground-floor chamber.

Hardy gave them a glance and shrugged. "Mary Queen of Scots's bedchamber—where her son was born—didn't see much in it myself."

At the top of the stairs they paused in a vaulted chamber where Danvers was obliged to pay the princely price of a shilling a person for their party to proceed. As those in front of them moved ahead, they entered the formerly walled-up room where the oldest complete regalia in Europe lay in state on a table heavily draped in gold-embellished red velvet.

Above its circlet of ermine, the pearl-and-gem-encrusted crown gleamed with the added adornment of five centuries since its beginning as a simple circle for crowning King Robert the Bruce. The golden scepter sparkled to one side of the table, and the mighty sword of state, its High Renaissance silver hilt ornamented with symbols of the risen Christ and the church, stood to the other side, a little apart in solemn majesty.

Antonia caught her breath as these visible manifestations of the strength of a nation made their impact. "Think of their being walled up—lost—for so long. How did they find them?"

With a slightly puffed chest that showed his pleasure at being asked, Hardy cleared his throat. "Sir Walter Scott it was—the very same who wrote all those fine books—got royal permission to search for them. Most folks thought they were gone, but Scott had the door unsealed." He pointed to the door of that very room. "The trunk had to be broken open—and a nice surprise it was for everyone."

With that conclusive bit of understatement, Hardy turned and almost stepped on one of the little boys that had caused the disturbance outside. He had apparently elected not to follow his mother. The child ducked under Hardy's legs, nearly upsetting him, and made a dash for the table, apparently with the object in view of hiding under the red velvet drape displaying The Honours.

"I don't care if your brother is in there. You are not going in without paying." The guard's voice sounded from the reception room.

Danvers snatched at the boy in their room and caught him by his tattered coat. Still holding the squirming child, he returned him to the ticket taker, who held the brother.

"If you'll allow me . . ." Danvers produced two more shillings. "I believe a history lesson might do these boys some good."

It was obvious from the looks on their faces that military strategy as translated into hide-and-seek was more on

148

the lads' minds than learning the history of their land, but the impressive size of the sword and the gleam of the gold and jewels in the scepter and crown were not lost on them.

". . . Then when Queen Elizabeth of England died childless, James the Sixth, Mary Queen of Scots's son, was her heir. He went south to be crowned James the First of England with an English crown, and The Honours became the symbol of the Scottish nation . . ."

The boys began wiggling. The younger one eyed the velvet cloth as if he still might make a break to hide under it.

Danvers turned them toward the stairway. "All right. Off you go then. Your mother's waiting for you."

They started forward.

"And don't pick on your sister," he added.

At that they seemed to remember their manners and turned back.

The older one grinned. "Ach, the wee lassie's nae sa bad."

"Ta!" His brother thanked their benefactor before clattering down the stairs.

Antonia smiled. When she saw the party outside she had thought they were there to see the sights. Now she realized they were local residents. That poor, harried mother of four was probably younger than herself and lived with her brood in the squalid Old Town. Tonia turned to Danvers. She was glad he had indulged the children.

The three adults made their way sedately back out to the bustling courtyard and across to a plain-looking rectangular block building.

"Saint Margaret's Chapel—oldest building in the castle."

Antonia smiled and nodded at Hardy. Now he had brought her to a site she knew something of. Her gaze swept up the unadorned stone walls, and she thought of the good queen who had done so much to feed the hungry, clothe the poor, and minister to the souls of her people that her sainthood gleamed through eight hundred years.

"But you'll be finding this interesting, m'lord."

Hardy's voice broke her reverie, and Antonia turned to view a massive iron siege gun.

"Mons Meg herself." And he launched into a tale of how, likewise under the hand of Walter Scott, the gun had been returned to Scotland from the Tower of London.

Danvers laughed. "Hardy, I'll soon be believing your Irish grandmother has been supplanted by a Scots progenitress."

"Oh, and have I not told you about . . ."

But Antonia was drawn to move inside the lovely old chapel. Its tiny, whitewashed walls gave it a sense of lightness and purity that seemed to reflect the life of the woman it memorialized. She crossed the worn stone floor to the vaulted arch framing the altar. A small vase of yellow flowers stood before the wooden structure.

Tonia paused. She knew little of Scots history, but what she had read of Queen Margaret impressed her. Loving her people, the queen wanted them to love God, so she lived in a way to show Him to them and—most important —to her own family. She was the mother of three kings, all of whom followed in her strong faith. Her son David I, who built this chapel in her memory and so many abbeys in the borderlands as well, was surely an example to all that, in spite of the scriptural warning that the sins of the fathers are visited on the children unto the third and fourth generations, just as clearly the righteousness of the mothers could be so visited.

But Hardy, with thoughts less devotional, was now behind her, suggesting, with as much deference as his ebullience was capable of, that they should move on to other sights.

Their carriage, raked sharply forward, rattled down the bustling Royal Mile, and on either side of the narrow, crowded way Hardy pointed out items of interest: ". . . And there's where James Boswell entertained Dr. Johnson . . . and Deacon Brodie's house—him that was for being the most upright of respected citizen by day and a thief and no-good by night—hanged right up there at the Tolbooth . . ."

Tonia turned her head to one side and then the other, nodding to Hardy's tales. As colorful as the past he recounted may have been—with such inhabitants as the countess of Eglinton and her seven beautiful daughters, whose procession of sedan chairs to dancing assemblies always drew crowds of ogling, admiring observers—it seemed that, by the midpoint of the nineteenth century, decay had decidedly set in.

Even the atmosphere emphasized the fact. The clouds that had threatened earlier now hung overhead as a reality, holding in the reek of coal smoke and brewery. Where women of fashion had once placed brocaded slippers en route to their balls, women of much lower class now tramped ill-shod, chasing muddy children from the gutter to make for home on a Saturday evening when their menfolk would be late in the pub.

"Has Edinburgh always been so crowded?" Antonia asked.

Hardy shrugged. "Excepting I suppose when it was cleared out a mite by the plague. But worse now, perhaps. Some still wandering in from the clearances. Those as don't fancy transporting to the colonies or couldn't succeed with kelp farming on the coast may come here or to Glasgow." He shook his head at the melee around them. "Clan chief's responsibility to take care of their people they say, but looks like somebody's not making much of a job of it."

A conglomeration of fruit barrows, old clothes hawkers, bannock vendors, and other assorted boskers blocked the way of the carriage. To their right a screaming child pulled the tail of a scruffy dog attempting to join a passel of snarling cats. Beyond them two women who had been merely yelling at one another suddenly erupted into a scuffle of scratching, screaming, and hair pulling.

Hardy suggested they alight. While Flanders sorted out the traffic snarl, he would just tell them a wee interesting tale. In a matter of a few strides they stood before an enormous stone monument with a statue on top.

"Here we are, the Mercat Cross. Now I've a fine tale to be telling ye." Unperturbed by the rowdy crowd around him, Hardy lectured. "It was 1513. One Richard Lawson, citizen of the fair city of Edinburgh, was returning home late one night when that very stone angel on top of the cross began to move. The scroll in its hand was unrolling, and the angel was reading aloud the names listed thereon: from King James the Fourth through most of the nobles and barons of the land, right on down. Richard Lawson listened until he heard his own name proclaimed . . ."

Antonia's attention wandered as she looked around at the bustling crowds, the tiny old buildings jumbled against each other higgledy-piggledy, the little dark passageways leading to tiny, yet more crowded closes.

". . . At that point"—a sudden drop in Hardy's voice made her turn to him again—"the laddie broke off listening and began praying. And mightily he prayed for all his sins. All the ones he knew of, all the ones he didn't know of, all the ones he'd committed, all the ones he might be going to commit, he repented them all . . ."

Tonia's gaze strayed again. The whole mile seemed like a rabbit warren pushed to the surface by an eruption not so much later than the one that threw up the massive castle rock. The dirty, somber-dressed people and their animals could even be seen as scampering hares hurrying down their narrow, curving ways to whatever cramped, dismal quarters they must call home.

". . . Then—" Hardy cleared his throat, calling her back "—thinking his best escape was to get right away from Edinburgh, the next day Richard Lawson joined His Majesty's forces and marched clear down south across the border to Flodden Field to engage the forces of Henry the Eighth. Not a very wise choice, as King James and all his nobles and barons—those whose names Richard Lawson had heard the angel read out—were killed that very day. But Richard Lawson, him who prayed so mightily, he was spared. Now . . ."

All at once, one of the groups Antonia had been observing stood out from the rest—not another faceless, rabbity clutch, but a mother and children she could identify. It was the children from the castle. The boys, pointed hats long knocked askew and ripped, were still wielding their toy rifles, this time over each other's heads. The small sister, who had come in for her share of the blows, was howling, and the mother, with the infant nursing under her plaid shawl, attempted ineffectually to separate them.

Tonia started to point Hardy to help when a champion stepped from the shady recesses of a close to lend aid.

He was a young man, better dressed than most around him but dirty, as if he had been at a muddy task. He stepped between the rascals, held them at arms' length, and gave each a hearty, single-handed shake. The surprise, more than the jostling, silenced them. Set firmly back on the pavement, the two, chastened for the moment, turned toward nearby Rhum's Close.

In an effulgence of gratitude, the mother flung her free arm around the man's neck, her other arm still engaged in clasping her infant. In the commotion, the man's cloth cap fell to the ground.

When he turned to retrieve his hat, Tonia gasped. *"Gilchrist!"*

She grabbed Danvers's arm and pointed.

He saw too and called out. But apparently their friend didn't hear them above the noise of the street, for Gil had turned away and was making for a south-curving wynd with considerable speed, weaving in and out among children, beggars, and street hawkers.

Danvers seemed determined to learn the truth about Gilchrist's strange behavior, and Antonia followed him down a steep set of stairs between buildings so close together they were obliged to go single file.

Now rain started to fall, making the jumble of lanes and closes darker, the stones slicker. And the stench worse. Soon Antonia realized that they both had lost all idea of where their quarry had flown and were at a loss as to their own location.

It was fortunate that Hardy too had followed. "Sure and it was the young lad," he panted as he caught up to them. "And what the likes of him would be doing in a place like this I'd rather not be thinking on."

"Yes, and I'm not so happy about having Lady Danvers in the likes of this place either, Hardy." Charles kicked at a small scampery animal that might have been a kitten but looked more like a rat.

"Oh, well, but it's not so bad, m'lord. And me wanting to show you the kirkyard anyway—it's just a step or two on this way.

"Hardy, you're amazing. How can you find your way in this?"

"Well, now, there's some mighty unlikely parts of London that you wouldn't be knowing much about either, m'lord. Seems as one slum's about the same as another. Course, the fact that I walked around here yesterday is no hindrance."

A few more shadowy bends of narrow, steep passages and the trio emerged onto a widened street beside the patchy, green grazing ground of the Grassmarket. Here, below the southern crags of the castle, weekly cattle and grain sales were held. Judging from the piles of droppings, this week's market had not been many days ago and had been attended by large numbers of cattle.

Hardy led around to the West Port and pointed toward a particularly grim-looking tenement. "Tanner's Close. The very place that Hare fellow had his rooming house.

Where he and Burke lured their unsuspecting victims, then saw them off. Very convenient. Just a nip on down the hill to Knox's house—not too far even carrying a body in a bag. Don't suppose you'd be caring to see the place?"

"A hansom cab for her ladyship, I think, Hardy."

"And right you are, sir, I'm sure. Although there's some as would say it's a pity to miss it—being so close and all." Shaking his head, Hardy turned eastward in search of a cab.

None presented itself the length of the Grassmarket, however, and the walkers found themselves before a quiet, green kirkyard, sheltered from the noise and stir of the city by a gray stone wall.

"Greyfriars Kirk. You'll be wanting to see this," Hardy declared and stepped into the yard.

The church itself, perhaps the most historic in Scotland—for here the National Covenant had been signed— was now a roofless, gray stone shell with empty traceried windows. It sat behind its scaffolding as if in a cage, in the midst of restoration from a disastrous fire of a few years before.

But it was another set of cages that took Antonia's eye. She observed the black iron grillwork encasing large numbers of the graves. Some were protected with a grid of horizontal bars a few feet above the ground, some with metal fences as tall as the kirkyard wall, others were entirely encased in barred metal structures the size of a small building.

"They look like the monkey cages at the zoo. They can't be meant for animals?"

"Mortsafes. To foil the graverobbers," Danvers explained. "Families went to any length to protect their departed from the ravages of the resurrectionists."

"And yet they failed," Antonia observed.

She noted a particularly grim look on her beloved's face as he replied. "Always someone to come up with a new scheme. Something of a game at the time, I suppose—and yet afterwards . . ."

"Ah, here we'll be now." Hardy perked up his ears at the sound of an approaching carriage. He hustled toward the street to hail the cab, then turned back. "Sorry I am, it's only an omnibus. Not suiting for your ladyship."

Tonia shook her head impatiently. "Hardy. I am excessively tired, cold, and hungry. An omnibus will do admirably."

"Well, at least it's not very crowded. Looks like only one other passenger." Hardy whistled and waved to the driver atop the long, green and gold conveyance.

Antonia, her head full of the civilized comforts of Charlotte Square to which she would be most thankful to return, lifted her skirts for Danvers to hand her aboard, while Hardy reached to open the door.

She observed the situation with slight annoyance. The omnibus offered six rows of seats, but its lone passenger had chosen the seat by the door and in the solitude of the carriage had apparently dozed off. She would be obliged to brush past him to make her way to a seat. But there was nothing else for it. Hardy swung the door open.

Antonia put her foot on the step.

One of the omnibus horses stamped. It gave the carriage only a slight jerk. But it was enough. The passenger fell forward toward the open door and landed face downward at Antonia's feet.

15

Antonia's scream drew the attention of several passers-by, including a police constable.

"Here, here, and wha's all this then? An early hour to be sae drunk, is it nae?" The bobby turned the exceedingly rumpled fellow over. A stale stench of decay and damp earth pervaded the already heavy air.

Antonia covered her nose as Danvers drew her away.

The policeman made short work of examining the man. "Dead," he pronounced.

"What?" Antonia couldn't believe it. "You mean the fall *killed* him?"

The constable shook his head, perplexed. "Can't rightly say. What d'ye know about this?" He addressed the driver, who had now climbed down off his box.

The driver pushed his tall hat back on his full brown hair and wiped his forehead with a dark blue kerchief before handing the policeman a crumpled note. "A friend of his put 'im on—last stop, just t'other side o' the kirkyard by Flodden Wall. Said he warn't feelin' quite right and this was where he wanted to go. He paid the man's fare."

Hardy shook his head. "He must have been feeling a lot worse than his friend thought."

157

The policeman smoothed the slip of paper and read. "'Liston House, 3 Bristo Square.' Wonder what he wanted there—sounds a touch above the likes o' him."

The driver raised his eyebrows. "Well, if that there Liston were still alive, I'd allow as how the fellow wanted a doctor. Seems as though it's a mite late for both of 'em as it is." He laughed at his macabre humor.

But the policeman took all seriously. "Doctor? Suppose that could be it. Have to check on it anyway."

The driver, however, knew his territory. "Not there. Liston's been dead three years—more. Family still there, but no doctors."

The commotion in the street was now increased by the rattle of a briskly approaching carriage. Hardy was the first to recognize it. "Ah, and if it isn't the luck of the saints that you've found us!"

Flanders pulled the Raeburn landau to a stop.

Antonia thought no carriage had ever looked better as she sank into the softness of its quilted leather seat.

Danvers left their address with the constable, should he have further inquiries.

Antonia, though, firmly put the entire incident out of her mind for the full duration of their host's superb dinner in Charlotte Square.

It had been an interesting, but tiring, day amid the history and brawling life of Old Town. And there had been that highly disturbing incident of seeing Gilchrist in those strange surroundings with that unfortunate woman embracing him. She looked at Madelyn, sweet and serene across the table, telling the pale and proper Mrs. Raeburn that Mr. Gil Morris would be calling later that evening, and the former scene slipped into unreality.

Surely in that highly charged atmosphere, with the surging spectacle of Old Town life all around them, she had been mistaken. Still, Danvers had been certain enough to follow the man down that warren of wynds and lanes—

and to what end? Another body? No. There could be no possible connection.

Antonia smiled at Moraig, who was offering a shimmering lemon jelly. Surely an overactive imagination such as hers was a curse. She should endeavor forthwith to curb it. She took a large portion of jelly and nodded as it was followed by a heavy dollop of cream.

Later that evening, when a scrubbed, shined, and polished Gilchrist presented his attractively shy self at the Raeburn drawing room, Antonia was glad she had already cleared her mind of ridiculous notions.

The conversation, however, could not be kept from the topic of the man who had fallen dead at her feet.

"Poor fellow," Gil said after a sip from a rose-crested teacup. "Heart attack most likely. Undernourishment, overwork, a touch of grippe—life's a hard lot for most."

"So you think he was trying to get to a doctor too?" Danvers asked.

Gil shook his head. "No, the driver was right. Liston was one of the most famous, but the fellow's friend would have known the doctor was dead." He bit into a triangle of sweet, buttery shortbread, then laughed. "Sorry. Bad joke. I just thought, though—if the fellow's friend knew he was a goner, Liston would have been the right choice—best resurrectionist Edinburgh ever saw."

When no one offered any other line of conversation, Gil continued. "Enormous strength they say. And speed—in everything he did. Liston holds the record for amputation —thirty-three seconds through a patient's thigh. Only trouble was, he took three of his assistant's fingers in the cut as well. Of course, the trouble with such popularity in those days was always getting enough cadavers for the demonstrations.

"But Liston was a champion at it. 'The Corpse King' they called him. It was considered a great honor to go on a midnight raid with him. His only rival was Monro. Not unusual for brawls to break out in graveyards between competing groups of students claiming the resurrected body."

Gil paused for another sip of tea. "It seems that one dark night Liston and his students were on their third grave when they found themselves surrounded by a mob with shotguns and blunderbusses. The resurrectionists scattered in the face of whistling buckshot, but Liston delayed long enough to scoop up the two bodies, one under each arm. He laid them up them in a garden, and the next day he performed the dissections cool as a cucumber."

Fortunately, Mrs. Raeburn had excused herself from the drawing room some time earlier so was spared the grizzly images. Antonia felt she also could have done without them, although the subject raised such interesting questions. "The whole thing is so awful—simply unspeakable —and yet the medical people were in an impossible position, weren't they?"

Gil warmed even further to one of his favorite subjects. "It can't be done—simply can't be done. You can't learn about the human body without looking at it. Would you want to be operated on by a surgeon who hadn't studied anatomy? Don't know what people were thinking about when they required anatomy training but denied bodies to train on. Executed criminals—those were the only legal subjects. Ironically, it took the worst of all—Burke and Hare, who murdered rather than robbing graves—to bring about a correction. When people saw what resulted from denying legal access to bodies, Parliament finally passed the Anatomy Act so we could get corpses legally. Put an end to that grizzly grave-robbing business once and for all."

"Yes, I know the need for study specimens is essential, and yet the body is sacred. I mean, we're created in the image of God, and the dead are awaiting His resurrection, not some graverobber's . . . I do see the objections."

Gil plunked his china cup onto a side table. "Those are the very arguments for studying the body with reverence. God made it, we should learn from it. The more we know of the wonders of the human body, the greater our awe of its Creator."

Antonia felt the comfortable room and excellent dinner working a stimulating effect on her. She was about to launch into an exploration of further views of life after death when Danvers rose abruptly to his feet.

"It has been a long day, Tonia. Let us retire."

She was surprised by the shortness in her husband's manner and even more so by the coldness in his voice and eyes. But that was all the more reason not to protest. "Right, my love. And we'll all be up early for church in the morning."

She nodded a good night to her host, who sat reading stolidly on the other side of the room, and exited on Danvers's arm. Perhaps they could talk in the privacy of their room.

But that was not to be. Charles prepared wordlessly for bed and lay in the four-poster with his back to her.

Antonia was determined, however. She would make one attempt before she snuffed her candle. "Charles—" she touched his shoulder "—won't you share with me what's on your mind?"

He turned toward her with a groan. "Oh, Tonia. What a hash of a honeymoon. I'm so sorry. If the choice were mine I would talk for hours. But it's not my story." And he rolled back onto his side.

Tonia placed the cone-shaped brass snuffer over her candle.

The next morning it seemed the Raeburn carriage rolled up a far different Royal Mile than the one they had visited the evening before. Although the scene was far from pristine, a vigorous rain during the night had rinsed the top layer of dirt down the gutter. There was no snarled traffic, and the drunks and children were all Sunday-morning quiet in their dim cubbies of closes. The drive to St. Giles's in the High Street was pleasant and rapid.

A dim but determined sun shone on the pepperpot

tower of the High Kirk of Edinburgh, giving even its sooty brown stones an appearance of warmth.

Inside, however, was unadorned stone. The paintings were still whitewashed and all the altars still stripped, as they had been at the Reformation. Cold seemed to seep upward from the floor to the ceiling, where the white plaster vaults between the brownstone arches gave the effect of winter snow on bare branches.

What had once been a sweeping cathedral was now divided into four churches, but the separating partitions did nothing to stop the flow of cold air. Antonia pulled her shawl tighter around her shoulders and sat as close to Charles as was decent in church.

Nothing was done to increase the sense of warmth when the black-suited minister announced his sermon topic. Leaning forward from the carved stone pulpit near the middle of the building where nave and transept crossed and the dividing walls intersected, he pointed a long finger at each hearer while pronouncing every word. "For I the Lord thy God am a jealous God, visiting the iniquity of the fathers upon the children unto the third and fourth generation of them that hate me."

The next hour and a quarter were filled with a ringing recitation of the sins of the congregation, of the sins of the citizens of Edinburgh, of the sins of the people of Scotland. That was followed by graphic images of the children born and yet unborn to these sinners, hanging by a slim thread over a blazing pit.

As the cold of the stone floor continued to seep upward, Antonia found increased difficulty keeping at bay the irreverent thought that the whole atmosphere was conniving to make even the preacher's images attractive.

But later that afternoon, while the Raeburns observed an appropriately solemn Sabbath—in careful attention that no sins of the fathers might be rung on Madelyn's tender head or that of her someday children or grandchildren—

Antonia saw that her suppressed levity was not to be shared with her husband.

Indeed, the weight that she had sensed on him for days had suddenly become an almost palpable thing. He sat in the winged chair before a fire that could barely be credited with smoldering and read the slim black volume Antonia had observed his father giving him the day of their wedding. His head was bent forward, his brow furrowed deeply.

Antonia had long abandoned any pretense of reading. When she observed the length of time it had been since Danvers turned a page, she decided that he too was making negligible progress. "Charles, won't you unburden yourself? Was it that dismal sermon that has left you so sullen?"

"Oh, Antonia." He thrust the book aside and came over to take her hands. "You are too good, too sweet. You should never have married me. I was well enough aware of my faults. But I did not know of my father's—and now that sermon . . ."

Antonia returned his pressure on her hand but not his frown. "My love, you are too morose. Your faults—yes, I was well enough aware of your melancholy moods—and the off-key singing they produce—" she couldn't resist a bit of lightness "—but I'll not have you suggesting that the earl of Norville is a monster—or that, if he is, it will blight our lives irredeemably." She faced him with a new urgency. "Charles, you must tell me. Whatever it is—unless you're sworn not to, of course. I am your wife. I must hear it."

"No, I'm not sworn. Only in our marriage vows to love and protect you with my very life. So I would protect you from distress in this matter."

"And don't you think I've been distressed over your worry?"

He nodded and ran his long fingers through his already rumpled dark hair. "It's all in his journal." He nodded toward the abandoned book. "He said he would have told me before, but there seemed little urgency until I was married and like to produce an heir. At least Mother is gone, so he needn't worry about hurting her any longer.

"It seems that in the golden days after Waterloo it was considered excellent sport for young men to come to Edinburgh and aid their fellows at the medical school in their grave-robbing ventures. It was all great fun at first.

"He recounts one night of adventure where, after a particularly successful foray in a small village kirkyard, they found themselves ravenously hungry, so they stowed their bag in the bushes behind an inn and went in to eat. They had almost finished their venison pie when the inn-keeper's son entered with a familiar burlap bag over his shoulder. Thinking he'd found a smuggler's swag bag, the lad tossed the pack to the middle of the floor and proclaimed his right to its contents in front of all the company.

"My father and his friends didn't stay around to see exactly what he did with his loot, but when the grave watchers reported the corpse returned, Father and his friends dug it up again the next night." Danvers concluded the story in the same flat voice with which he had told it all.

Antonia gave a gentle smile. "My dear. I know that grave robbing was a terrible thing—it seems it's all I've heard of since we came north—but it's history now. The distressed families must be long over their worry—most themselves gone to undisturbed graves of their own. And you heard Gilchrist last night—the medical knowledge was vital. You distress yourself far too much. No sins are to be visited on you or our children for your father's youthful pranks."

"If only it were so simple, Tonia. It seemed so to me at first, as well. But I have read on in my father's journal. Now I see why he felt it necessary to inflict the thing on me, even on our honeymoon, when he knew we were going to Loch Leven.

"It seems Sir Graham was his confederate in the whole mad affair. It was the summer following the business in the inn. A young sailor from Leven had returned to his home and sweetheart only to die of a fever the day before their wedding.

"So the wedding became a funeral and the grave watched over by the bride was watched by resurrectionists as well—my father and Sir Graham. They waited until the girl, still in her white gown, had finished strewing blossoms and tears on the grave, then moved in quickly. Strong, efficient workers like they were could usually accomplish their business in sixty minutes or less. But time ran out on them. The grave was empty, the daisies still scattered wide, when the sweetheart returned.

"They made it with the body to their rowboat waiting in the loch, but Father would not let his friend push off. Instead they watched while the distracted maiden ran among the tombstones mourning her twice-lost lover. At last Father could stand it no longer. He went ashore to comfort the girl. She was receptive to his comforting. He continued to comfort her throughout the summer.

"She died in childbirth, but the child flourished. Is still flourishing with his own burgeoning brood and a wife that is pushing him to claim his rights as heir to the earl of Norville."

"What!" Tonia jumped to her feet. What had been a tale of long-ago sowing of wild oats suddenly fell into focus with immediate sharpness. "Heir of Norville? You mean your father married this girl?"

Danvers ran his fingers over the calfskin of the journal. "Father is notably vague on that point. My . . . er . . . half brother apparently is not." He turned the book over and pulled a letter from under the cover.

Tonia took the missive as she might have reached to touch a garden snake. The surprisingly high quality paper, however, did not writhe but opened smoothly at her touch. She read silently, then looked up, more confused than before. "But I don't understand. This is a very proper letter. He writes with a well-formed hand. His command of the language is excellent—if it is his own."

Danvers again rumpled his hair before replying. "Oh, yes, I'm quite convinced it's his own. Don't you see, Tonia —that's the fiendishness of it. If he were some low-life upstart, there would be far less justice to his claim. But my father did a thorough job of seeing to his education. From a distance, of course—Father then came back to London and married my mother—but the earl of Norville was never one to do his duty by halves."

"Yes, yes. Of course, that's admirable. But the question of marriage . . ."

Danvers's long fingers flicked toward the letter Tonia still held. "You see the fellow claims to have examined the entry in the parish registry. I had intended to get to the bottom of it all before now—as my father asked me to— but there have been so many distractions." He paused, then concluded, "He seemed a nice enough fellow."

"You mean you've met him?"

"Hardly avoidable at Leven. He's Grahame's factor."

Tonia stared, then looked back at the signature on the letter. The tall, quiet fellow she had mistaken for Danvers. "And Ross Dalkeith, Sir Graham Grahame's factor, claims to be your elder brother and the rightful heir?" The facts were plain enough, but she felt the need to hear them.

Danvers turned and paced around the room. "The vexation of it is that under any other circumstances I would have liked him enormously and wished him every success." He strode back to the fireplace and flung himself into his chair, his long legs extended to the weak flame.

"But won't he be reasonable? Surely you can come to some understanding?"

"Doesn't matter how reasonable he might be prepared to be. The estate is entailed. By law it goes to the eldest legitimate heir. There's no breaking it."

He stared long into the fire. "How could my father . . ." Danvers looked up. "I'll tell you, Tonia, when that parson this morning started in on the sins of the fathers, I almost froze. I thought he saw directly into my

166

soul and was preaching his whole long-winded sermon straight at my head as if I were guilty as well and would go right to perdition for my father's sins—and take our progeny with me. I've never felt such despair in my life. The title be hanged—there are immortal souls at stake here."

Tonia settled quietly in the chair next to his and touched his arm gently. "I think you have no need to fear for your soul, my dearest. Since you gave it into Christ's care, it is in quite good keeping in the hands of your far higher Father. But, of course, in a temporal sense, the Scripture is quite right. Children suffer every day for the sins of their parents, just as the fortunate benefit from the good their parents do. But you must see that it can be turned around as well."

"What do you mean?" Danvers put his hand over hers and held it tightly.

"I mean, can't the good of the children be felicitous for the parents? Matters of good and evil needn't flow only one direction. It is often for the children to correct and improve on the mistakes of their elders."

"Yes, as it's in my lap to clean up this mess. Oh, Tonia, what have I gotten you into? And what Agatha will have to say I can't imagine. And Aunt Elfrida . . ." With each new thought he slid deeper into the folds of the chair.

"Take heart, Charles. I have every confidence in your ability to undo this tangle. And you mustn't make the same mistake the preacher did this morning."

"What's that?"

"He overlooked the next verse. Of course, it didn't fit his theme so well, but the penalty of sin is only unto the third and fourth generation—the Lord's mercy is for a thousand generations."

Danvers lifted her fingers to his lips and kissed them.

Antonia smiled back at him in the wavering firelight. She just wished she felt as confident as her words sounded.

16

The next morning Antonia and Danvers were quite settled on the matter. They would stay in Edinburgh another
day and in the evening attend the play Hardy had so urged
upon them. Then they would return to Leven Lodge and
get to the bottom of the Ross Dalkeith matter. It all seemed
perfectly ordered and sensible.

A pale sun shone on the spring flowers in the garden
beyond the breakfast room window, and birds sang in the
larch trees. Tonia handed the maid a half-finished cup of
chocolate. "Where is your mistress, Moraig?"

"I believe Mrs. Raeburn has gone out, ma'am. But
Miss Madelyn is in the morning room." She turned at the
door. "With Mr. Morris."

Tonia smiled and adjusted the drape of a ribbon in
her lace cap. "I must say, our Gilchrist isn't one to let any
grass grow under his feet. On his way to a lecture, I suppose he'll say—as if anyone would believe Charlotte Square
were on the way between the Meadows and Surgeon's
Hall."

When they reached the small room at the back of the
second floor, however, Tonia thought it empty, until a delicate sniff drew her attention to a huddled figure in sprigged
muslin in the alcove.

"Madelyn, my dear. Do we intrude?" Antonia crossed to her.

Madelyn dabbed at her eyes with a lace-edged handkerchief and attempted a wavery smile.

"We had thought to find Gilchrist here as well."

Madelyn's clouded countenance told Tonia she had hit on the source of the tears.

"He was. Until a moment ago. Then the police came . . ."

"Police?" Danvers stepped forward. "Don't tell me they've taken him?"

"No. That is, I don't know. They went somewhere to talk. Papa's library, I suppose . . ." She waved a hand in that general direction.

Danvers nodded a bow to his wife and departed.

Tonia sat beside her friend. "I take it that it is not the appearance of the law that has reduced you to tears?"

"No. Quite the contrary. They rather rescued me from hearing more of what I had no wish—no thought—ever to hear. I believed . . . I was so certain . . . Gil and I. I mean, I hope I was never unladylike in assuming . . . but I was so confident that he felt as I did."

"Madelyn, has Gilchrist been ungentlemanly?"

The beribboned head jerked up so quickly that a brown curl slipped from its mooring and dangled over one ear. "No. That's quite impossible to imagine. No, it must have been my own silly imaginings. I have presumed too much. Dreamed . . ."

"Can you tell me what he said?' Tonia spoke as gently as she could but felt she must urge some coherence on the girl's speech if she were to be of any help.

"His words were the gentlest possible. But his meaning was quite clear. He said he must be fair. He mustn't raise false hopes about our future. That as matters stood there could be no future, and I must consider myself completely free." She paused for another sniff. "Oh, he said all the proper things—about how high I stand in his regard and

169

how he prizes our friendship, but that I must understand very clearly that he has obligations—involvements . . ." She stopped with another gentle sniff.

Tonia pulled a fresh handkerchief from her pocket and handed it to Madelyn. "What a ridiculous muddle. Obligations? Involvements? Whatever could he have meant?"

"It's perfectly obvious. He meant that he does not love me."

"Now that is the most nonsensical thing I have heard all morning. Whatever he meant, he certainly didn't mean that. Compose yourself, my dear. I shall see what Lord Danvers has learned. Do not fear—we shall get to the bottom of this."

Brave words, but the scene in Harry Raeburn's library did little to assure Tonia of their fulfillment.

"And so you deny digging that poor fellow out of his grave in Greyfriars Kirkyard and placing him on an omnibus?" Inspector Futter's clear words brought Antonia to a halt inside the library door.

Gil stood before the cold fireplace, his head up but his shoulders slumped. Danvers, his long arms making perfect triangles, stood with his hands on his hips before the tall window. The constable who had come at Antonia's scream when the body landed at her feet in the Grassmarket stood behind Futter, scribbling earnestly in a notebook.

Futter took another step toward Gilchrist. "In spite of the fact that two witnesses have described you as being in the area at the time that evening and the fact that Constable MacRoy here found the grave-digging tools in your study carrel at the university, you still deny all knowledge of the happenings?"

Gil nodded. "I do."

Tonia gasped when she saw the tools the constable referred to—a sheet of canvas, a crowbar, and that strange, crooked spade with a blade like a plowshare. She knew where she had seen such an implement before. Surely there weren't many such outside the Isle of Skye.

Futter seemed to be thinking the same. He held up the odd little shovel. "Now I'm not a native of these parts, so someone will correct me if I'm wrong, I'm sure. But I'm told that such awkward instruments as this are unique to a very limited area in the Hebrides—and perhaps to just some Highland areas—such as perhaps to Lochiel, where I understand your family comes from, Mr. Morris, is that correct?"

"Yes. No." Gil shook his head. "My mother's family is from Lochiel. But I've never seen the spade or one like it before."

"And—" Futter advanced until he stood shoulder to shoulder with Gil "—you refuse to tell us what you were doing in Old Town at the time the body was dug up?"

Gil stood his ground. "I do."

Antonia pushed on into the room. "Do you mean to say that the man who fell off the omnibus in the Grassmarket was already a corpse—dead and buried?"

Futter turned to her. "That's right, your ladyship. Old Mackelby he was. Had done odd jobs around the medical school for as long as anybody could remember. Died of pneumonia a couple of days ago. Apparently some young sprig thought it'd be a fine prank to send him on his way back toward the school one last time. Gory sense of humor." He looked back at Gil. "But I've heard tell medical students often have just that."

Gil shook his head helplessly.

Futter was clearly weighing matters. There appeared to be no doubt in his mind that he had sufficient evidence to arrest Gil on grave-robbing charges. Yet the problem was obvious. If he arrested the young man and Gil persevered in his silence, what would be gained? A fine levied for grave robbing would not answer any of the questions surrounding this bizarre case—or cases, if the mysterious corpses proved to be linked, as it seemed they must be—if only for the oddity of their circumstances.

Antonia considered. She had believed Gil in the matter of his involvement with the tartan. It made sense to her that he had recognized the description of Madelyn's design in the papers and had gone to rescue it for her. It was typical of him to engage in a rash, gallant gesture. She had believed that all cleared up with the return of the tartan to the mill. But was there more? What if Gil was more closely associated with the corpse than simply recovering the shroud?

And then what did go on in Old Town Saturday evening? Who was that woman with the children who seemed so closely associated with Gil? What was he to them—or they to him? Was that woman somehow the reason for his refusal to explain his alibi for the grave-robbing charge? If so, the woman must have a powerful hold on him. Was that the entanglement he had referred to in his muddled words to Madelyn?

And now this new charge—by her own eyes and footsteps Antonia knew Gil had been in the Greyfriars area. But grave robbing? Gilchrist Morris a sack 'em up man? He had defended the activities of a generation ago in the name of medical science. But now there was no need.

Still, somebody had done the grisly deed. Surely someone very, very sick. Not the brilliant, gentle Gilchrist. That wasn't possible.

Inspector Futter, however, obviously thought it not only possible but also entirely likely. He gave Gil a warning before turning away.

Antonia, Danvers, and Gil sank into the nearest chairs when the police exited the room. Tonia's first urge was to repeat the questions that had just whirled through her mind—to demand answers from Gil. But she knew such demands would only drive his silence deeper. Whatever his reasons for keeping his own counsel, he considered them good ones.

So instead she asked, "How did they identify the old man?"

Danvers answered, "Coroner recognized him when they took the body in. He'd seen him just a few days before."

"But why would anyone dig him up? And why give the driver Liston's address?"

Gil remained sunk in silence, so Danvers continued. "Nothing more than the medical school connection, perhaps? He probably had worked for Liston. Could be some student's idea of a joke, as Futter suggested."

With the mention of students, Tonia glanced at Gilchrist, but he didn't react. She shivered. "A rather sick joke. I could see it, perhaps, if Liston were still there and some student he'd failed wanted to get revenge . . ." The thought hung in the air without comment, so she asked. "How is it done—digging up a grave?"

Danvers drew his hand over his face and sighed. "As a result of my more recent reading, I seem to have formed a rather clear picture of the technique of the more adept in the field—such as those who had the honor to work with the renowned Liston. It seems that the preferred hour was between six and eight o'clock of an evening, before the kirkyard watch went on duty. The students cleared rubble, flowers, and such-like off the grave first—they were often placed in a certain order so the family could tell if the grave had been disturbed—then they spread out a canvas sheet to hold the earth and dug straight down beside the coffin to where the head and shoulders lay. When they reached the coffin it was the work of three prizes with a crowbar to pry a hole in the lid.

"The body was fished out with hooks—a jerking movement said to have been more effective than violent dragging—the subject stripped, the shroud replaced in order to avoid a charge of theft, the body doubled in half, trussed, and put in a sack. The earth tipped from the canvas sheet back into the grave and any telltale pebbles or twigs re-

173

placed." Danvers brushed his hands with an air of finality. "All right and tight. Very efficient and done in well less than an hour. One fellow is on record as having dug up twenty-three bodies in four nights."

An ironic edge to Danvers's voice belied the academic detachment he affected. Antonia knew the bitterness was for his father's involvement in the distasteful activity and the complications that were now being visited on his family as a result of those long-ago iniquities.

"Right." Tonia came sharply to her feet. "We've had quite enough of the dismals for one morning. This is our last day in Edinburgh, and I have no intention of spending it moping about. We all need a change of scene. Charles, my love, I recall hearing of a quite charming island in the Firth of Forth to which you rashly promised to take me. I can imagine no better time than the present. Gilchrist, I left Madelyn in a state of shockingly depressed spirits in the morning room. I believe she is much in need of some fresh air."

Before either of her companions could answer, Hardy entered the room.

"Hardy—the very person," Antonia said. "You may drive us."

That Hardy agreed to do with even more than his usual gusto, apparently taking his cue from his mistress, who was determined to raise the spirits of her friends.

Madelyn, her perky little chin equally determinedly set so as not to quiver, entered fully into the plan. "Yes, that's the thing—a picnic. I shall tell Cook to prepare a hamper."

The carriage ride to Queensferry was the most quickly accomplished of any Antonia had yet made, partly because Hardy continued to regale them with yet more stories of the area's seamy past.

The village of Barnton drew forth the tale of the man whose dead wife was resurrected by Liston's graverobbers. But they were interrupted in their work by Monro's contin-

174

gent. When both groups were set upon by the watch, the warring factions ran, dropping the corpse, still in her shroud, in a secluded lane—as it happened, right outside the grieving husband's house. The next morning the man discovered her. Nothing would convince him that his wife had not attempted to return from the grave to get back to him.

And then there was the burglar from up Aberdeen way. In the course of justice he was hanged. But so terrified had he been of being dissected that his friends took him from the gallows and buried him at sea. "An unfriendly sea, it would be seeming, for the unhappy fellow was washed back ashore, and the authorities handed his remains over to the anatomists.

"And have ye not heard of Half Hangit Maggie?" It seemed that not even the locally bred Madelyn had, so Hardy continued. "Maggie was a fish hawker in the High Street who was no better than she should be, as the saying goes. When she discovered that she was . . . er . . ."

Hardy looked from Antonia to Madelyn, blushing to the roots of his hair. He had obviously not thought ahead before he launched into this story. "Er . . . begging your pardon, m'lady, Maggie was found guilty of concealing her 'interesting condition' and sentenced to death by hanging." He got over the difficult part quickly, then settled again into the rhythm of his story.

"Well, now, Maggie being a popular local girl, a right large crowd turned out for her hanging. Some friends even brought a cart and coffin so they could give her a decent burial. But when the body was cut down by the hangman, a group of medical students tried to seize the body for dissection. They were run off with a sound thrashing from Maggie's friends.

"Pretty soon, though, it was Maggie's friends that got the fright. They started hearing groans coming from the coffin. When they lifted the lid, sure enough, Maggie was still alive. The lawyers decided she would have to go free since she'd already been pronounced dead by the magistrates. She lived another forty years, known until her dying day as Half Hangit Maggie."

As they entered the busy town of Queensferry, Hardy had to pay more attention to his driving, so the stories ceased. But Tonia's consideration of them didn't. Again she thought of how cheaply life was held—life so important to God that holy Scripture said He knows each one. Even the burglar? The babe Maggie concealed? Apparently so.

It had to be that way, didn't it, or there wouldn't be anything wrong with murder? Murder was wrong because to kill a person was to kill one made in the image of God.

Only when the carriage lurched to a halt did Tonia realize they were at the pier. Now their speedy ride was followed by a period of inaction while Hardy scouted the waterfront for a boat to take them to the island. Several fishing vessels sat idle at the dock, and it was likely that Hardy could have induced any of their owners to ferry them for a consideration, but the comfort and convenience, not to mention odor, of such conveyance left much to be desired.

Tonia was beginning to despair for the success of her plan when Danvers drew her attention to a tidy craft bearing the crest badge of a mermaid holding a comb in one hand and a mirror in the other. "The earl of Moray's boat."

"Don't tell me—" she shook her head "—another crony of your father's."

"Not only that. This particular crony happens to own Inchcolm Island. I believe I'll just have a word with the captain."

Danvers returned in a few minutes, accompanied by a gray-bearded man in a red and black plaid kilt. "Captain Lindsay will be happy to welcome us aboard."

"Aye, the earl's not in residence at the moment, but he's that happy to welcome visitors to Saint Colm's island.

176

And a wee pretty isle it is when the sun's shining on it. Not but that it can't be driech enough in a winter's storm."

On the way to the island in the middle of the Firth of Forth, the captain recounted for them the story of King Alexander I, another son of the sainted Margaret and brother to David.

"Aye, that's the one." The captain puffed on his black bogwood pipe and nodded when Tonia identified who he was talking about. "And a terrible fierce storm it must have been that drove Alexander and his men off course to shelter on the island in the winter of 1123. For they sheltered on the stormbound island for three days in the tiny stone cell of a good hermit, who shared his scanty food with them. In gratitude, Alexander—who was also identifying Saint Colm with the blessed Saint Columba who brought Christianity to all of Scotland—vowed to build a fine abbey on the island. And true he would have been to his vow, I'm thinking, but the good Alexander died before he could fulfill it."

A large shipping vessel passed close to them and rocked the smaller launch in its wake. The captain turned his attention to his wheel for a few minutes. When they were steady on course again, he continued. "A place of great and ancient sanctity you'll find it if you're looking. Many come here—most to see the sights, but some to pray. You're my third load of visitors today, plus a boat from the university—over here digging for bones of ancient Danish kings they say. Macbeth defeated the lot of the Norsemen, and their kinfolk paid handsome sums of gold, so it's said, to have their dead buried on the holy island."

Captain Lindsay paused to give a hearty chuckle. "Makes ye wonder whether the archeologists are digging for bones or gold, doesn't it now?"

He would undoubtedly have continued with more of the island's history had not a cry of delight from Madelyn interrupted him. She jumped from her seat and ran to the rail, leaning far out toward a cluster of rocks jutting up through the water. She pointed. "Seals!"

177

Gil was beside her in a moment, more to be sure of a firm arm around her waist than to observe the wildlife, Tonia was certain, but equally obedient to looking where she pointed. Indeed, on second look it was clear that the entire surface of the tiny island was covered with the soulful-eyed creatures, sunning themselves on the shiny black rocks. Here and there a seagull or wigeon stood sentinel on rock or sealback, watching for fish.

Only a few more minutes of sailing took them to Inchcolm. When the boat was fastened at the dock, the captain handed all ashore and gestured up the green slope toward the impressive stone structure. "The earl keeps his residence in the abbot's house to the southeast, but ye're welcome to visit the cloisters—best preserved in Scotland they are—and the abbey. Course, the abbey's not sae well preserved. Seeing as its vulnerable position in Forth made it prey to devastating attacks by English forces . . ." He looked at his English visitors and cleared his throat. "And then the fine thick stones were sold to the Edinburgh city council for rebuilding of their Tolbooth. Still, it's a grand sight."

As they thanked their guide and started up the path to the ancient monastery, threatening clouds rolled in from the North Sea.

"Oh, our picnic!" Madelyn eyed the depressing black sky.

"We shall have to eat in the cloister," Danvers said, holding out his hand to the first drop of rain. "With luck, the marauding English and Edinburgh city fathers will have left its roof intact."

In fact, it would have been impossible to have imagined a more watertight building than the cloister. Its roof had been built in the Irish style of stone-vaulted ceiling, supported by six-foot-thick stone walls. They found seats in an arched window opening, and Madelyn set out Cook's sumptuous veal and ham pie, Orkney cheese, and oat-cakes, with assorted pickles and last year's little tart apples, wrinkled but still sweet, for their feast. They sheltered cozily in the snug setting while heavy rain dripped on the green grass just a few feet away.

It was when all were on a second slice of pie that Gilchrist turned to Danvers and inquired whether he had been following the advance of Ashley Cooper's Public Health Bill in Parliament.

Danvers shook his head. "Something to do with housing for the poor, I understand. To provide for licensing and inspection of all common lodging houses. Not enough, I'd say. They need a much more sweeping measure. Something on the scale of his bill a few years ago to provide for drainage, water supply, destruction of slums and cellar buildings. Goodness knows London needs it."

Gil nodded. "London's not the only place."

"I hear his father, the earl of Shaftesbury, is not well. Maybe Cooper'll be inheriting the title soon. Perhaps he'll be able to marshal more support then."

With no more room for Cook's excellent repast, the men moved a little apart, still talking of politics, and Madelyn began packing the hamper. Tonia gathered the cutlery, wrapped it in a linen towel, and handed it to her. "I didn't know Gil was interested in politics."

Madelyn shrugged. "I don't think he is particularly. I suppose it's the public health issue—being a doctor and all."

Tonia murmured agreement, but she wondered. Had Gil brought up the subject to keep the conversation from anything closer to home? What was he hiding?

Carrying the repacked hamper, Danvers led them down the east walk of the cloister to view the excellently preserved octagonal chapter house and its magnificent vaulted ceiling, then on to the tower of the old church. Since this building was not in as perfect repair as the cloister, it was fortunate that the rain had lessened now to a mere drizzle.

It was a somewhat ambitious climb, but one Antonia would not have missed. At the top she stopped to catch

179

her breath, dropped the full skirts that she had been holding out of harm's way on the uneven stairs, and looked out over the stone railing. "Oh, it's magnificent!" The rain had intensified the greenness of the already emerald grass. Daffodils growing in sunny clusters nodded to the dancing water of the Forth as it lapped the shiny rocks on the shore.

She walked to another side of the tower and looked at the tiny paths running from the monastery to the far side of the island. She moved to still another side and saw the rugged, stone-piled bay where seabirds sheltered on the rocks. Activity on the hill above now took Antonia's attention. That must be the group from the university, looking for the ancient Danish burial ground.

Then she went back to the east. Two figures proceeded slowly down the winding path that apparently came from the hermit's stone cell. She watched for some time as they approached. An old man, bald and stooped, leaned heavily on his stick. Seemingly near blind, he felt the path with his cane in spite of the supporting arm of a younger man.

Tonia caught her breath. What was there about the scene that made her feel for a moment as if she were back on Skye? A shiver ran down her spine.

That younger man—he seemed to remind her of someone she had seen in the islands—one of the mourners or crofters? A passenger on the boat? No, the impression was too vague.

Then, as the pair moved closer, the identity became clear. Not the Hebrides, but the university. It was the assistant from the dissection. What was his name—Warden? Warrington? Warrender, that was it.

But what was Warrender doing here? Had he come with the archeology group? Even though he worked in the medical school, perhaps his interest extended to archeology—a knowledge of skeletons would surely be useful to one who dug for the bones of medieval dead. Or were

180

these two merely another of the tourist groups Captain Lindsay had referred to? Perhaps this was Warrender's father, and he was giving him a treat. They did rather resemble each other. And Warrender seemed appropriately solicitous of his senior.

On the boat trip back, the couples stood at th rail in the moist air. Tonia lifted her face to the breeze and considered, but resisted, the impropriety of removing her bonnet and letting her hair blow. Instead she turned to Gil and told him of seeing the medical school assistant on the island.

"Noah Warrender? Odd. I wonder what he was doing there? Hope he had a good time. Seems he has few enough of them. Poor fellow, they say he was a brilliant student in his day."

"You mean he was going to be a doctor?"

"The story is he was top of his class until that Burke and Hare thing. He just couldn't go on after the scandal."

"Why?" Tonia could understand that learning one had been studying murder victims would be unsettling, but to give up a whole career over it . . . "Did he fail his exams?"

Gil shook his head, and they laughed when the gesture flung silver drops of sea spray from his hair. "I don't know. I think he just quit. Interesting about exams, though. They say that Monro failed Knox when *he* was a student."

"Knox? I thought he was brilliant." Danvers joined the conversation.

Again Gil shook his head, but more gently this time. "That's what they say. Maybe that's why he worked so hard later—to prove Monro wrong."

"Yes. And then it all went wrong for Knox." Antonia paused thoughtfully. "Maybe he worked too hard."

"I don't suppose we'll ever know who was really to blame. After the trial Burke made a couple of statements clearing Knox. But then Knox's doorkeeper, Paterson—the fellow who received the bodies for dissection—turned completely against the doctor and denounced him publicly." Gil paused. "Bad business all around."

The topic was abandoned as they approached Seal Island and the playful creatures took their attention.

Captain Lindsay offered to idle the boat so that the ladies could enjoy the seals longer. Madelyn looked eager, but with apologies Danvers asked that they decline. They must return speedily to Edinburgh, or they would be late for the play.

17

That evening while she enjoyed the red and gold splendor of their box at the Adelphi Theatre, Antonia wished the playwright had chosen a more congenial subject. Of late, she had had more than her fill of burking and resurrectioning, but the splendid audience in one of the most elegant theaters in Edinburgh did much to divert her from her somber thoughts of earlier in the day.

Hardy had been right in arranging this entertainment for them. Now if only Charles could relax. Tonia longed for the carefree times they had shared before he read his father's journal. Would they ever know that joy again?

The director and his cast made the most of the billing that this was to be a lamentable comedy and played every scene to its broadest possibility, adding a much-appreciated lightness to the evening, if not to the authenticity of the actual event.

The scene opened with a weaselly appearing William Burke pacing the squalid parlor of his boarding house in Tanners Close. Rubbing his hands, he bewailed the fact that Old Donald, a boarder, had died owing him four pounds. The solution appeared easy enough when William Hare, another lodger, suggested that he collect by selling the old man's body to the anatomists at the nearby medical school.

In a scene full of slapstick and pratfalls, the two men removed the body from its rough coffin, bundled it into a bag, and managed to bustle it out the door. Almost. Hare, having forgotten his hat, returned, still dragging the bag. Burke, in a frenzy induced by the riches they were to attain, followed him in, tripped over the bag, blundered into Hare, and knocked him off his feet. The two bunglers were in a heap on top of Old Donald when a cat, which had crawled into the empty coffin, chose that moment to emerge with a banshee shriek.

The audience erupted with startled laughter and applause. Antonia stole a sideways glance at her companion in his well-starched evening wear. She breathed a sigh of relief for the smile she saw lurking among the lines at the sides of his mouth.

In the next scene the ne'er-do-wells staggered down a dark alley to the university quadrangle. There they met a student returning late to his rooms. After considerable tomfoolery with the body and roundabout inquiries to the student, it became clear what information the men sought.

"Ah, Dr. Monro's rooms you're asking for?" Now the student looked at the lumpy bag with more understanding. "Well, and isn't this a piece of luck that I've crossed your path! It isn't Monro you're wanting. The high and mighty Chair of Anatomy won't be paying you nearly as much for your services as those in more need and—I might add—those of more talent."

At the mention of money, a confused dialogue broke out, but in the end the student made clear that he was a loyal and leading member of Dr. Knox's privately held anatomical class, which ran in competition to the officialdom of Dr. Monro, and that Knox would be happy to prove his gratitude if these fine gentlemen would care to step around to Number 10 Surgeon's Hall.

The scene ended with Burke and Hare triumphantly waving their seven pounds ten shillings profit from the evening's adventure.

But for two scalawags who loved their labor less and their whiskey more, waiting for another such windfall was "awfu' tedious," as they declared in song between acts. They considered the life of the resurrectionists and quickly rejected it when Burke reminded Hare of the terrors of a graveyard at night—and Hare reminded Burke of the heavy work of digging up a grave. Finally Hare hit on a solution. They could form a removal business: invite the old and infirm—"such as wasn't doing anything anyway"—into his lair and "do for them."

> "Do for them, do for them.
> We'll do 'em up right and tight,
> Swill 'em up, fill 'em up,
> Sack 'em up tonight,
> We'll do for them tonight."

Burke and Hare were joined by their women: blonde-curled Mrs. Hare, perennially carrying a small child in her arms, and square-jawed, hard-eyed Helen McDougal, who ushered in an assorted cast of imbeciles, streetwalkers, widows, and orphans, all of whom ended with a pillow over their faces before landing trussed up in a sack to be delivered to Paterson, Dr. Knox's doorkeeper.

The macabre merchandising was brought to a halt when Mr. and Mrs. Grey, poor but honest former lodgers of Hare's, reported discovering the body of poor old Madgy Docherty under a pile of straw in the boardinghouse.

The scene then shifted to the dissecting room of Dr. Robert Knox, where with great exaggeration of gesture and maneuvering to gain credit for the discovery, the police cut the ropes on the tea chest in which Madgy's body lay.

A tangled courtroom scene followed, where justice was more or less seen to be done. William and Margaret Hare saved their necks by giving evidence so that they could not be sentenced. The audience hissed its disapproval. But Antonia, recalling Hardy's identification of the blind beggar of Oxford Street, felt that perhaps the mills of the gods did not grind so altogether unjustly. Helen McDougal was ordered to make her way back to Ireland from whence she had come.

Then, with a mighty wielding of the judicial gavel, the judge in solemn countenance placed a black cloth atop his stiff white wig. "Hang him!" the judge shouted. The audience applauded. "And then dissect him!" At that stroke of poetic justice the audience came to its feet in cheers.

The final scene, with full accompaniment of the stage manager's art, showed a grim crowd gathering throughout the night as a scaffold was built under the pelting of a pitiless January storm. All the closes and stairs of the crowded terrace filled with upright citizens determined to see justice to its ghastly end, as hammers clanged on the gallows, lurid torches glared, and shadows danced weirdly.

Finally Burke arrived on the platform. Curses against him were mingled with even louder shouts of "Hang Hare too!" "Where is Hare?" and then the loudest of all, "Hang Knox!"

The final scene depicted not the dispatch of the murderer but the mob from the streets of Old Town, carrying sticks, stones, and an effigy of the once-lauded physician, as they marched toward Knox's house demanding his neck on the gallows.

Antonia applauded with the rest of the audience. As a theatrical piece the production deserved the acclaim it was receiving. And it had been an enlightening evening for her. She had been hearing about Burke and Hare for weeks.

It was intriguing to have all the bits and pieces played out before her in a cohesive whole—especially now that she had been confronted with an example of the gruesome act of grave robbing at her very feet and since she had learned of the far-reaching consequences of such activity in her own husband's family. Surely, as Charles had said, the sins of the fathers were making themselves felt.

And how interesting to note that Hare had been a father. If only the puzzle of it proved to outweigh any personal application in Charles's mind, the evening might be counted an enormous success. She smiled at her husband.

"You enjoyed the play, my dear?" Danvers placed her cashmere shawl around her shoulders and offered his arm to escort her from the box.

"Indeed I did. Good entertainment and thought-provoking too. I had not realized Mrs. Hare had a child. One wonders what effect such a start in life must have had on him. And where he might be now?"

The jets of gaslight lining the theater wall flared under their frosted crystal globes and made the red, flocked wallpaper shimmer like the silk dresses of the ladies leaving the hall before them.

Danvers followed up on her question as they descended the broad stairway to the lobby. "Yes. If he was portrayed of an accurate age he would only be a few years older than myself now. It gives one pause for thought." He placed his tall, black beaver hat on his shining, if unbridled, macassared locks. "I also found it interesting to note that Monro—not Knox—was the intended target for their first sale. If the men hadn't been directed to Monro's rival, the hereditary high priest would have been the one to have his career ruined, and Knox would have flourished."

Antonia smiled again. That was her Charles, his curiosity piqued, tangling with the mystery as a great game. She sought to encourage his questioning. "Instead of living in ignominious isolation where he can still see his competitor's glory."

The thought stayed with her as the carriage rolled up Broughton Street. "Charles, you don't suppose . . . no, I can't see any sense in it . . ." The thought was too vague to put into words, but after a moment she tried again. "You don't think Dr. Monro might be in any danger? I mean— suppose the body from Greyfriars and the one that wound up on his dissecting table in place of the tartaned corpse

187

—suppose someone connected with all this old affair were trying to make trouble for Monro. Or Liston. Or—"

"I'd say he left it a bit late. Liston dead, Monro retired—it doesn't make sense."

Tonia sighed. "No. Nothing makes sense. And yet there's a pattern here, I'm sure of it."

"A pattern—or the work of a madman?"

"A madman perhaps, but one with a design." In spite of her sense of triumph over diverting Charles from his worries to the murder puzzle, it was more than the damp night air that made Antonia shiver.

18

The next morning when the *Scotsman* arrived folded neatly beside Danvers's cozied silver eggcup, they found few answers to their questions of the night before but more pieces that needed to be fitted into the puzzle somewhere. Only the pieces wouldn't fit.

"ANATOMY CHAIR A RESURRECTIONIST?" the headline ran. As Danvers read the front page piece to her, Antonia tried to fit the startling revelations into place. Acting on an anonymous tip, the police had exhumed and examined the body Monro had dissected in lieu of the tartaned corpse. Although it was still unidentified, the police surgeon clearly established that the subject had been dead for many days and that splinters of wood and streaks of dirt on the remains were consistent with its having been ripped from a broken, buried coffin as had been done to resurrected bodies a generation ago.

"So Monro was maneuvered into dissecting a purloined body?" She interrupted his reading. "But why?"

Danvers dipped his paper to look at her over its top. "To know why would probably be to know who. But one guess I might offer is that someone might have wanted the identity of the victim destroyed—a thorough dissection could do that quite effectively, I imagine. Another, not so

189

vague, guess is that someone seems to want to discredit Monro. Listen to the rest of this."

Tonia listened. The same informant who provided the hint about the body had also delivered to the newspaper a copy of Monro's lecture notes, charging that they were of spurious, outdated scholarship.

It seemed so unlikely. And yet Tonia recaptured a fleeting memory of her own glimpse of Monro's notes. It had struck her at the time how ancient and shabby the lecture manuscript appeared.

But Tonia could give no more consideration to such thoughts, no matter how intriguing she found them, for today she and Charles were to travel back to Loch Leven. The journey was one of mixed emotions for her. She was delighted to be traveling once more through the beautiful Scottish countryside, away from the noisome, malodorous city with its alarums and worries. And yet, what would they be facing in the matter of Mr. Ross Dalkeith?

She looked across the seat at her husband and knew by the tight set of his jaw and the iron look in his eye that he was wondering the same thing. She placed her hand over his with a small pat. The title was not a major concern to her—she was a lady in her own right—although she realized that, as Agatha had warned her, she might feel differently on the subject when she had children and their inheritance to consider. Certainly the money was of minor consequence. Danvers had quite a large fortune of his own, and she was her father's only heir.

But she knew that the intangible things were the most important. That Norville had behaved with youthful ardor toward a pretty young girl could be forgiven—must be forgiven if he were repentant, as indeed he was. And the fact that the man had stood by the consequences of his rash act and seen to the boy's education and establishment in life was admirable. But that now, after all these years, the family name was to be scandalized, its honor besmirched, was a shattering of all the ideals for which

190

their world stood. The strength of the family was the strength of the empire.

She also knew it was a measure of Danvers's deep concern over these issues, and of his high regard for their host and his position as one of their oldest family friends, that he talked openly with Sir Graham that evening at dinner.

Their host waited until the tureen of steaming Scotch broth had been covered on the oak-leaf-carved sideboard, and Molly had departed, before he picked up the conversation again.

"Yes, yes, so long ago, and yet—funny how one's memories can move closer through the years. There have always been several points about that particular night— never thought it made much difference until now. I mean, everyone seemed to be quite content. Content and quiet, if you understand me. But now, perhaps some further inquiry . . . Just what does your father have to say on the matter?"

"About the night of the grave-robbing? Oh, his journal account is quite complete. I think I fully understand the emotional attachment."

"No, no, that's not what I mean. The critical point now is the matter of the marriage."

Danvers nodded. "Quite. There seems to be little doubt that the ceremony took place. What sort of records can be produced is the question I'm here to explore. Of course, if I'm convinced of the right of the matter, justice must be done."

"Ah yes. Truth and justice. Always. But sorting them out is the difficult part, what? Takes time. Mustn't rush these things." Sir Graham fingered his flowing red mustache as he returned to his favorite theme. "Take your time. Still, about the wedding—I remember being there, standing at the altar right beside your father I was—I can still remember how golden the candlelight was in that little stone chapel."

He paused so long Tonia started to comment, then Grahame drew his hand over his eyes as if seeing it all again. "Pretty little maid that Linda was—had a sweetness and innocence that was really irresistible. Made a fellow feel he'd do anything to protect her. All golden in the candlelight she was too. Funny how you can remember some things and not others. Course, we'd had a wee dram or two." He paused for a sip from his own glass. "A wee dram or two too many if the truth's to be told. Still, sure we can get to the bottom of this. I'll go around to the church with you tomorrow. Didn't suppose it made much difference after all this time—but of course if there's an entailment . . ."

After breakfast the next morning their host was as good as his word in spite of the longing looks he gave the trout jumping in the lake. "We could take the boat across. Just be wetting a wee line on the way." Then he looked at Antonia's pale muslin skirt and pink bonnet and retracted his suggestion. "Er . . . perhaps tomorrow. Fish will still be there. Plenty of time for angling. Plenty of time." He offered Antonia his arm. Danvers walked behind, keeping his own thoughts.

It had rained earlier in the morning. The leafy boughs over the narrow lane still dripped with heavy mist, freshening the air while spotting their garments.

The tidy stone manse was tucked behind a vine-covered stone wall next to the kirk. The minister's sturdy wife greeted them after carefully wiping her hands on the starched white apron covering her dark green dress and tucking three errant strands of hair back into her cap.

"Well now, come ye in, come ye in. The Reverend Ogilvie's gone to see about the repair work in the kirkyard. Sit you down. I'll just put the kettle to the boil. Won't take me a minute."

She bustled through her polished parlor to the kitchen beyond and returned before her guests were fully seated. "No, no, and don't you be getting up, gentlemen. I'll just set myself down right comfortable over here."

She took a seat in a small rocker that creaked with each backward and forward motion, giving a new punctuation to her words as she picked up where she had left her subject. "New drains. I'm certain that's what they'll say. And how the tithes are to be stretched to it I'll not be saying. But then, it's all the Lord's work, so the Lord will have to provide. And as I told Reverend Ogilvie himself before he left this very morning, worried as I could see he was, if the Lord hadn't wanted to provide for new drains He could just have kept the kirkyard from washing out. After all, it's all in His hands. That's what we all are—in His hands—and He can just provide new drains anytime He sees fit. It's all one to Him."

With that comfortable assurance she bounced to her feet on the next forward swing of the rocker and went off to see to her whistling kettle.

The pot was empty, and the subject of the Lord's provision of drains long exhausted, however, and the Reverend Ogilvie had not yet returned. So Danvers suggested that perhaps they might proceed over to the church on their own. "The parish register, that's what we've come to see. Perhaps we could just have a look. No need to bother Reverend Ogilvie when he has so much else on his mind."

His good lady sighed. "It's always something, and that's the truth of it. Before this it was the roof. Three great slates came down in that storm ten years ago. And no telling how long the roof had been leaking before that. We'd just come here then, Reverend Ogilvie and me, and here we were, water standing two inches deep in the vestry. Then there was the crack in the bell tower. But if the Lord didn't mean for us to learn by it all, He wouldn't bother letting us go through it. That's what I always say.

"What that good family will say about the water undermining the grave of their dear departed and him barely cold in his resting, I can't say. So I just told Reverend Ogilvie the only thing to do was to get it all repaired and fixed right and tight before they're any the wiser and thank the good Lord that it's not like in those days when the families had to worry about graverobbers."

She paused long enough to take breath. "Just wait snug and cozy in God's good Scottish earth until it's His time to come and take the rest of your earthly remains home—that's the Christian comfort, and no resurrectionists or bad drain systems should say anything to the contrary."

She came suddenly to her feet again in an exceedingly agile movement for one so stout. "But here's me rattling on again with you fine folk just waiting to take a peek at the register. I'm sure there's no problem. No problem at all. The key to the records box should be right in Reverend Ogilvie's desk. It's all the Lord's, he always says, all the Lord's—just ours to take care of as best we can. So we do our best."

Mrs. Ogilvie removed her bonnet and shawl from the carved hat stand in the hall and led the short distance across the grass to the church.

On the way Antonia noted the watch house where she and Danvers had sheltered their first evening at Loch Leven. She also noted Grahame's eye moving to the tombstone bearing his family name and wondered again what relation that "Jonet" had been to her bachelor friend.

As Mrs. Ogilvie promised, all the parish records were locked securely away in the heavy oak chest where Reverend Ogilvie preserved the written record of the Lord's work. The key turned in the well-oiled lock. The Reverend Ogilvie was a man worthy of his charge. It took Danvers only a matter of minutes to find the pertinent volume.

Light was dim in the small study so he took the heavy, leather-bound volume to the window, where pale white light fell through the leaded panes. His long fingers turned the thick pages backward. Antonia moved to stand quietly at his side.

At last he came to the page headed 1817. Two years after Waterloo. Tonia remembered the stories she'd heard of Norville in those days—the gallant young Hussar who had been left for dead in the field and rescued by his friend. Surely the recovery had been long and painful— quite understandably followed by the outburst of high spirits that had produced this potential disaster in their lives.

She followed Charles's finger as it moved down the list of births, deaths, baptisms, burials, marriages. The signatures, many of them, were hard to read or were mere X's. And as they came to the bottom of the page and turned over to the next, the difficulty increased. Perhaps it was from the leaky roof Mrs. Ogilvie had alluded to, but, whatever the cause, the registry had been exposed to an excess of damp. Some signatures were merely blurred, others blotted beyond all recognition.

Danvers's finger stopped two-thirds of the way down the page. Antonia, who hadn't realized she had been holding her breath, let it out. There was no difficulty reading this signature. "Norville." As distinctive as the title itself. The signatures around it, minister, bride, and witnesses, had succumbed in varying degrees to the ravages of water seeping under loose slates, but "Norville" stood.

"As you said, my dear. He never did anything by halves."

She touched her husband's arm. Whatever this meant for them in the future they would face it together.

"At least it appears the bride was capable of writing her name." Danvers spoke in a flat voice.

Sir Graham came forward. "Oh, yes. Good yeoman stock. Educated to read the Bible." He took the book from Danvers's hands and moved closer to the light to examine the signatures. At last he turned to Reverend Ogilvie's desk. A brief rummaging produced what Grahame sought, and he returned to the window with a magnifying glass. After another lengthy perusal he returned the book to Danvers.

Charles took one more look, shook his head, and handed the closed volume to Mrs. Ogilvie.

"Did you find what you wanted all right, then? Great pity about the water getting to it. Like I said, we'd just come, had no idea about the condition of the roof. Of course Reverend Ogilvie got right on about the repairs and locked all the books up as tight as could be immediately. Nothing like that has happened to any of the Lord's property since my husband has been in charge. Well, nothing except this matter of the drains, of course, but the books are all right."

She turned to the last page written in the book. "See, there it is—Monroe. Jacob Monroe, buried just one week today. Pity to be disturbed so soon, and him just settling in, like. But at least the register's all fine."

Antonia stepped to her side. "Monroe?"

Danvers was right behind her. "The name is Monroe, and the grave has been disturbed?"

"Yes, large clan hereabouts, but the weather's no respecter of persons, and that's a truth."

"Could we see the grave?"

"Why certainly. Kind of you to want to pay your respects. It's just a step across the kirkyard." She led the way.

In a minute Danvers stood beside the grave, nodding.

"Rabbit hole is what I say." Mrs. Ogilvie pointed to the cave-in beside the partly exposed coffin. The sweep of her gesture led Tonia's gaze on down the sloping yard to where a good deal of excess water had indeed washed toward the little stream that tumbled its way to the loch.

Danvers considered. "Rabbits? Possibly, Mrs. Ogilvie. Possibly. You probably know that Sir Graham here is something of an expert on soil in this area. Perhaps he could advise."

The goodwife clapped her hands. "Oh, if you would be so kind, sir. The Reverend Ogilvie would be right honored to have you take an interest—he's that worried he is—it being the Lord's work and all."

196

"Right. Quite right. Glad to oblige. Plenty of time. No hurry at all." He looked around. "If I just had a spade, that is."

Mrs. Ogilvie pointed them to the little gardener's shack at the corner of the wall, then had to search the Reverend Ogilvie's office for the key, but in the end all obstacles yielded to her enthusiasm, and Grahame set to work removing careful shovelfuls of dirt from beside the coffin.

It took only six or seven scoops to bare the side of the fresh pine box.

Mrs. Ogilvie gasped. "Oh, that poor man! Surely no rabbit did that?" She searched the possibilities. "Beaver? Could it be a beaver?"

"A somewhat larger animal, I believe. And two-legged." There was no need to return to the gardener's shed for a crowbar. The nails of the coffin-lid had not been replaced.

Mrs. Ogilvie was pliant to Sir Graham's leading her away at Danvers's signal, but Antonia stood firm.

Danvers lifted the lid.

There was no alarm at the sight. Tonia had seen the man before. He was considerably more shrunken and decayed this time. And he smelled worse. But the missing tartaned corpse was missing no longer.

19

And so, in spite of the variation in spelling, it's the same clan? That means Monro unwittingly dissected his own relative?" Antonia sat before the fire at Leven Lodge, sipping a cup of tea. In spite of her claim to strong nerves, she had accepted a far more vigorous fortification of sugar in her cup than usual.

"The annals of grave robbing are full of such stories," Danvers replied. He sat on the other side of the fireplace in his characteristic position, long legs extended before him. "There is the case of the student who delivered a body in a bag to his professor, then discovered that it was his own sister's son. Another, memorialized in an oil painting, of a resurrectionist who was led with a group of his fellows to dig up his own mother's tomb. And another account of a doctor who removed the sheet from the specimen his assistant had prepared for him only to find laid out before him the body of the sweetheart he had buried the week before."

Sir Graham moved to refill his guest's cup and discovered the pot was empty, so gave three sharp tugs to the tapestry bellpull beside the fireplace.

"Horrible stories." Tonia shook her head. "But it's hard to see what bearing they might have on the current situation. I wonder what kind of inquiries Futter has made around the medical school?"

Whatever further observations Danvers held, they were not made known, for at that moment Molly entered with the required pot of tea carried for her by a familiar round figure in a green coat.

"Hardy, what—?" Danvers began.

"I hope you didn't expect me to travel alone." An imperious female voice accompanied by sharp raps of an ebony walking stick turned all heads to the doorway.

The men snapped to their feet.

"I need a cup of tea. With some of your infamous Scotch whiskey in it. The discomfitures of this country are all worse than I remembered. The Minister of Public Roads should be boiled in oil."

The dowager duchess of Aethelbert took the center chair as if ascending a throne. Danvers and Grahame resumed their seats.

"And sheep. On the roads. Everywhere. If you can't run your roads properly I suppose it should be no surprise that you can't run your university properly." With that she dismissed Sir Graham and rounded on Danvers.

"But I did expect better of you. You're English. I suppose, though, that one must make allowances for the Norman blood. At least my family is Anglo-Saxon. Full-blooded Anglo-Saxon. I should have known you'd bungle it. Should have come myself in the first place."

Antonia bit her tongue. She wanted to point out that, whatever failings they may have had, the Normans were famous for their organizational skills. Instead she meekly held out a cup of tea, duly doctored by Sir Graham. "Is there a problem, Aunt Elfrida?"

"Problem? Certainly not. There's a catastrophe. While you've been lollygagging up here with those odious sheep, my nephew is apparently about to get himself sent down from university. That even the Scottish should show such a marked lack of respect is quite unthinkable. I have brought Norville to deal with the authorities."

"Father?" Danvers came upright in his chair. "Here?"

"In Edinburgh. I left him to deal with the authorities, as I said. I have come to remind you of your duty."

A smile flickered at the corner of Danvers's mouth, but his bow, even from his seated position, was punctilious. "Yes, Aunt Elfrida."

Antonia, however, had not missed the import of the dowager duchess's call. "Gilchrist. Sent down? The police . . ."

"Police!" This caused the dowager duchess's silver lorgnette to be brought into service from the end of its black ribbon around her long, lace-swathed neck. "Police. I should think not. Whatever should the police have to say about Gilchrist involving himself with some tatterdemalion woman? It's not the thing. Not the thing at all. I said there would be trouble when his father married a Scottish woman. I don't care if her father is a chief, I said. Blood will out. That's what I said at the time, and that's what I said a week ago when I received Gilchrist's letter. Responsible for this woman. And her brood of children. Impossible, that's what I say. The infant, maybe, but not the older ones. Simple mathematics. He hasn't been in Scotland that long. It's all nonsense anyway."

A short time later, in their room, Tonia and Danvers had to agree that they could make little more sense out of whatever tangle Gil was in. "I knew he was mixed up with something unsavory when we saw him in Old Town that night. Something to do with that woman. And whatever it is must be what he was trying to explain to Madelyn the morning I found her in tears. Charles, you don't think he could have *married* her, do you? "

"Out of some excess of youthful gallantry—like my father did?" Now there was no incipient smile around Danvers's mouth. "Is there anything in Scripture about the folly

200

of the youth becoming the sins of the fathers?" He ran his fingers through his hair as he paced. "I can imagine no reason for it; yet I can see no other explanation. It seems that human nature is capable of far greater imbecility than I had believed possible."

"But would he be dismissed from university for an unwise marriage?"

Danvers shook his head. "He would be dismissed for *any* marriage."

Seeing no more to be accomplished in that direction, Tonia moved to the dressing table and removed her lace cap before the beveled looking glass. She took her time pulling out each of the long, tortoiseshell hairpins holding her smooth, amber locks in place. When the clustered curls had been freed to fan across her shoulders, she picked up her silver hairbrush and held it out to her husband. "Here, love."

This time the craggy features lit with a smile.

The atmosphere shattered, however, when after a most satisfactory brushing of Antonia's tresses, accompanied by several kisses on her smooth, white shoulders, Danvers thrust the brush down with a thud and strode to the door. "Do not wait up for me. I have matters to discuss with Grahame which will not wait."

The dawn chorus was barely under way when Hardy bustled in with their coffee the next morning. "Oh, and it's a fine day for traveling. I'm thinking even the elements don't dare disobey Her Grace." He placed the tray on the bed and turned to open the drapes.

"Hardy, what do you know of Gil's troubles?" Antonia asked as she poured hot milk and coffee together.

"Pitying little, and there's the truth of it. But the old . . . er . . . that is . . . Her Grace seems to have the essence of it. Guess the boy meant to warn her—soften the blow, as you might say. I'm certain he never expected her to hot-foot it all the way up here. But what any of us can be doing to help is a deep question."

That and far weightier questions filled Tonia's mind as the carriage rattled southward later that morning. She felt almost dizzy with the comings and goings between Leven Lodge and Edinburgh. And she had to admit that the sheep in the road didn't speed their progress, no matter how much she delighted in the pastoral scenery.

Antonia was not at ease. Aunt Elfrida was an irresistible force, but they were leaving far too many unsolved problems behind them in Fife.

Sir Graham had summoned the local constabulary to deal with the matter of the mixed-up corpses, and they had probably already gotten on to the Edinburgh police to sort the matter out. So perhaps there was little need for Tonia and Charles to remain for that.

But the larger issue was that of Ross Dalkeith. Antonia was certain Danvers had intended to interview the fellow, to attempt to reach some sort of arrangement. Of course, in the face of the legal complications of the entailment there might not be much to be accomplished in that direction either.

For some reason a snatch of popular poetry came to her mind: *I am the master of my fate; I am the captain of my soul.* She gave a rueful smile. That was, indeed, the popular philosophy. Mechanized men could build bridges anywhere, run trains anywhere, accomplish anything with steam power. But they couldn't manage their own lives.

So it was with a sense of being borne forward by an irresistible force greater even than the dowager duchess of Aethelbert that she at length felt the familiar jostling of the carriage wheels on the cobbles of Charlotte Square.

The tall, distinguished, silver-haired earl of Norville came down the stone stairs to greet them.

The dowager duchess took his extended hand to alight from the carriage but made no acknowledgement of his courtesy. "I trust you've made progress here, Norville.

As you can see I've succeeded admirably. But I can't do everything myself."

"I'm pleased that you realize that, Your Grace," the earl murmured not quite under his breath.

She passed by with her head up.

Sir Graham stepped out, and Norville clasped his old friend's hand. "Good to see you. Thank you for coming. My son has explained our . . . er . . . difficulty?" He pumped his hand again. "So glad you came."

Grahame clapped his friend's shoulder with his free hand. "Certainly I came. Certainly. There is much to see to. Much. I hope I haven't left it too late. Always seemed there was plenty of time . . ."

With a flutter of lavender and white skirts, Madelyn flew out the door that the stiffly proper Jeffers was holding open for their guests. A furious yapping and bouncing accompanied her springing step.

Tonia started forward to greet her friend, then threw out her arms in delight. "Tinker! How did you get here?" The dog bounded into her arms.

Norville bowed to his daughter-in-law. "I am exceedingly pleased to know that you are happy to have him back. I'll admit that it was almost worth the rigors of the trip north to get him out of Grosvenor Square."

"Oh, has he been very bad?" She fondled the soft golden ears.

"Quite the contrary. He has been entirely silent and still. My complete staff has devoted their undivided attention to trying to cheer him up—to the considerable cost of the attention I received from them, I might point out."

"Oh, thank you so much for caring for him for me." She looked up and saw clearly the kindness and concern behind the man's stern facade. She spoke so that only he could hear. "You needn't appear fierce for my sake. I know your son learned his consideration from his father."

Harry Raeburn, head and shoulders forward, muttonchop sideburns flowing, led his guests up the stairs to where Mrs. Raeburn, in a champagne-colored gown that so blended with the pale afternoon light as to affect near invisibility, was supervising the arrangement of what must have been hastily ordered refreshments.

One guest was already sitting in a far corner with an untouched cup of tea in his hand. From the look on Gil's face Tonia could tell that there had been no improvement in his circumstances.

She crossed to him. "Gil. Is there no hope?"

He shook his head, and a quantity of cold tea sloshed into its saucer. "None. I must see this through. Whatever folly others call it, family honor must be upheld. If only I could make Madelyn understand, it would ease the pain somewhat."

Tonia patted his arm. Amid the confusion of introductions and refreshment-serving in the large drawing room beyond them, she tried to talk to him. "You've talked to Madelyn? Explained everything to her?"

"I've tried. But it's always the same thing. I won't deny how much I love her, so she can't see that there are any impediments. You see how happy she looks in spite of everything."

Tonia looked to the other side of the room where Madelyn was performing her hostess duties with becoming grace. She understood how Gilchrist felt. Such blissful confidence was more heartbreaking than tears would have been. Tonia gratefully accepted a cup of tea and one of Mrs. Raeburn's excellent shortbread biscuits.

The room was so full that it was a matter of several moments before Tonia realized that there were yet more arrivals. Moraig bobbed curtsies at the drawing room door but without achieving success in securing her mistress's attention.

The sharp-eyed dowager duchess, however, was not so long in noticing. The entire focus of the room was turned at her single, ringing word. *"Alexander!"* The duchess stood in the center of the room, looking at the newcomer.

A tall man with a leonine mane of white hair thrust his high, black silk hat into Moraig's hands and pulled his gloves from his long hands, finger by finger. Then he undid his flowing black cape and swirled it from his shoulders in a billowing sweep before handing it to the servant. But he retained his silver-tipped walking stick as if he would have need of it for dueling with the dowager duchess, toward whom he advanced with long strides.

He bowed over her outstretched hand, then raised it elegantly to his lips. "Elfrida."

If Antonia had not seen it with her own eyes she would not have believed it. Having seen, she still barely believed. It was a very near thing. The dowager duchess of Aethelbert came within a hair's breadth of swooning at the feet of Dr. Alexander Monro *tertius.*

He led her to a chair and assumed for himself the center stage that she had held.

Tonia found the entire performance fascinating, but the one beside her was less entranced.

Gilchrist groaned. "My nemesis. Why did he have to come here? Couldn't he deliver the blow in private?"

Antonia was proud of Gil, however, as he rose firmly to his feet. The blow might be public and painful, but he would receive it standing like a man.

"Gilchrist Morris" —Monro turned to him— "I have come personally to take charge of your case. The staff at the school are a bunch of lenient nincompoops. There has been far too much scandal attached to the school of late. It will not do. You young radicals must not be allowed to besmirch the reputation of the world's finest medical school —a reputation which has been built by generations of my own family." His slight pause was not filled with the applause he seemed to expect, so he continued. "Warrender."

The figure who had apparently accompanied Monro up the stairs still remained in the hall.

"Noah Warrender!" Monro thundered.

The assistant now came forward.

Antonia looked at the bald, bespectacled man with his fringe of sandy hair and prominent nose. This was definitely the man she had seen on Incholm. This was the man who had prepared the body for dissection the day she had accompanied Gil to the medical school—the day Monro had unknowingly dissected his own relative. If the police had now informed Monro of the truth, the great man appeared to be unaffected by the news.

With Norville and Grahame, the Raeburn family, the dowager duchess of Aethelbert, and Lord and Lady Danvers all looking on, Alexander Monro addressed Gil as if they were alone in his office. "My assistant here has brought to my attention certain facts concerning your activities in Rhum's Close, Morris."

Warrender held out a packet of papers loosely tied with brown string. "Such doings compliment neither a student nor my school."

Tonia would not have thought it possible that attention could be wrested from Alexander Monro, but this was a day for amazements.

Hardy entered, both hands full of sandwich trays, followed by yet another newcomer. With his usual force of purpose, Hardy headed across the room to deposit his sandwiches on the sideboard and presumably inform Mrs. Raeburn of the presence of an additional guest. Then Tinker spotted his old friend and bounded across the room. Hardy saw him coming and sidestepped.

At the same moment Tinker apparently saw the newcomer—or the bundle he carried—and changed course. In an amazing feat of agility, Hardy managed to leap over the hurtling projectile of golden hair, pirouette to the sideboard, and deposit both towering trays without dislodging so much as a single slice of salmon.

"Thank you," Mrs. Raeburn murmured as if her maid had recovered a misplaced embroidery thread.

All eyes followed Tinker to his target, a short, shiny-headed man who peered around near-sightedly.

Harry Raeburn was the first to turn his attention from Hardy's exploits to the man standing just inside the door. "What in tarnation are you doing here, Warrender?" Harry Raeburn thundered toward his mill foreman and seized the parcel he carried. "Quiet! Confounded animal." Raeburn's command sent Tinker scampering backward toward his mistress's skirt but did not make the terrier take his eyes from the heather and gold tartan Harry Raeburn now held.

"Just finished the cleaning and reweaving." The mill foreman's smooth, projecting forehead beaded with sweat. "I gave it my personal attention seeing as how it's Miss Madelyn's birthday so soon. I thought you'd be wanting it. I am sorry, I didn't realize—didn't mean to intrude." He began backing toward the door.

When the foreman reached a level with Monro's assistant, Antonia felt as though a candle had suddenly been lit in her head. That day at the mill she had known the foreman reminded her of someone. But the name was wrong. Raeburn had just now called him "Warrender"— but that was Monro's assistant's name. The man from the mill was called something weaselly. Ferret—was that it?

"Oh, my plaid!" Madelyn took the bolt from her father's hands and turned to the foreman. "Thank you for bringing it by, Ferral. I've been asking Papa for it. I couldn't imagine why it took so long to have it woven. My dressmaker will be most pushed to get it finished." She ran her hand over the soft surface. "It is beautiful, is it not? My very own special design." Her smile was radiant as she passed the bundle to Moraig.

"At least I could do that for her," Gilchrist said, and, even with her mind on other things, Antonia noted the satisfaction in his voice.

"Wait." Tonia moved quickly toward the retreating mill foreman. "Ferral—or Warrender—what *is* your name?"

"That's it, ma'am. Ferral Warrender, at your service." He bowed in her direction, although it was obvious he didn't see her clearly. He dug for a moment in his vest pocket, then hung a pair of round spectacles on his hawk-like nose.

Antonia blinked, thinking the fault was with her vision. But there was no mistaking. She looked from Monro's assistant to Raeburn's and back again. "Brothers?"

Monro's Warrender—Noah—answered. "That's right. So is there a law against having a brother, even if he only works in a grubby mill in Leith?"

Harry Raeburn was not the man to let such a slight pass. "What's that? I'll not be insulted in my own drawing room. I'll have you know Raeburn Woolen Mills is Scotland's finest. So fine that we draped the bed for the Scottish Exhibit at the Crystal Palace, *and* Her Majesty the Queen noted our work and has honored us with a commission. And what do you have to say to that?"

It was Noah Warrender he challenged, but it was yet another arrival at the very busy Raeburn drawing room door who answered.

"That's just the question I've come to ask you, sir." Inspector Futter entered, accompanied by an elderly, bald man leaning heavily on a cane. For all the man's frailty, Antonia drew her breath at the striking resemblance between him and the Warrender brothers. And she felt she had seen him before too.

The policeman turned to Mrs. Raeburn. "Sorry about imposing on your drawing room, ma'am. I'll try not to take more time than necessary, but this is official business, and I'm afraid it won't wait."

Mrs. Raeburn rose to her feet. "Please. Everyone be seated." It was probably the longest public speech she had ever made in her life, and Tonia could have hugged her. The effect of her soft voice on the large and varied crowd was amazing. Everyone turned and looked obediently for a chair.

When all were sitting, feet on floor and hands folded in lap as if in church, Futter nodded. "My friend here has made a most significant identification." He held up the police sketch of the tartaned corpse and handed it to the man who accompanied him, clearly giving him the floor.

Antonia leaned forward in her chair. This was the man she had witnessed Noah Warrender attending to with such solicitude at Incholm Abbey. But who—?

"Ladies and gentlemen," Futter announced, "Dr. Robert Knox."

20

Antonia blinked.

Dr. Robert Knox—twenty years ago one of the most successful men in Edinburgh. A man of superior intellect and unusual industry, whose numerous books on anatomy were still valued in spite of the fact that he was personally reviled. Was this the face she had seen at the window of the isolated house? When she saw him on Inchcolm she had felt a vague sense of recognition.

A short man, his round head shining bald, thick spectacles perched on a large nose above heavy lips—Tonia had heard that childhood smallpox had left him blind in one eye—Knox still exhibited signs of the vigor that had driven him to the height of achievement.

He brandished the picture of the corpse. "Yes, yes. I knew him well. Much changed after all these years, as we all are. But some things don't change: shape of the head, bone structure. Note the high cheekbones, the elongated jawline."

In all those years Knox had not lost his lecturing skill. His audience leaned forward to see the portrait better.

And now Antonia was sure she knew. The idea had been growing for several days, ever since the play had re-vealed to her the fact that Hare had a son. The identity of the tartaned corpse was obvious. The Hare child, now an adult, had been murdered to avenge the crimes of his father, who had escaped the hangman's rope. The sins of the father had been visited on the son.

Knox, in his old-fashioned blue coat with wide lapels and high, stiff cravat, turned suddenly from the picture to sweep his audience with the piercing gaze of his good eye. What an effective technique that must have been in the lecture hall! It was equally effective now. "And so, I am faced once again with the perpetrator of my disgrace. I thought never to name his name again. And yet I am called from retirement to do so—to drag forth old, painful memories that would better lie forgotten were it not for the hand that has moved against this one in an act of vengeance." The elderly man's energy flagged. He bent further over his cane, thrusting his heavy head toward his listeners. "And yet I will not name him. Others here can do so."

The firelight reflected off the lens of Knox's spectacles, making Antonia feel he was singling her out. Before she realized what she was doing, she had spoken. "Hare. It is Hare's son. Someone has taken it upon himself to punish the son for the father's wrongs."

Across the room she saw Danvers move. It was a slight shifting of position only, but enough to place him beside Noah Warrender. And she saw that Warrender was laughing—laughing at *her*.

"Hare! Ridiculous. The brat died before his mother could rabbit back to Ireland with him."

Antonia's perfect theory shattered.

"This was a man who deserved to die. This was *Paterson*."

The silence in the room was not one of shocked recognition. It was of confused anticlimax. From the blank looks and questioning frowns it was apparent that none knew a Paterson.

Except those from the medical school.

Knox nodded. "Yes. That is the name. My doorkeeper. Paterson, the most energetic receiver of anatomical material a lecturer could have wished for. Always my lectures were supplied. But in the end he turned against me— undoubtedly because he couldn't face his own guilt in the matter. Even when Burke made statements exonerating me, Paterson pointed blame." The old man paused for breath. "But you remember, Noah Warrender. You know the truth. You, the brightest of my students. I thought you would follow in my footsteps. You would be the son I never had. People even said we looked alike."

Student approached master. "And you were the most eloquent, most versatile, most thorough teacher of anatomy that Scotland ever produced. That you should have been dragged into disgrace by the happenstance that those murderers crossed your path—it is intolerable."

In a sudden change of mood, Warrender lifted his chin and puffed out his chest. "But I stood by you. I never turned against you like Paterson did. I cared. I couldn't even go on with my studies afterwards. And after I fought my way up from nothing." He rounded on Antonia. "You saw what it was like on the island—sheep and rocks. Nothing . . ."

Tonia gasped. "You! I thought someone was watching me. It was you."

"Gave me a nasty turn, it did, when I saw you— thought you'd come after me—but I watched, and I could tell you didn't know a thing. Nobody knew anything. I fooled everyone. I was the only one who knew!"

"But what were you doing on Skye?"

"Old Malcolm's funeral—my father's youngest brother —last of the family. Not that it matters much now. But we had our pride. We had our family loyalty. And he'd always been so proud of me. When the parson took me up to educate because I showed promise—then when I went off to university. Of course, my brother came with me—but not to university. I was the one with the brains. The one who would be a great surgeon. But after they ruined Knox I couldn't go on. No one else cared. They all went right on."

Warrender's round face was now red bordering on purple. He spoke in a rising voice. "They all went right on to greater and greater success. Do you know who Dr. Knox's assistants were? The men who shared in th advantage of his brilliant dissections and took none of the blame? Wharton Jones and William Fergusson, that's who."

Tonia felt confused, and Gil whispered in her ear, "Wharton Jones has done brilliant ophthalmoscope work. Sir William Fergusson's a distinguished London surgeon."

"They should have been punished. All of them. Liston—he robbed graves himself and was lauded for it. Dr. Knox never sullied his hands. But I got even with Liston . . ." The frenzied speech faltered. "Well, it was too late to punish Liston—but I could let his family know they hadn't gotten away with it. A resurrected body on their doorstep was just the thing. Serve them right. The Bible says iniquity is accounted unto the third and fourth generation—so let them pay. That's the key—let them pay."

"That strange spade—it was the one from Skye! You used it to dig old Mackelby's grave—then stuck the evidence of your crime in Gil's carrel. You were jealous of Gil because you could see he was going to make the success you never made—"

But Warrender was too far gone in the frenzy of his outburst for Antonia's insight to interrupt his flow. He obviously now knew no difference between boasting and confessing. How long had his reason been so decayed? she wondered. What had pushed him over the edge?

Sweat dripped from Warrender's forehead as he rounded on Monro, consumed by his madness. "But you were the worst. Monro the great. The man who should have received the bodies in the first place."

Monro sat perfectly still, yet seemed to grow in height as the raging Warrender took another step toward him. "But it started long before that, didn't it? You saw Knox's originality when you rejected him on his first examination for Doctor of Medicine, didn't you? You, who had never had an original thought in your life—spent your whole life giving outdated lectures—you saw a man who would write volumes on anatomy. You feared him, and you failed him."

"You quite overrate my powers of perception, sir."

But Warrender ignored Monro's remark, if he heard it at all. Now beyond all reason, Warrender pulled a knife from his pocket.

Danvers and Futter on each side darted forward to protect the doctor.

Their protection, however, was unnecessary. Warrender's feint had been successful. While all focused on protecting Monro, Warrender turned and sprinted out the door. He was better than halfway across the inner hall before Danvers and Futter sprang after him.

Antonia was never quite sure whether she grabbed Gil or he grabbed her, but the two of them raced hand-in-hand across the room to the stairs while the others still sat seemingly frozen. Antonia hadn't followed every step of this case, from finding the body through Warrender's frenzied confession, just to sit quietly in a drawing room and miss the outcome.

The rattle of carriage wheels just turning out of Charlotte Square hit Tonia's ears at the same time as prickles of icy rain reminded her that she had come out without shawl or bonnet. Then the sight of Danvers and Futter springing the horses of the police carriage took all thought of personal comfort from her mind.

At that moment a light landaulet shot from among the carriages waiting in front of the Raeburn residence. "And you'll be wanting to go too, I'm thinking."

At Hardy's words she didn't wait for Gil to hand her into the conveyance, and they were off before she was seated. The rain splashed harder in Tonia's face as they clattered down the quickly darkening streets, forcing her to close her eyes at times in spite of her fear of losing sight of the carriages they pursued. She managed an occasional glimpse of the shadowy black vehicle Warrender drove, careening around yet another sharp corner and down a steep, narrow road beside the castle ravine.

At times it appeared that Futter and Danvers were closing the gap. At others she could see nothing and despaired that their quarry had entirely escaped. At the narrow Stables Road that cut through the edge of the ravine she caught sight of them again. Then she cried out as she saw what Futter, in closer pursuit, could not. Warrender had taken a sudden, sharp left turning and disappeared under the trees. In the shadows and driving rain, the police carriage now appeared to be following another vehicle that had happened along the nearly deserted streets.

"Oh, thank goodness!" Tonia almost jumped to her feet as the police van made a split-second turn after Warrender, wobbled on its left wheels, then straightened to continue.

It would be hard to say what all at once gave Tonia the impression that they were chasing an empty carriage: something about the wildness with which the leading horses ran, perhaps, or the absence of a snapping whip urging them to greater speed. But she knew. Warrender somewhere had abandoned his gig and taken to his feet. Somewhere in the shadowy, rain-soaked ravine a killer was running free.

The men in the second carriage must have realized this at the same time she did. Without bothering to slow the van, a dark form sprang from each side and disappeared into the rugged terrain.

Hardy took time to stop his horses, but Tonia gave no thought for her best dove wool traveling dress as the hem caught on a spring and let go with a ripping sound. She was forced, however, to have consideration for the slippery wet rock underfoot or she would tumble to the bottom of the gorge.

With a sudden, unwanted flash of common sense she halted. What was she doing? A lady didn't go dashing off chasing a killer and his pursuers across rocky ravines. Not even if her whole happiness depended on the safety of one of those pursuers.

She started to turn.

Then she froze. A figure moved ahead of her. The dark form of Warrender crept from the shelter of a bush and sprang up the path. And she saw something else. Only the briefest gleam of reflected light told her something had fallen from his pocket. Something shiny. The knife? A small gun? Whatever it was, if there was the slightest chance it could be of use to Charles she must find it.

She moved forward carefully, scanning every inch of ground beyond the bushes for the object. Then her foot kicked a small bottle. She picked it up.

What a disappointment. Not a weapon. She read the label in the dim light. Chloroform. Then she remembered. Puts the patient out with a single whiff, Milton had said. Or you can soak a rag and clap it over the nose and mouth— but you have to be careful—too much can be deadly.

Had Warrender been using it in the course of his work? Or did he foresee the possibility of using it as a weapon? Either way it offered hope.

Here was indeed something the unarmed Danvers could use against Warrender. If she could get it to him.

She turned to face the rock wall.

Going up was even more treacherous than crossing the ravine. In spite of the fact that it was never truly dark in Scotland in May, shadows were deep and dark on that side of Castle Hill. And the volcanic pillar seemed a sheer cliff. Yet she found footholds. As long as Warrender found them, so could his pursuers, and so could Antonia. An occasional dislodged stone or muttered curse told her their quarry moved ahead.

And then all was silent save for the splatter of rain and the howl of wind on rock. Tonia held her breath. She

216

felt a sinister lurking presence but could not locate it. She inched ahead, then stopped. The tall, thin form that was her beloved Charles moved from behind a rock above her on the cliff face and crept forward.

She more sensed than saw a slash of wet, cold steel as Warrender leaped from ambush. She closed her eyes and prayed. *Not Charles. Don't let him be hurt—or worse.* Her mind balked at the thought. They hadn't even begun their life together. It couldn't end here on the face of a cold, wet cliff at the thrust of a madman's knife. If only she could get her weapon to him.

Another movement brought her eyes open. Futter lunged forward. A scrabble of blows followed. Surely such struggling would send them all crashing down the slippery, jagged rocks.

But only one figure fell. Antonia screamed as the body dropped at her feet—one sharp, fierce outcry. And then she was silent as she bent over Futter, tugging at his torn coat to get to the wound and staunch the flow of blood. Tears and rain ran down her cheeks as she worked in a frenzy, aware that the struggle continued on up the hill.

She allowed herself a quick upward glance. Warrender was climbing again—with Danvers close after him. And then Gil was at her elbow, pulling his cravat from his neck. "Here, Tonia, use this for a tourniquet."

"Gil, you use it. You're the doctor." And she was off. Her petticoats dragged in the mud. Her rain-soaked skirt slowed her further. Yet she must keep up. Now it was only Charles and the murderer. Charles must have whatever aid she could take him.

In only a few yards her feet felt the blessed smoothness of a roadway. But that meant the going was also easier for the men again moving ahead of her, and the distance stretched until she feared she would lose them.

She realized now that the killer was not continuing up the crag to the castle. He was heading southward toward the back side of Castle Hill and Old Town. If he could reach that rabbit warren of stairs, closes, and wynds he could go to earth there and never be found.

Tonia's breath was coming in sobs, her ears pounded, and she felt as if her burning chest would burst. She couldn't stop now and let Charles pursue that madman alone. But she couldn't go on.

"And why would you be running when you could be riding?"

She heard Hardy's welcome voice and the clatter of horse and carriage almost at the same time. She held up her arms, and he swung her to the seat. She pointed in the direction the men had gone, more slowly now after the exertion of the struggle on the cliff.

It was a few minutes before Tonia recognized their location. Tanner's Close. The very site of Hare's boarding-house where all this long struggle began a generation ago. Now, if they could just bring this final malefactor to justice, history could put "Paid" to one dark era.

The light glimmered in Tonia's mind, but ahead of her, in the increasing dark, Danvers continued his pursuit. For a time the two in the carriage lost him, but then an angry, drunken shout from some observer led them on down the Grassmarket. Unlike New Town, whose streets had been virtually deserted in the late evening, Old Town was thronged with those who had no place else to be. And their cries guided the pursuing carriage.

Then they swung around a familiar, gray stone church, ghostlike and hollow in the center of its kirkyard, and came to a sudden halt at an ancient stone barricade.

Flodden Wall had been thrown up hurriedly to protect Edinburgh after the defeat at Flodden Field. It was intended to keep out the English King Henry, seeking to ravage their city, not a Victorian English lady seeking to clear the city of a later ravager. The wall was never tested against King Henry. It did not hold against Lady Antonia.

The fact that Flodden Wall had crumbled somewhat in its near-to-four-hundred years did not contribute to her scaling of it nearly so much as did the sight of Danvers's pursuing his target along the top and the fact that buildings along the wall provided a natural access.

But it was still a sheer drop on the kirkyard side. Antonia saw the dark, heaving form of Warrender stop. She saw the risks. He could leap to the ground and, if he landed unscathed, likely escape his pursuers. But if he miscalculated and fell askew among the tombstones and mounded earth, a broken leg would bring the chase to an abrupt end.

Instead, Warrender took the unlikely choice of running along the wall.

Tonia didn't understand. This was the greatest risk of all. One misstep, a loose stone, a renewed wash of wind and rain, anything could bring disaster. And yet the madman plunged forward.

Then she saw his object. Out of the shadows to the left loomed an escape hatch. Shining black in the rain were the iron bars of a mortsafe, one built to the dimensions of a small house, only slightly lower than the wall, and offering a smooth slide to the ground.

The certain peril of a moment's carelessness necessitated that Danvers pursue more slowly. If Warrender made this, it could easily mean freedom for the killer. If only she could get the chloroform to Charles. Could he pull the stopper and splash it in Warrender's face from that distance? Would the anesthetic work that way? What had Milton said? She couldn't remember. Her only hope was to try.

Warrender reached the wall beside the mortsafe. An easy spring would land him on the top. He hesitated.

"Charles, here! *Catch!*" Tonia threw the bottle. "Chloroform . . . make him breathe it . . . try . . ." Her jumbled instructions ended in a sob-choked scream.

219

She had thrown wide, and in reaching for the bottle Danvers overbalanced and fell from the wall.

Warrender leaped for the mortsafe.

Both hands clapped over her mouth, Tonia heard a groan as Charles hit the dirt of the cemetery. Seconds later came the thud of Warrender's landing on the top of his escape hatch.

They had come so close only to lose it all now. And it was her fault. Warrender would slither off into the night and escape to freedom. All because of her.

But that was nothing compared to her vision of Charles lying crumpled and broken at the foot of Flodden Wall. Why had she interfered? If she had stayed in the drawing room like a proper lady, he would undoubtedly have overcome Warrender by now.

The bars of the mortsafe creaked like an unoiled hinge.

She couldn't stay here wallowing in self-recrimination. Stiff with cold and fear, she forced herself forward, inching toward the place where he had fallen from the wall. *"Charles!"*

Her cry was answered only by a sharper rasping creak from the iron bars of the mortsafe—the sound of Warrender escaping. She heard him drop to the ground.

Antonia fell to her knees on the wall and crawled the remaining few feet. She peered into the shadows. "Charles? Can you hear me? Can you speak?"

She was answered by a shout of laughter. "Tonia, my love!"

"Charles, are you all right?" She leaned farther forward. "I'm so sorry. I ruined everything. But if you're all right . . ."

"Don't be a silly goose. You were brilliant! See . . ."

She followed the thrust of his arm. Then she saw a dark shape inside the mortsafe. "Is that Warrender? But I thought he escaped."

` "Would have, if you hadn't landed me where I could see the loose railing in this cage. It only took the slightest push to spread the bars so he would fall through."

She looked at the still, crumpled body. "Is—is he dead?"

Again Danvers laughed. "Dead to the world. It's that chloroform you flung at me. Bottle broke. He landed with his head in it. He'll sleep peacefully for hours."

Now it was Tonia's turn to give a gurgle of laughter. "He's already jailed."

"Which could save the good ratepayers of Edinburgh the not inconsiderable cost of dragging the scoundrel through the courts." Danvers grasped the top of the barricade and levered himself up to a sitting position beside her on the Flodden Wall. "However, I suppose the law will wish to have its hand in this."

He looked up as Hardy arrived. "Hardy, Lady Danvers and I shall await your return with the proper authorities."

Antonia was dimly aware that a curious crowd was gathering at their feet, that her bare, disheveled curls were getting yet more soaked in the continuing drizzle, and that the stone structure on which she sat seeped four hundred years of cold. She was in Danvers's arms, and that was all that mattered for the moment.

21

Hours later they were back at Charlotte Square. Antonia, swathed in the warmest woolen undergarments and rugs the best textile miller in Scotland could supply, sat by the drawing-room fire sipping yet another cup of Mrs. Raeburn's tea, so silky to the tongue, brewed as it was with soft Scottish water and free, as she insisted it be, of Scotland's stronger brew, in spite of the dowager duchess's advice.

Except for the absence of Noah Warrender and Knox, whom Raeburn had had escorted home by a servant, the company was unchanged from what it had been earlier in the evening. Danvers stood beside Antonia with Mr. and Mrs. Raeburn seeing to their comfort. The dowager duchess sat firmly upright in her chair on the other side of the fireplace next to Alexander Monro. Gil and Madelyn had chosen the sofa best screened by Mrs. Raeburn's prize potted palm. Norville and Grahame remained quietly in the far corner. The one newcomer was Sergeant MacRoy who stood by Inspector Futter questioning Ferral Warrender.

Constable MacRoy, constant ever to his beat, had been near to hand when Hardy sought the services of the law and, having duly delivered Warrender to the jail, had returned with a pale but well-bandaged Inspector Futter to complete their records.

In deference to Gil as his physician, however, Futter conducted his statement taking from a seated position and fortified with a mug of Harry Raeburn's steaming grog. "So it appears that Warrender had brooded on this for twenty years, waiting his chance to avenge his mentor."

The miscreant's brother, head hanging, spoke from a dark corner where he appeared to be attempting to hide himself. "I feel so guilty. I should have watched closer. If I'd reported Paterson's disappearance—but night watchmen are notorious for going off drunk. When he didn't show up, I just hired another fellow in his place." He shook his head. "My own brother."

Futter turned a page in his notebook, found the motion painful to his wounded arm, and handed the pad to MacRoy as he continued the questioning. "So you hired Paterson and told your brother about him?"

Ferral nodded. "Paterson didn't make any secret of his past connection with Burke and Hare—almost bragged about it. And he hated Knox. Blamed him for their all losing their jobs. Although to be fair, Knox was a busy man, and no one in his position vetted their specimens closely in those days."

"I think we can leave that issue to posterity," Futter said. "What I'm more concerned about is how Paterson ended up in the Great Exhibition."

Ferral shook his head. "My brother will have to tell you about that. Best I can do is guess. He said he came by that night to share his good fortune—his old friend Knox had given him a bottle of whiskey, so we'd have a wee dram together. I was working late to finish Miss Madelyn's plaid. I remember Paterson coming in—didn't think anything about it at the time, though. When I'd finished my bookkeeping, I went to find my brother. He was gone. Didn't see Paterson again either, but didn't realize he wasn't around. That is, I didn't realize he was still around, so to speak. The next day I supervised the shipping of the bed from the Port of Leith. Didn't see Paterson or the plaid again after that." He looked at Gil. "Until that fellow showed up with the plaid. I suppose the chest was the handiest hiding place, and my brother wrapped Paterson in the first thing that came to hand to keep the body from shifting around." He sat shaking his head.

Antonia shuddered. "And I'll bet I know how he killed him. Chloroform."

Danvers took her hand, and the shivering stopped.

"One thing I still don't understand." Antonia spoke into the silence in the room. "Why did your brother feel so strongly about Dr. Knox? There may have been an injustice done, but Dr. Knox had hundreds of devoted students. What was your brother's attachment?"

"Oh, don't you understand?" Ferral's weak eyes blinked at her. "He was the one. My brother. He was the student that told Burke and Hare to go to Knox instead of Monro."

The coals shifting on the grate made the only sound in the room while that revelation registered with all present.

At length Alexander Monro cleared his throat.

"Right." Futter rose a bit unsteadily to his feet. "I don't think we'll need to bother these good people any longer, Constable."

Gil hastened to support his patient, helping Futter toward the door behind Ferral and MacRoy.

The dowager duchess stopped his progress with a rap of her walking stick. "That's far enough, young man. The Inspector here may well have cause for gratitude for your medical training, but your case is far from settled."

Gil stopped in the middle of the room. MacRoy took his place supporting Futter. When the three were gone, Gil rested a long look on Madelyn before giving himself a little shake and turning to Monro. "Sir, I realize I have blotted my copybook even further as you were drawn into all this unpleasantness tonight by coming here to deal with my case. I know I have broken university rules and must bear the consequences, but I cannot see that I could have done otherwise."

"State your case." The Anatomy Chair Emeritus was unsmiling. He needed only black crepe on his white hair to sit in the place of a hanging judge.

"Thank you. It will be with the greatest relief. I have had nothing but arguments and interruptions every time I have attempted to do so." This time he carefully did not look at Madelyn. Instead his eyes sought the dowager duchess.

"As some of you know, my mother is the daughter of Lochiel. His only child. My grandfather is not well. The title will pass to me one day. Although not yet legally so, I feel morally responsible for the people of our clan."

He nodded at the dowager duchess's snort. "I know it's a rather old-fashioned notion. Most of those ideas went down with the last Jacobite rebellion. But my mother raised me on stories of chiefs seeing to the welfare of their people, and here was this Lochiel woman with four children and no decent place to live."

He took a gulping breath and plunged onward. "Well, Old Town has lots of old closes sealed up ever since plague days—what with ghost stories and other things to keep folks away—and probably just as well too, with all the disease they've seen. But now with Prince Albert leading the way in slum clearance—I saw his model village at the Great Exhibition. And Ashley Cooper working for public health in Parliament. And there's a professor in London, Lister by name, who believes that cleanliness can prevent disease. Well, I had to try. Fumigating and whitewashing Rhum's Close was a small enough thing to do—there's so much to be done."

He turned to Madelyn with his palms turned outward. "I'm sorry, Madelyn. I had to try. Even if I'd known how great the cost would be."

This time the rapping walking stick was Monro's. "Yes, yes. Well, I think we've heard enough twaddle for one night. Washing out Old Town for the rabble—even if they are of your clan—all nonsense. You'll have to do better than that to keep your place in the university. A lot better. What's this world coming to—a lot of radical thinking. Not what we want to foster in the world's greatest medical school." He swooped the papers of Gil's record from a side table and took a long stride toward the door.

"I believe you should think again, Alexander." The dowager duchess of Aethelbert faced the Anatomy Chair Emeritus of Edinburgh University. "It's a fair trade. Your family honor for mine. There have been hints, Alexander. Broad hints. I don't believe you would wish them to become any more distinct. But I have always known that you repeated your grandfather's experiments and read from his lecture notes and passed them off as your own. And I know why."

From under his bushy white eyebrows, deep dark eyes held her pale blue ones. "Because I was too busy courting you to see about my lectures properly. And when you left I was too heartbroken. And then the pattern was set. Why did you choose Aethelbert, Elfrida?"

"Because he was an original thinker."

Alexander Monro cleared his throat. "I see. Quite. Well, I do admit that it wasn't quite the thing, using Monro *primus*'s notes. But they were rampling good lectures. A wee mite out of date, but my students never seemed to mind."

The dowager duchess raised her lorgnette.

He cleared his throat again. "Quite. Well, I suppose the least I can do is make the way clear for an original thinker here." He took the papers he held in his hand and tore through them, top to bottom, then turned with a flourish and placed them on the fire.

He paused in the door of the drawing room. "I shall see you before you return to London, Elfrida?"

She peered at him long through her lorgnette. "If you behave, Alexander."

Monro exited with a sweeping bow to the ladies.

Moments later Harry Raeburn returned from ushering his departing guest to the hall. "Well, if he isn't a rum one. Don't quite know what to make of all that." He looked at Madelyn. "But you look happy enough, my lass."

"Oh, I am, Papa. Gil's going to marry me." A little sidestep took her to Gil and the hand he was holding out to her.

Harry Raeburn looked the two of them up and down. "Aye, and about time too. As soon as he finishes his degree. He's a fine lad, and it's Harry Raeburn that says so. Right, Mrs. Raeburn?"

Madelyn's mother simply smiled and took the arm her husband held out to her. "Yes, Harry."

"You youngsters come with us. I've a thing or two to show you."

Madelyn and Gil followed her parents.

"And I'll just have a word with you, Mr. Raeburn." The dowager duchess exited behind the others, yet managed to give the impression she was leading the procession.

"Happy ending," Harry Raeburn said from the hall. "Happy. Only thing. Can't abide anything else."

"For them, that is." Norville, who had sat without stirring throughout the preceding events, turned to his son. "I must apologize. No, there's more needed. I must repent. I behaved irresponsibly in my youth, then dumped it on my son in my old age. I have no excuses."

"Nor have any of us for our misdeeds, Father. That is what forgiveness is for."

"Yes, but to bring ruin on the family. Unborn generations . . . your own children . . . my grandchildren . . ."

"Unto the third and fourth generation," Antonia said under her breath.

"I think not, Father. You're quite forgiven, you know."

"By you, and by God, as I hope for eternity," Norville said. "But not, I fear, by the law. The entailment is very clear."

Tonia nodded to herself. Unlike God, the law did not offer grace to thousands of generations.

"Our time in Fife was cut short, Father, but I quite believe I got to the bottom of the matter. Or perhaps I should say the heart of the matter, for that's truly what it is, isn't it, Grahame?"

Sir Graham, who had sat silently across a small table from Norville all evening, inclined his head. "Aye, and that's the truth of it. The lovely Linda lassie held my heart from the beginning. But Norville was my friend, and she seemed most content to be marrying him. And he the decorated war hero still limping romantically, with so much more to offer her than my little holding by the loch.

"But then when the groom had a bit over his head before the wedding, and I learned the true state of things, and Linda agreed most happily . . . of course I should have spoken up immediately, but it was all just a matter of form, of signing records for the sake of the child. And then Linda fell ill right afterwards. And I did care for the child all those years, with the assistance of Norville's money. Had the boy reared by that fine Dalkeith couple on my estate—couldn't have had a better home. Should have spoken up, I know, but my father was still alive. He would not take as good news the story of his son's folly. It was so much easier to remain quiet. There was plenty of time. Didn't seem any need to hurry."

Norville looked from Danvers to Grahame and back again. "I don't understand."

"Afraid you're making a hash of it, Grahame. You've left out the key point." Danvers turned to his father. "I suspected it when I examined the parish records, but it wasn't clear—they'd been damaged by water. But when I questioned Grahame he was much clearer with me than he's being now.

"The short of it is, Father, you were too foxed to know the difference, so the happy couple married, and you signed as witness—a rather unreliable witness in this case."

In her rush of relief, it took Tonia several moments to ask Grahame, "But why didn't you just say so the next morning? Why keep it all a secret? You could have raised the boy as your own."

"Don't think I didn't want to. But it wasn't that simple. I was engaged to another as well. Jonet Macintyre. My father had lost our estate to hers in a horse race. Marrying her was the only way to restore my family fortunes. The next morning I had to face those facts and thought the best course was to stay quiet and let time take its course. In the end Jonet died in childbirth a year after Linda."

Tonia was still sorting through it all when the dowager duchess swept back into the room with the Raeburns and their future son-in-law. "Well, that's all settled then. I have commissioned a tartan. The Aethelbert plaid. There shall be nothing else like it. All London is quite mad for the fashion, and there's no sense in having a royal supplier in the family without taking advantage of it. Gilchrist, I shall wear plaid to your wedding. And you may dance with me, Norville."